MASTERS OK ROAD · LEGENDARY RACE

THE DUTCHMEN
MOTORCYCLE CLUB

THE PRICE OF
FORGIVENESS

ML NYSTROM

HOT TREE PUBLISHING

THE PRICE OF FORGIVENESS

ML NYSTROM

HOT TREE PUBLISHING

ALSO BY ML NYSTROM

For information, contact the publisher, Hot Tree Publishing.

WWW.HOTTREEPUBLISHING.COM

EDITING: HOT TREE EDITING

COVER DESIGNER: BOOKSMITH DESIGN

EBOOK ISBN: 978-1-922679-15-4

PAPERBACK ISBN: 978-1-922679-16-1

To Sharon Stogner, Adrienne Wilder, and Christopher Kingery. You might not know it, but you three taught me a lot about the art of writing, and I'm forever grateful for your mentoring.

PROLOGUE

HE RAN FAR AND FAST THROUGH THE SNOW-COVERED fields. When he came to one of the dividing property fences, he climbed over it and ran farther. His lungs labored hard, sucking in great gulps of the cold air as his skinny legs pistoned. The thin soles of his shoes were no protection against the wheat stubble underneath the white blanket, but he didn't feel that pain, nor did he feel the cold. At least not yet. He had no idea how far he ran. He should have collapsed in the field from exhaustion or the beginnings of hypothermia, but somehow his body kept going, powered by something he couldn't name. If they were going to find him, they'd be smart about it and get the farm trucks to chase him. He ran faster and watched for telltale headlights coming across the empty plain.

He came to the wooded area on the other side of

the fields. He needed to get through the trees. There was safety on the other side. At least he hoped so. He didn't stop when he got to the tree line but ran straight into the dense growth. He half expected to smack into a trunk, but he was able to see enough in the dim moonlight to avoid them. It was as if a path had appeared to guide him through the dark forest. He knew when to dodge right or left, where to put his feet, how high to jump to avoid being tripped by a log or root. He didn't dare stop to think about it; he just ran.

He finally came to another fence. It was thin, wired, and high. On the other side was the paved road. In his short life, he'd never been beyond it, but he couldn't go back.

A loud engine startled him, and he crouched down to hide. Lights came closer, and he was confused as to why they would use a dozer to find him. The heavy vehicle swept past his spot, clearing the paved road of snow and leaving a pile of white in front of him. Air sawed in and out of his aching lungs, the cold making it painful. But he had to keep going. His body pulled energy from somewhere deep inside, and he climbed, the links and barbs of the fence cutting into his hands and legs.

He fell from the top, tumbling into the soft white mass and crawling to the center of the cold asphalt.

There he lay. Whatever reserves he'd managed to find had drained, and his body was spent. Maybe he would die now. Just another boy to be buried somewhere in the fields. His bones would be discovered someday, like all the others, when spring plowing began. He wondered if God cared at all.

A pair of headlights shone over him from a distance. He struggled to his feet to run again, but he couldn't move fast enough. He stumbled and pushed himself, but he had nothing left to give. His legs gave out, and he landed hard on the cold, icy road. He imagined they would make short work of him and simply run him over with the heavy farm truck, then toss his body in the back to bury later. He closed his eyes and awaited his fate.

CHAPTER
ONE

GRETCHEN INHALED THROUGH HER NOSE AND BLEW OUT slowly through her generous lips. *Patience, patience, patience,* she chanted in her head. Her blue-gray eyes took in the time on the old-fashioned cuckoo clock on the wall. Both hands were nearly pointed straight up at the elaborate twelve on the carved face. Midnight.

Gretchen sighed and rubbed her eyes that were tired from staring at the computer screen for so long. The deadline for this edit loomed close, and the author wasn't making the job any easier. There were so many grammar mistakes that Gretchen wondered if the writer bothered to try. Classic mix-ups between your/you're and their/they're/there were bad enough, but add in the content editing, and the piece became one big, massive mess. The name of one character changed from Kane to Cain with regularity.

The point of view jumped from first person to third omniscient, which made Gretchen's head spin hard enough that she needed another Tylenol hit. The sex scenes were long and complicated. She wondered how anyone could get off in the described twisted positions.

"Cain grabbed her hair in his hand and grabbed both her breasts to pinch and play with the nipples."

Gretchen bit her lip. "Cain has three grabby hands, eh?" She made another note on the already long column of notations in the margin.

"Bart entered the room and joined in the fun. His boner stood tall and straight as an arrow pointing to the sky."

"Who's Bart, and does he always walk into a room naked with an erection?" Gretchen leaned back in her desk chair. "Nope. I'm done with this."

She typed out a quick email to the author stating that the book needed so much work, it would be best to do a few rounds of self-editing before sending it to a pro. Another glance at the clock showed her that it was five past midnight. Her back protested as she stretched it while pushing away from her desk, and it tightened up as she suddenly lost control. She grabbed at the chair to keep it from moving, but something else overpowered her effort. A gasp left her lips as the big rolling chair jerked around, and she nearly spilled to the floor. Terror flashed through her body as several thoughts hit her at once.

Four large men towered over her. All of them wore black leather vests that pegged them for what they were rather than who. She knew about motorcycle gangs since her brother, Ezra, was a part of one. Well, half brother, whom she hadn't seen in years.

Her eyes darted to the logo. The Dutchmen. She'd heard the name mentioned by her friends up in Red Wing. They radiated cold menace, and she cowered in her chair. One of them was shouting at her, his face red and his mouth wide open as he pointed at her face. Two of them grinned and stared openly at her breasts that were covered only by a thin tank top she used as nightwear and was wearing with a pair of her favorite hipster briefs. She crossed her arms over her chest and clutched at herself in fear.

The fourth one stood back with his arms folded and seemed to be observing. His eyes were a dark bluish, almost charcoal, gray and only slightly lighter than his long black curls. Gretchen caught herself in the gaze of his cold, emotionless snake eyes that held her in thrall. Her body started shaking. She couldn't break away from it. It felt like she was being pulled into his power, into him, and nothing she did would stop her from being absorbed. If she had the ability to scream, she would start and never stop.

A rough jerk from the yelling one rescued her from the locked stare. The red-faced one grabbed the arms of her chair and shook the piece of furniture violently as he leaned into her face. Her hands came up, and she gestured wildly at him, over and over again. Tears poured from her eyes to flow over her cheeks as she did the best she could to make them understand. To tell them….

The black-haired man unfolded his arms and grasped the red-faced one's shoulder. Gretchen's attention flew back to him, and she trembled with fear as he crouched down in front of her, putting them at eye level. She noticed he had two parallel scars running down his cheek that cut through a close-trimmed beard. The depths of his eyes glowed with dark fire, and the muscles of his jawline moved as he gritted his teeth. Gretchen covered her breasts again, desperate for some sort of protection.

He glanced down at her useless attempt and back to her face. Gretchen knew if he wanted to do anything to her, anything at all, she was powerless to stop him or the others. In this northern residential area in the small town of Wabasha, the houses were spread out with some distance between them along the banks of the Mississippi River. Her neighbors tended to keep to themselves and rarely paid her any attention. These men could beat her, rape her, and kill her, and no one would hear a thing. Her vision grayed as her head tried to shut down in the only escape route she had left.

The man before her snapped his fingers in front of her eyes, bringing her back. He was the most unlikely person in the world to offer her a lifeline. But he did. With very slow movements, he signed a question to her. "Are you deaf?"

A frisson of relief flowed through her. Fear still permeated her body, but at least someone understood the dilemma. She clutched her fingers together and nodded.

"FUCK!" REBEL EXPLODED, POUNDING DOUBLE FISTS ON the delicate desk. A white cup holding several pens fell over, and they rattled as they fell to the floor. The woman didn't move at the enormous sound. Her dilated eyes darted to the raging man and back to Railroad, who stayed in his crouch in front of her. He watched the rapid pulse beat in her neck and the fast breaths between her parted lips. *Pretty*, he thought as she licked them nervously. *Pretty, but going into shock.*

He slowly signed. "Breathe slower. All the way in. All the way out. We're not going to hurt you."

Her eyes went back to Rebel.

"He won't hurt you either. Promise."

Railroad noticed her skeptical expression, but she did take a few deep breaths and relaxed the rigidity of her shoulders. Fuck, it had been a long time since he'd done this, and he was rusty as hell.

"Who are you, and why are you in my house?"

Railroad followed the movements of her graceful hands and noticed they were bare. No rings. That was good. The blue was coming back to her irises, but as soon as she finished signing, she covered her chest again. The golden blonde hair didn't help cover anything, as she had it bound to the back of her head in a big clip. He kept his eyes on hers as she followed his gestures. "We're from the Dutchmen Motorcycle Club in Red Wing. We're looking for Piglet."

She followed his spelling, and her face grew more confused. "Piglet? That's someone's name?"

Railroad ignored the impatient noises behind him. "Road name. Your brother. Where is he?"

Shutters came down over the cerulean color, and the pretty woman's mouth pressed into a thin line. "Ezra and I haven't seen each other in years. I have no idea where he is now."

"He's your brother."

"Really? Only half, and he's the bad half."

The woman made such a disgusted expression,

Railroad nearly laughed. He didn't need her to speak to hear the sarcasm in the words.

"Deaf and mute, or just deaf?"

A pissed-off expression now showed on her face. "I can speak. I choose not to. Are you going to leave?"

"What the fuck did she say?" Rebel's agitated voice sounded behind him, but Railroad kept his position.

"Says she doesn't know anything."

"Fuck!" Rebel's hands hit the desk again, and this time the woman frowned.

"Please ask your friend not to tear up my desk or break my computer. This is my workplace, and I have deadlines to meet."

"You're a writer?"

"Editor."

"Never met an editor before."

"I wish you weren't meeting one now."

Rail chuckled at the woman's wit. Her hands were strong, with long tapered fingers and short nails. When she signed, her movements were fluid and precise. Dance-like. Her breasts swayed gently with each gesture, and Rail could see the darker outline of nipples under the thin white cloth before she covered them again. Pink? Peach? Or a color in between? Her robe was close by, and he could have snagged it for her but chose not to.

He stood up to leave. "She doesn't know anything."

Rebel sniffed hard and pulled at his red nose. "Ask her again. She's lying."

Rail frowned at the man. Rebel's drug use had gotten worse the closer his woman came to giving birth. Peebles had been a club sweetbutt for years and was happy to be one, until she fell in love with wild man Rebel and found herself pregnant. Since then she'd cleaned up her act and had made a home for them. Rebel started out strong in becoming a family man, but he'd fallen off the wagon lately. More than once.

The Dutchmen MC was only a remnant of what it once was. The latter part of the previous year had seen the club go through a big stinking pile of shit. Club rivalries between the Tiger Clan MC and the Dutchmen, with the added bonus of a Greek crime family, had led to massive upheaval in their little Minnesotan world. Many people were killed, and the Dutchmen lost their president, Iceman. He'd been the glue to hold the club together for many years, and without him, the MC was a thread away from chaos.

The remaining members voted Railroad in as president because it made sense. That mantle lay heavy on Rail's shoulders, and he hoped he could be at least half the leader Iceman was.

Rail borrowed a page from Ice's book and turned to stare coldly at Rebel. "Did you just give me an order?"

The lanky man dropped his shifting eyes and sniffed again, but he remained silent.

Rail put his attention back on the seated woman. She had re-clamped her arms tightly over her breasts and banded her generous thighs together. Her drawn-up legs made her soft lower belly pouch out a bit. Rail saw the pale skin beneath her belly button flush red under his perusal, and she moved one hand to try to cover that part too.

He chuckled again and raised his eyes to meet hers. "I'm sorry we disturbed you," he signed, hoping he remembered the correct ones. "It would be best if you didn't tell anyone about our visit. If Piglet makes contact, you've never heard of the Dutchmen, yeah?"

She blinked at him as if coming out of a trance. He watched her press her full lips together, and she raised her chin. Her gaze didn't waver, but she nodded sharply in affirmation.

"Good." He didn't feel the need to say goodbye and really didn't want to. He wished he had more questions. She would have to uncover those rounded breasts again to answer him.

Wishful thinking. He turned to his frustrated brothers and pointed to the door. "Let's go."

Nutter and Duke kept their silence, but Rebel cursed and yelled as he left. Rail sighed. Rebel skirted the edge of control, and it was only a matter of time before that ticking time bomb went off.

He glanced back at the woman and noticed the blush had faded. He leaned over her, bringing his face close to hers. Her eyes got big, and her lips parted. Rail nearly laughed again at how fast the color came back. Nice to know he had some effect on her like she did on him. Maybe it was his scars that alarmed her, but if he got a chance to see her nipples again, he bet he would find them puckered into little points.

Deliberately taking his time, he reached behind her, bringing his mouth inches from hers, and picked up one of her business cards. If he could have gotten away with it, he would have released her hair clip to see how long those golden waves would fall. When he stood back up, she let out the breath she'd been holding in a short rush. One half of his mouth rose in male triumph. He looked at the card.

"Nice to meet you, Gretchen Davonsky. I'm Railroad."

CHAPTER
TWO

The ride back to Red Wing was a short thirty minutes for the four bikers but a warm one, as the beginnings of summer were upon them. Minnesotans joked that their state had two seasons: "winter is coming" and "winter is here." Truthfully, the summer was typically hot and filled with festivals, fairs, and as much outdoor activity as possible. The Harbor Bar and Marina did a lot of business year-round, but summer was the boom time. Every chance they got outside of work, people spent their time on the Mississippi River, fishing, cruising, and lazing.

The doors to the clubhouse were open to allow air to circulate. It sat farther behind the Harbor Bar in its own fenced compound. The Dutchmen converted the old warehouse into their private place, but like many other buildings, it didn't have cooling units and only heaters for the long winter months.

All four bikes pulled into the gravel courtyard with muted roars. Rail glanced at his phone. Almost one in the morning, and there were still people inside partying. Light spilled from the open door, and bass-heavy music thumped in the air. Rebel had barely parked his ride before he dismounted and hurried into the noise. Rail frowned at the man's negligence and disrespect. Rebel probably didn't even realize what he did in his search for a drug hit.

Duke and Nutter followed him inside to their usual spots on a ring of mismatched sofas. The people occupying them moved, as it was understood this area was reserved for officers. Rail sat back on the "throne" and let out a huge sigh as fatigue set in. A club woman hurried over with three beers, her braless breasts moving freely under her crop top with every step. Not even the glimpses of her cherry nipples aroused his interest. He rubbed his thumb and index finger over his tired eyes.

"Fucking waste of time. We're back to square one." Nutter swallowed half his bottle in one go and burped out loud. "Why the fuck are we doing this again?"

Rail wanted to throw something at the man's head.

Duke saved him by interrupting. "You're a fucking moron. We've talked about this for weeks. There's a good chance Piglet stole a big pile of cash during that fucked-up FBI raid. Money that belongs to us from all the skimming Bookie did. Money we need back. Piglet played us all and got a lot of people killed. You remember the Dark Horses, right? Their club is wiped out. Gone because a brother betrayed them. The Dutchmen have to answer back and make sure that fucker pays in blood."

Nutter grumbled and put the bottle to his lips again. Rail wouldn't admit it out loud, but he did see the big man's point. Their archenemies in the Tiger Clan MC had also been decimated not long ago, the few surviving members scattered to the four winds. The Dark Horses MC was destroyed completely. Some of them patched over into the Dutchmen, but many had simply given up on the life and gone legit. The landscape had changed drastically for the club, and a few months later they were still recovering.

But their life had survived. The Dutchmen were in okay financial shape for now. The discovery of revenues and other money from Bookie's hidden accounts helped them get back on their feet and kept everyone with income so far. Camo had taken over the books, and the club had invested in the expansion of the marina and bar. That expansion had benefitted the entire membership as the revenues steadily climbed. So far, the only illegal thing they kept was the private poker games, but the drug smuggling hadn't started again. Rail didn't see a reason to go back to those lines, as the club's legal businesses were making enough money. As far as he was concerned, Piglet could keep whatever he stole. The risk was no longer worth the reward.

Not everyone agreed with him.

Rail leaned his head back and closed his eyes. These were the times he really missed Iceman. The former president had an aura of power and leadership that Rail could only hope to live up to. Ice had a way of speaking that made people pay attention, and he always swayed everyone to his point of view. Rail wondered for the hundred thousandth time what Ice would do in this situation.

A squeal pierced Rail's wandering thoughts. He cracked open his eyes and turned his head to see Rebel in a corner, his bare ass on display as he pounded away at a club girl. She had a huge smile on her face as she was pinned against the wall with her legs wrapped around the lanky man's waist.

"Oh, yeah, baby, give it to me," she gasped, not caring in the least that she had an audience.

Irritation surged through Rail's veins, and he

opened his mouth to yell, but this time Nutter beat him to it.

"For fuck's sake, take that shit to a room. We built the damn things so we don't have to watch your skinny humping ass!"

Nutter turned back around. "Stupid mother-fucker. Got a pregnant woman at home and can't keep his dick under control."

Rail wanted to laugh. Duke had no problem letting his mirth escape. "That's rich coming from you. Mama J still freezing you out?"

Nutter burped again and ignored Duke. Nutter had been one of the most notorious cheaters in the club. He had Janice, his ol' lady, at home, and Mimi, who had been his regular club piece on the side for years. Both women had produced children, and Mimi was about to pop with another one. Somehow he managed to cheat openly on both of them with other club women. Mama J finally drew a line in the sand and kicked him out. The sticky situation was made worse in that Nutter and Mama J were never officially married under the law, but she'd been given his patch. In their world, wearing a patch was the same as marriage, and a biker divorce could get just as ugly as a courthouse one. The biggest problem was Nutter still claimed he loved Mama J, but he couldn't leave Mimi.

Rebel ignored the yell and thrashed harder. The woman's shrieks of pleasure grated on Rail's last nerve.

"I'm done with this shit." He stood up and felt his back muscles seize up from the ride and from the tension in his body. Fuck, he was only thirty-nine but felt like an old man creaking through life.

He made his way to the expanded back hallway where new rooms had been added for club members to crash. Before, there had only been four available to officers, but now every member had a space. Rail went into the room he had inherited from Ice, which was the biggest and still the only one with a private bathroom. It was weird to him to occupy that space, but he enjoyed the privacy as well as the location. It muffled the noise from the main room.

He stripped and lay back on the bed, placing his hands behind his head to stare at the ceiling. A knock on his door disturbed his thoughts.

A club woman cracked open the door. "Hey, Rail. Thought you might like some company."

"Not tonight."

She hummed a little before closing the door and leaving him to his thoughts. He resumed his upward gaze, but his focus traveled elsewhere. Piglet was definitely a loose end, but the possibility of him doing any more harm to the club was little to none. All his allies were gone, including any connection to the Galanos family, from the debacle this past winter. Rail had no problem dropping the search for the man and letting it go, but the rest of the Dutchmen hierarchy wanted blood. The only lead they had was a rumor he was headed to Wabasha to hide with his sister. At least that's what Spider assumed when he spoke to the woman he'd been seeing in that sleepy town. From Gretchen's obvious distaste, she'd be one of the last people to harbor her brother.

Half brother, that was, and the bad half.

He reached into his pocket and pulled out the card. It was a pale cream color with an image on it of a river of pink ink flowing from a fountain pen. *"Gretchen Dolansky, line editing, proofreading, and formatting services."* The woman had a website, Facebook, Twitter, and Instagram pages promoting her business. He pulled out his phone and found her profile. The headshot appeared to be from a few years ago. She had quite a number of followers and what seemed to be a thriving trade. Apparently, her services were well in demand. He scrolled through the posts, skimming the recommendations and other bits about her life. *"Single, likes bowling, hates broccoli, loves taking cruises."* A selfie appeared under his thumb of Gretchen and two other women at a bar, all three grinning widely at the phone camera and holding up mixed cocktails. From the abundance of tanned skin on display and ocean view, it was clear they were on a ship in some tropical location. She looked radiant.

Rail ran his finger over her image. He recalled her plump thighs and belly showing in the plain pink underwear she'd been wearing. His taste tended to be for women on the larger side. He'd been with plenty of skinny ones too, but his favorite type had more meat on their bones. Gretchen had stayed seated throughout the encounter, but he could picture her ass. Nice and wide.

His dick stirred at the thought, but if he really wanted pussy, all he had to do was call the sweetbutt back, and she'd oblige. As president, he got his pick of whoever came to party in the clubhouse. Women vied to be in his bed, even the ones who shied away at his scarred face. He got nightly offers for sex or blow jobs, and most of the time he turned them down. It wasn't because he was a monk. He'd fucked plenty of women in the past, but the temporary release held no appeal for him anymore. Hell, he couldn't remember the last time he had a woman in his bed. Maybe that's why he was so fascinated with the pretty editor. He reached up and ran two fingers along the thin raised lines and wondered what Gretchen thought of them.

He scrolled through more posts. Memes, announcements, and more pics. There were more from the same cruise, including one of her in a bikini showing all that gorgeous flesh as she lay sleeping on a lounge chair with dark sunglasses covering her eyes. The next pic was of her and her friends in cocktail dresses, dancing on a big dance floor. They appeared to be humping each other. He swiped faster. Pic after pic appeared on her feed. At a conference with her hair up and glasses on her face. Throwing a bowling ball while sporting a look of deep concentration. Behind a podium signing while her friend stood next to her interpreting. He stopped on one that took his breath. A selfie of her lounging in an Adirondack chair, wearing a denim shirt and torn jeans. This was taken outside her house at a sunset with golden light gleaming from the slow-moving river in the background. Her face didn't have a provocative expression but rather one of contentment. He found it sexy as hell.

It didn't matter that he thought so, as she would never know. In all his weekly trips to Wabasha, he'd never seen her in that tiny town and likely never would again. He regarded the card and, on impulse, programmed her number into his phone.

The noise filtering from the main room sounded muffled back here, but it didn't stop the fatigue that stole over him. He reached over and clicked off the lamp, resigning himself to only fantasizing about the pretty deaf editor.

CHAPTER
THREE

"WATCH OUT, GIRLFRIEND. BEER COMING THROUGH."

Gretchen didn't have to hear the words to know what Penny's hip bump meant. She lifted her hands to take the giant bulbous glasses from her friend's hands and set them on the table between the hard plastic seats. A long shiny bowling lane stretched out in front of them with more on either side.

Once seated, Penny started signing. "I'm so glad you finally got out of that house. You've been holed up in there ever since you got here."

Gretchen sipped her beer and made a face. "I had deadlines to meet. Summer is my busiest time. That's why I come here every year—to check on Mom and Dad's house and get some downtime to get work done."

"Connecticut not treating you well?"

"Connecticut is fine. I just get more done here. No one bugs me, except you."

Penny laughed. "I bug you only because I'm one of the few people around here who can communicate with you."

Gretchen wrinkled her nose at her friend. "I can read lips, you know."

Penny picked up her own beer and took a healthy swallow. "Yes, but you said yourself, it's hard to do. People mumble or you have an unclear view, and even when you can watch a person's mouth, you can only pick up on so much." She put a wry look on her face. "I'm doing a piss-poor job of convincing you to move here permanently. Why in the world you would want to keep paying outrageous rent for that tiny postage stamp apartment when you can have a whole paid-for house is beyond me. I'm sure being in the big city is great, but this town is not so bad, especially considering what you do."

Gretchen turned her attention to the screen and typed in their names. "I've thought about it. There are advantages in both places. In Connecticut, there's a lot more for me to do and see, and a lot more resources, but you're right about the rent. It gets harder every year to make ends meet. If I lived here year-round, I could afford to be pickier about which gigs I take." She sipped her beer before continuing. "I like watching the river. The solitude. There's a kind of peace here that I haven't found anywhere else."

"Thus, a golden opportunity for you to move here. A nice big four-bedroom house with a big yard and docking pier. A view of the river every morning. All the peace you'd ever want. No rent or mortgage, and best of all—" Penny paused and threw up her hands like a game-show host. "—you'll have me."

"I've had you since the third grade. Go throw your balls so I can beat your ass."

Penny laughed and got up from her spot. "Such a delicate flower."

Penny hit a split and picked up the spare. Gretchen managed a strike. In the second frame, Penny cleared the pins while Gretchen knocked down eight. They traded back and forth for several rounds, laughing and poking fun at each other. Gretchen was happy and easier than she had been in a while. The pressure from several deadlines was over, and any more fears over her biker home invasion had dissipated. She hadn't seen a motorcycle on the road in just over a week. Only the lumbering farming tractors as they made their way to the fields of growing crops. The first few nights after seeing those bikers in her home, she didn't sleep well. She thought about calling the police, but what could she say? "Yes, they broke into my house. No, they didn't steal *anything. No, they didn't hurt me. No, they didn't damage my house, only somehow bypassed my security lights."* Wabasha wasn't exactly a hub of criminal activity, and Gretchen imagined the small police force would roll their collective eyes at her.

The only vivid memory of that night that stood out was the man with the scars on his face. Railroad, he called himself. The depth of his eyes as he gazed into hers was not easy to forget. He could be the villain or the hero in any one of the books she edited. She gave a little shudder as she recalled when he leaned in close to pluck one of her business cards from the desk. His mouth came within inches of hers. A deliberate move on his part? Maybe, but for that suspended moment, she'd wanted to move in and meet him halfway. She always did like the bad-boy antihero characters. Too bad they weren't real. Men in books were always sculpted like Greek gods and never had skin tags or bad breath or dandruff.

A scribbled note appeared in front of her eyes, breaking into her reverie. It read "Stalker alert. You have an admirer next door." She glanced up to see Penny picking up her ball and winking. Gretchen stuck out her tongue at her friend and, as best as she could, casually glanced over at the group of men setting up their game in the adjacent lanes. They wore blue league shirts, and their bowling shoes were actually nice.

Sure enough, a cute guy was staring at her. He was tall and had a nice body, from what she could tell. Probably maintained it from working one of the surrounding farms. He wasn't overly handsome but wasn't bad to look at either. If he was in a story, he'd be the sidekick or best friend of one of the main characters. He smiled big when he saw her looking back, and he gave a finger wave. She waved back out of reflex. He took that as encouragement and turned his attention to her.

His lips moved, and he stuck out his hand. Gretchen imagined he had just told her his name and gave her a greeting, but the movement of his lips was so shallow she couldn't make out anything. *Better now than later*, she thought as she signed to him. "I'm sorry, I don't understand."

The man's face dropped in a fascinating combination of confusion and horror. His mouth opened, and he spoke with overexaggeration that no one could miss.

"Are. You. Deaf?"

Gretchen didn't flinch. This wasn't the first time she'd met a hearing person who found communication difficult. She simply nodded. The man looked at her like a third eye had suddenly erupted from her forehead. He smiled awkwardly and nodded back at her before returning his attention to his league group.

"Another one bites the dust?" Penny signed as she sat down.

"He was yelling, wasn't he?"

Penny's eye roll affirmed Gretchen's suspicion. "Yes. If anyone had any doubts about your hearing, they know for sure now. Boggles the mind that someone would think shouting at a deaf person is going to do any good."

Gretchen smiled and laughed as she stood up to make her next round. "There are assholes everywhere. Best part about signing is he has no idea I just called him an asshole."

Penny blew her a raspberry.

Gretchen scooped up her ball and faced the lane. At one time it disturbed her when men rejected her because of her deafness. It wasn't her fault she had this disability, but she'd adapted to the challenges of the hearing world. "Deaf doesn't mean stupid" had become one of her favorite phrases. She traveled by herself, ordered food at restaurants, shopped, and attended festivals, conferences, and movies. She made a good living at editing, paid her bills, and saved for a future retirement. What else did she really need?

A man would be nice but wasn't necessary. The

last boyfriend she had was deaf, and they got along great, but their relationship lacked passion. Gretchen came to realize they were together out of convenience rather than love. She and Gary were still friends and FaceTimed once in a while, but for the most part, their breakup had no effect on either of them. Last she heard, Gary had found a hearing woman who accepted him, and they planned to get married this fall.

She took three steps and sent the ball rolling smoothly down the waxed wood surface. Out of the corner of her eye, she saw her admirer let loose his own ball. All ten pins fell on her side while only three went down on his. Gretchen couldn't help but smirk just a bit.

She and Penny finished their game, then left the bowling alley to go home. They'd switched to Diet Coke earlier as they were both driving. Gretchen spotted the police cars hiding in the next lot over from the bowling alley.

She pointed out the vehicles. "Sharks waiting for the minnows."

Penny nodded her acknowledgment. "Most excitement they ever get on a weekend is pulling over a drunk driver to give them a breathalyzer. Good night, girlfriend. Sleep well."

They hugged briefly and made tentative plans for

their next bowling night. Penny once again mentioned joining a league, and Gretchen responded with her usual "Someday."

The drive home was uneventful. The headlights from her car flashed over the front of the house. She'd left on the porch light that now had a halo of miller moths flying around it. After locking up, she walked into the large kitchen at the back of the house and poured a glass of wine. The wide window in the dining area showed moonlight sparkling on the lazy moving water just beyond the private boat pier at the bottom of the shallow hill. Gretchen remembered only once during her childhood that the river swelled high enough to flood the house's partial basement.

That was the first time her parents discovered Ezra's drug stash. A pile of wet baggies filled with what looked to her like tea leaves. She'd been six at the time, and Ezra had been sixteen. There was a lot of yelling, finger-pointing, and tears. Gretchen's memories of Ezra consisted of him always being angry, constantly arguing with their father, and being mean to his stepmother. Gretchen, he simply ignored. It wasn't long after the drug incident that Ezra disappeared. He came back a few times over the years, mostly to ask for money. The last time she saw him was after their father's funeral when he'd come to find out if he had inherited anything. When he found out there was nothing for him, he cursed and left. She hadn't seen or heard from him since.

Why the Dutchmen MC wanted him was a mystery—one she didn't care to find out. Many of the books she edited were motorcycle club romances, and she loved them, but seeing a club up close and personal was much different from seeing them on paper. Hot-bodied, gorgeous-haired bad boys who set women on fire with want were a far cry from the men who had invaded her house.

Except for Railroad. He could be in a book with his good looks and piercing dark gray eyes. Perhaps he had a touch of Native American in him with that rich black hair swept back from his forehead and those high cheekbones. His intense expression burned behind those eyes, and she found herself thinking about him. A lot. Add in his knowledge of sign language, and he had the perfect combination of attributes for a book hero.

Or at least the look of one. He might be the biggest asshole in the world, for as much as she knew about him. Keeping the other bikers from hurting her or tearing up her house didn't mean he was a good person. She would put him down in the category of intriguing for now. *I wonder what he would have done if I'd kissed him?*

She sipped her wine and stared out into the clear

night. Whatever trouble Ezra had gotten into wasn't her problem, and she had no plans to change that. The chances of running into Railroad again were slim to none; therefore, she could file his handsome face away as fodder for another time. She placed the empty glass in the sink and climbed the steps to her bedroom.

CHAPTER
FOUR

PIGLET WIPED THE SWEAT FROM HIS BROW AND STUCK HIS trembling hands in the pockets of his work pants. He was on edge and ready to explode, mainly from a forced withdrawal from smoking. Here on the farm, no one was allowed to drink or smoke. His gut twisted again, but he kept his breakfast down. This time. He wondered why he stayed.

Because this place offered the sanctuary he needed. The farm was almost totally off the grid and isolated. Way too many people were searching for him, and he didn't want to be found by any of them. The remnants of the Tiger Clan MC; the FBI and authorities; the former members of his own club, the Dark Horses MC; and, of course, the Dutchmen MC. All of them wanted a piece of him or simply to kill him.

He had no illusions as to why. His actions as a double agent between the clubs had led to the deaths of many of his biker brothers, including Musicman, the late president of the Dark Horses. Betrayal like that could not go unanswered, and Piglet knew his days were numbered. He might have had a chance at surviving if he had faced the Dutchmen head-on and confessed to them. Perhaps Railroad might have only blacked out his ink and excommunicated him. If Iceman was still in charge, he'd be dead the moment he set foot in the Dutchmen's compound.

Instead, he had run the night the world exploded. The Tiger Clan had been on the brink of destroying the Dutchmen and cementing an alliance with a Greek crime family when Iceman brought a bomb to the party. Actually, he'd ridden it in the form of his big black Harley right up to the front door of the Tiger Clan compound. Some dumbass moved it to the courtyard, smack in the middle of the complex, and set it off. What followed was total chaos filled with choking smoke, fire, and flying bullets that took out most of the key players. Coupled with a botched FBI raid at the same time, the shit show hit the national airwaves with an aerial view of the ruined building. Months later, the authorities were still picking through the debris and searching for those who had escaped.

Piglet had been in the Quonset hut, watching the slow torture of Iceman at the hands of Grizzly, the Tiger Clan president, when all hell broke loose. Somehow, he got out with his skin hole-free and found his way into the only part of the building still standing. He spotted Carrie, Grizzly's private whore, running away with a bulging duffel bag. A brick of money dropped from it as she dashed through the hazy air. On impulse, he ran to Grizzly's room and started jerking open the drawers. He found one stuffed with stacks of cash and figured Carrie had grabbed as much as she could carry and ran. He followed her idea, seizing handfuls of money and shoving whatever his hands landed on into his pockets as fast as he could. The *rat-tat-tat* of automatic fire echoed, and he snatched up one of the handguns Grizzly left out.

It was a miracle he made it to his bike and an even bigger one that he got away. One man tried to stop him, and Piglet shot him in the face. Might have been FBI or Tiger Clan or a client from the club's whorehouse. He didn't know or care.

Later that night, he sat in the seediest motel ever created and watched the news of the burning compound. The footage was playing on repeat, and he strained his eyes for a glimpse of himself that might leave a clue about his escape. There was a split-second image of Carrie, but that was all.

Piglet reached for his customary pack of cigarettes and cursed when his fingers touched empty air. "Fuck!"

"What seems to be the problem, Brother Ezra?"

Piglet looked up to see Matthias walking toward him. His old-school friend had appeared out of the blue one afternoon a few weeks after the explosion. Piglet had been riding around the southern part of the state, staying in one cheap motel after another, trying to figure out a direction or an ally. The money he stole seemed substantial at the time but was almost gone. He had come up with nothing until running into Matthias at the docks in Hastings. Matthias offered him a place to stay for a while, and here he was, at this giant farm complex.

He'd been surprised at how primitive it was compared to the rest of the world. Very few people had cell phones. Most of the men lived in barracks, while others were in huts scattered around the property. There was a large farmhouse for the owners, but he hadn't been inside yet. Matthias told him it was by invitation only. Something about separating wheat from chaff that made no sense. He'd been given a "guest hut," which wasn't much more than a small one-room camping cabin, but it was free and private.

A shudder ran down his body, and he clenched his teeth. The nicotine withdrawal had his head pounding in tandem with his belly.

"Evil still working its way out, eh?"

Piglet growled. "I don't think I'd have come here if I knew you would take away my cigarettes."

Matthias laughed. "You said yourself it's a bad habit and an expensive one. Besides, we didn't take them away. You smoked your last pack and haven't gone to get another one."

"My bike is out of gas, and I don't have any more money."

Matthias *tched* his teeth. "That brings me to what I wanted to talk to you about. Everyone here works with their given talents, and I think it's time for you to earn your keep. You mentioned you were a good mechanic, and we need someone to do some maintenance on the farm equipment. We have tractors that haven't moved in years, and with the size of this harvest, every vehicle has to be used. We'd like you to help with that. In return, you can stay as long as you like. You'll have to move into the barracks with the other men, but you'll have a bed, plenty of food, and other privileges."

Piglet's stomach flipped as he nodded. "Sure, I can do that. You guys got me out of a real mess, and I'm grateful to you."

Matthias's smile resembled that of a used car salesman. "No problem, brother. We just want to live our lives without interference from anyone else. The more self-sufficient we are, the less reliant on government handouts we become. Way too many people are letting the government take control, and that's not going to happen here. We take care of our own, and if the world stopped tomorrow, we'd still be here."

Piglet didn't understand half of what Matthias was saying, but at the moment, his head was hurting too bad for him to care.

"You look terrible, Ezra. Maybe you should visit one of the comfort women."

Piglet frowned. "What are you talking about?"

Matthias smiled again. "I can't believe I didn't tell you about the comfort women. That's one of the privileges of the single men who work and live in the barracks." He pointed behind the long building. "All those cabins back there? They belong to a group of women we keep for relief. We have so many hard-working men toiling in the fields, working the sheds, and keeping the grounds up. It's a lot of effort, and at the end of the day, they need a way to relax. If you become a working part of the farm, you have the right to visit those women."

Piglet chuffed with humor. "You keep a stable of whores to fuck?"

Matthias's face dropped, though he somehow managed to keep his smile. "Everyone has a role to play here. The men work, and the women provide ease. There aren't enough of them to give every man a wife, therefore we have comfort women whose job it is to provide ease to the men who don't have wives. But they're not whores. They don't get paid. It's simply another form of work that benefits the farm."

Piglet snorted. In his mind, it sounded a lot like the whorehouse kept by the Tiger Clan for revenue. Whatever Matthias wanted to call it, he didn't really care. "Sounds good to me. When can I go?"

"Anytime you wish. Now, in fact, but I'd rather you take a look at the tractors first. Makes it look better to the big boss that you're willing to be a part of the farm operations, yeah?"

"Yeah, I get it. Work before play."

Matthias clapped a hand on Piglet's shoulder. "Great. I'll tell Brother Zachariah you're willing to help us. When you go visit the cabins, ask for Leah. She's my favorite."

Piglet watched Matthias walk away before heading to the large building that housed the farm machinery. There was something both creepy and appealing about the man. It was weird how he talked about "brother this" and "brother that," kinda like one of those crazy TV preachers.

There was still a lot Piglet hadn't yet seen on the farm. The main complex was surrounded by a variety of massive crop fields, and from everything he'd learned these past weeks, Matthias was heir apparent to the whole enchilada. The mysterious Brother Zachariah remained the head honcho, but he was sick or something. He rarely came out of the monstrous farmhouse.

Piglet entered the garage area and saw several men examining a broken tractor. "Matthias asked me to help out. I know a thing or two about fixing engines."

One of the men greeted him with a firm hand-shake and a laugh. "Welcome, lay-brother. We need an expert mechanic bad."

Piglet preened a little. He liked being called an expert, and in truth, he was good at this kind of work. He found the problem in less than ten minutes. The engines fired up with a rapid chugging sound, and the men around him cheered.

For the first time since he ran from trouble, Piglet found himself wanted and happy.

CHAPTER
FIVE

Rail cut off the engine of his bike, and the rumbling machine fell silent. He took in the columned façade of the Hidden Acres Retirement Home. There was lots of color, with blooming flowers, plants, and greenery decorating the outside. The inside was filled with nice-looking furniture, decorative carpet, and more flowers in vases. The air was scented with lemon polish, as the place got spit shined on a daily basis. His jeans, riding boots, and club cut were clearly way out of place in this posh environment as he approached the front desk, but he didn't care. The only reason he ever came to this loathsome town was to see the one person in the world he loved outside of the club.

Scratch that. He now had a second reason to take a ride to Wabasha. His mind pulled up the picture of the blue-eyed woman sitting in her underwear, defiant even when trying to cover her breasts. Then he thought about the beautiful shot of her sitting outside and watching the river. If he showed up at her house a second time, what would she do? Invite him in? He indulged himself in a brief fantasy in which he settled in one of the Adirondack chairs and watched the fading sun with her. He'd have a beer, but she'd be drinking wine. Too classy for beer. They'd sit side by side for a while and just listen to the water and the night sounds starting up. Well, at least he would hear them. She would sip her wine and admire the sparkling water in the golden twilight. Then she'd stand, take his hand, and lead him to her bedroom, where he'd ride that fine ass of hers until they were both exhausted from coming so many times.

He gave a mental laugh. Who was he kidding? If she had a gun, she'd probably shoot his ass before he lifted a foot onto the first porch step.

He leaned on the front counter. "Railroad to see Flora Jones."

The cute receptionist smiled and blushed as she dropped her eyes. "Hi, Rail. Flora is in the courtyard if you want to join her."

Rail couldn't remember her name but figured it wouldn't take much for him to get her into bed. This wasn't the first time she'd reacted this way when he spoke to her. It wasn't hard to see the schoolgirl crush directed at him. Not going there. "Penny with her?"

"Yes. She's got everything worked out for you."

He nodded and walked down the hallway to the huge lounging area and through the french doors that opened onto a wide brick patio and lush green courtyard.

A tiny African American woman sitting at an umbrella-covered table raised a thin hand and called out to him. "Railroad, my boy! I'm so glad you've come to see me." A huge grin burst across her wrinkled face, and she pushed her wheelchair back to turn and face him.

"How are you doin', Grams?" He leaned down to hug the frail woman. At one time in his life, Flora had been a larger-than-life powerhouse. Now in her mid-nineties, she had shrunk with age but was no less aware of the world around her. Some people thought it odd that he called the woman his grandmother, as it was obvious there was no blood relation between them. Still, this was the woman who raised him. He'd never known his birth mother and had forgotten most of the memories he had of his early childhood. Flora had been a grandma to plenty of boys in the group home, but with Rail, the relationship was special.

"If I was any better, they'd tax me or make me illegal. Now, whatcha got in the bag for me?"

Rail chuckled at the old woman's enthusiasm. "*Lefse*. A friend of mine bakes them from time to time. I asked her to make some extra to bring to you."

He'd gone by Mama J's house to drop off a set of shelves she needed and to check on her. He'd found her at the stove making the traditional Norwegian sweet treat while the horde of Nutter's children ran around her legs and through the house. Several cabinet drawers had broken tracks, and the kitchen faucet had a continuous drip. Rail made a mental note to go back and fix those things for her if Nutter didn't.

"Is she single?" The old woman's eyes glittered at him.

"Separated, but even if she was, we're friends. Don't get your hopes up."

Flora blew a raspberry. "Friends make the best lovers. You should try it sometime."

Rail laughed. "I don't have time for that right now, Grams. I got a lot going on at the club and at the marina. No time for anything else."

"Child, you need to stop worrying about every-thing and everyone. God's got this under control."

"God doesn't live in my neighborhood."

"He's there if you let him in."

Rail's heart clenched. He had it in him to respect other people's ideas, but he didn't like having conversations about them. "Grams, we've talked about this. I'm not convinced there is a God out there, and if there was, where the hell is he when bad shit happens?"

Flora picked up a *lefse* roll and bit into it. "Mmmm, this is so good. You're right that bad shit happens to people, but that's not God's fault. What He does is give us the strength to get through those times and find some good in them. You remember my friends from Detroit? Maudie and her son? She lost her husband to cancer, and those medical bills were eating her alive. Worked her fingers to the bone to keep what she did have, and through it all, she kept smiling. Even when her house burned to the ground. Lost everything. But"—she held up a thin finger—"the community came together and raised the money she needed. Even better, it was enough to send her son to school. Now that man is a doctor and takes care of his mama, plus a whole lot of other people in the neighborhood that loved and supported them in their time of need. That's my proof God exists."

Rail fell silent. Experience taught him long ago that his Grams's faith was unshakeable. She didn't preach or beat him over the head with it, but she never hid her belief from him. He knew better than to get into a debate with the woman, as many things she said made sense and often disturbed him.

He crossed his arms and tried to give the old woman a stern Dutchmen stare. "Are we going to lunch or not?"

She cackled. "Look at you, being all serious, trying to put me in my place. Yes, I'm ready to go anytime."

Penny walked up in her scrubs with her purse. "The van is waiting outside." She spun a set of keys around her finger.

Rail saw the sparkle in her greeting. Penny was no stranger and often accompanied him and his Grams. She'd been in the clubhouse a few times over the years and even shared his bed on a couple drunken nights, but she never became a regular. He liked her, but not enough to pursue anything else. He didn't do relationships or want an old lady in his life. The only woman he might have considered was happily married and living in the Outer Banks of North Carolina. He wished her well.

Rail hated riding in the van, but with Flora bound to a wheelchair now, that was his only option of transport. Penny was the only person authorized to use the awkward vehicle, so she drove while his Grams regaled him with commentary on the retirement home food service, the fine weather, and the latest gossip of who was doing what with whom.

"Mrs. Cara Kelly's been widowed three times already, and it looks like Mr. Andrew Folson is gonna be number four. Ms. Becca Ridenhour caught sight of him coming out of her room several mornings in a row."

Penny giggled and slapped a hand over her mouth as she pulled into the parking lot of Slippery's Tavern, a riverside restaurant with a beautiful view of the moving water. "Oh my God, are you serious? He's been getting it on with Ms. Reba, and now he's added Ms. Cara to his harem? Way to go, Andy."

Rail blinked as he lowered the power chair lift to the ground. "Aren't they too old for sex?"

Flora blew out a raspberry. "If he can still function, I don't see why."

Rail laughed and shook his head. "That's a visual I could've gone my entire life without thinking about."

Flora cackled and clapped her hands. "Now, don't you try to play Little Mr. Innocent. I remember walking in on you spanking the monkey more than once."

"Jesus, Grams, keep it down. Do you have to remind me?" Rail looked around at the other patrons waiting to be seated. They seemed to be occupied with their phones, but a couple of the women sent snickers and glances his way.

"Weird to hear a ninety-some-year-old woman talk about masturbation, eh?" Penny's eyes gleamed with amusement. "I'll tell you, Rail, working at the retirement home is better than any soap opera plot."

Rail groaned and did his best to ignore the two women. It amazed him that he, a badass biker, feared by so many men, ruthless in nature, craved by women, would revert back to a ten-year-old boy around his Grams. The old woman maneuvered her power chair to an outdoor table on the deck to wait for the waitress.

The river flowed easily and deceptively smooth. Rail watched the peaceful movement and thought with some irony about the secrets this long tributary held. His club had used the river for smuggling and transporting illegal prescription drugs from Canada for years. Bodies had ended up in the depths as the Dutchmen fought wars with other MCs to keep their trade. Some of those bodies were ones he'd helped put there, and now he would be the one to try to bring the MC out of the criminal world to go legit. The world around him was rapidly changing, yet the water kept flowing.

"Pretty, isn't it?" Flora remarked. "That river's been here since the world started, and I bet it will be there when it ends."

"Oh, so it's going to be one of those philosophical lunches, eh?" Penny sat down on a wooden chair and squirted hand sanitizer into one palm.

"Not really. I'm just making a comparison. There's no end to the Mighty Mississippi, but I can feel it's coming for me. My time on this earth isn't for much longer, and I'm hoping heaven has a spot like this for me. Somewhere I can watch the water flow forever."

Rail turned away from the view. He was no stranger to death and had helped more than one man on his way to the Grim Reaper. This past year had been filled with people in his life dying, but hearing Flora talk about it disturbed him. "Don't talk like that, Grams."

Her face wrinkled even more as she smiled. "Railroad, my precious, come sit with me." She took his hand and gripped it as hard as she could. "I'm gonna pass from this world into the next someday. It's part of life everlasting, and every living thing that draws breath will face that same reckoning sooner or later. I have no regrets in my life, and I pray that when I stand before my Savior, He looks down on me and says, 'Well done.'"

A bug-like premonition burrowed into Rail's mind, and his heart jumped. It sounded like his beloved Grams was trying to warn him of the near future. He wasn't ready for it, but he recognized it would happen whether he wanted it to or not. He squeezed her small hand lightly. "If there's a heaven, Grams, I'm sure you'll be there."

He was sure that with all his sins, he'd be going in the opposite direction.

"Oh! Oh! Oh!" Penny's eyes widened, and she started gesturing and waving like crazy. "That's my best friend over there. Wave at her so she'll see us!"

Rail glanced over to see a tall blonde woman. Awareness hit him as he identified the pretty editor who had wormed her way into his mind. She spotted Penny's wild movements and waved back. The nurse made several come-here motions, and Gretchen complied.

Rail stayed still as the woman approached, wondering how she would react when she saw him. She was dressed in what he guessed was business casual. A navy pencil skirt stretched across her generous hips and ended just above her knees. The outline of a plain bra showed beneath a thin sleeveless white blouse, and her hair was twisted up into a roll at the back of her head. She wore light makeup that enhanced her eyes and full mouth. Rail's groin tightened. She was even more alluring in clothing than when she sat in front of him half naked. She held her head high and gave off an aura of confidence with her long strides.

Two distinct realizations hit Rail. First, he wanted this woman. Second, she was way out of his league.

As she approached the table, her eyes and smile shone, and she signed a greeting. "Hi, Penny. Nice day." She stopped, and her face fell a bit as she realized who else sat at the table. Rail saw it in her eyes when she decided her play was to ignore him. It bothered him, but he let it go. At least for now.

"Hi, yourself. This is Flora from the retirement home and her grandson, Railroad. And yes, that's his real name, or at least the only one he claims. What are you doing here all dressed up?"

Gretchen tore her eyes away from Rail's and wrinkled her nose as she answered. "I was supposed to meet a new client here, but he just texted me to say he has to reschedule."

"That sucks. It would be nice if he could have canceled before you got here, but since he didn't, how 'bout joining us?"

Gretchen shook her head, but Rail signed this time. "Stay. Please."

Her eyes met his, and for a moment, he thought she would sneer at him and walk away. He wouldn't blame her, since their first and only meeting consisted of her being half naked and him looming over her in scary biker form. Instead, what he saw in the blue depths was speculation.

Flora reacted with delight. "Oh my goodness, it's been such a long time since I used my ASL skills. This is wonderful. Sit down and tell me all about yourself, child."

Gretchen smiled. The old woman's gestures were feeble, but Gretchen clearly understood them. She smoothed her skirt and sat next to him across from Flora. Rail let out a breath he hadn't known he was holding and caught a whiff of the light perfume Gretchen wore. Something floral. He inhaled deeper.

"Gretchen is a thirty-six-year-old woman, Flora." Penny laughed as she signed while saying the words out loud. "Hardly a kid."

Flora blew a raspberry at Penny. "And I'm ninety-seven. Everyone is a child when you're as old as I am. Now, talk to me, sweetie. Are you single?"

Rail choked a bit. The waitress came up and took everyone's order, but that didn't stop Flora for long.

The information kept flowing just like the river, and Rail found himself fascinated as well as embarrassed.

"An editor! That's wonderful. What an interesting job. What do you work on?"

"Mostly line and content edits for romance novels and novellas. The client I was supposed to meet today has something else for me. He is writing his father's memoirs, and I thought it would be nice to do something different. Your signing is very good."

"Thank you, child. I learned it when I was in college to become a specialized caregiver for children. In fact, I taught my Rail when he was a boy. When he first came to the group home, he didn't say a word to anyone for almost two years. Doctors couldn't find a thing wrong with his hearing. He just didn't talk. Came in malnourished and so underweight, we all thought he was seven or eight when he was closer to ten. Took me weeks to get him to trust me, but when he did, he started signing and never stopped. Starved for attention as much as nourishment for his body. We did just fine, keeping to ourselves, didn't we, precious?"

Rail growled a low "Grams," but his warning might as well have been silent for all the attention Flora paid to it.

"Grew up to become a wonderful man. All my other boys graduated and left, but Rail comes to see me every week and takes me out to lunch sometimes. Always been special to me. I never had kids of my own, but all my boys called me Grandma. To Rail, I'm Grams. That's my favorite."

"Thanks for embarrassing the shit out of me," Rail groused as he leaned back and did his best to ignore the avalanche of information pouring from Flora's mouth and hands. "You can stop sharing my entire history anytime."

She tapped his hand and signed as she spoke. "There's nothing you need to be ashamed of, child. Had a rough start, that's for sure, but look at you now. Doing good and living your life. The only shame is not sharing that life with someone."

"Don't start, Grams."

Flora pealed with laughter. "Look at my boy, trying to be all tough with me. Love you to the moon and back, precious."

Rail couldn't stay angry at Flora. She was right, as she had been the anchoring rock that held him together for years. Her steady faith kept him sane and opened the world to him at a time when he was in his most vulnerable state.

Thankfully, the waitress came back with their food. He got his usual walleye sandwich basket. Penny ordered the fish tacos, and both Flora and Gretchen had bowls of Slippery's signature jambalaya. Rail noticed the shakiness of Flora's hands as she spooned up the spicy stew, but no one minded the mess.

Gretchen sat to his right, and he was aware of her every movement, every gesture, every facial expression. He glanced at her lap, where a paper napkin lay spread over her thick thighs. He recalled what they looked like bare and imagined himself peeling up that tight pencil skirt to free them from the constraint. Then he would bend her over and view that luscious ass high in the air before....

Fuck, he could feel himself getting hard and needed to shut this shit down. "I need to get back to the marina soon. There's work that needs to be done, and I can't trust anyone there to do it right." He signed everything he spoke, mainly because he didn't want to be rude, but he didn't look at Gretchen again.

Flora nodded. "I understand, precious. I'm getting tired and need my afternoon nap. I love going places with you, but I get winded more and more each time I do."

Rail's gut twisted. As much as he didn't want it to be true, his Grams was getting older and frailer at every visit. He vowed to be more careful with her in the future.

The waitress came, and he paid the bill for all four

of them. Gretchen tried to protest, but he waved her away. "I owe you. My Grams means the world to me, and I appreciate you keeping our business private. Thank you," he signed discreetly.

Penny and Flora were fussing with the power chair's maneuvering and didn't see it. Gretchen looked at Flora, and her face softened. Rail's breath caught. She simply signed back, "You're welcome," and didn't elaborate.

Flora dozed off on the trip back to the retirement home, and Rail had to push the power chair into the facility.

Penny checked them back in at the reception desk and handed the van keys to the girl behind it. "I've got her if you need to go," she said to Rail.

"I'll see her to her room."

The tiny room wasn't much bigger than one found in a college dormitory, but the walls were full of pictures. Rail recognized many of them, as they were of the boys he grew up with in the group home. There was one of him and Tiny M playing soccer in the yard with Iceman and Carter. Another one of Flora smiling as she read to a group of boys seated on the floor around her. His favorite was the one she kept by her bedside: a framed picture of him as a young boy wrapped in her loving arms and snuggled into her bosom, her head resting on his as if nothing in the world could separate them. He remembered the day that photo was taken. It was the moment he finally spoke aloud and named Flora "Grams." She'd hugged him close and told him how much she loved him.

"I'm not sleeping. I'm just resting my eyes a bit," Flora grumbled as Rail transferred her from the chair to the bed.

"Rest your eyes all you want, Grams. I'll come see you next week." He kissed her gray head, but she was already asleep.

Penny nodded at him as his lengthy strides carried him down the long hallway and out the front door. The finger wave from the receptionist went unanswered as he left. The roar of his bike as he fired her up helped keep his emotions at bay. Once his helmet was on and he got on the road back to Red Wing, he could let the tears fall, as there was no one to see them.

GRETCHEN STOPPED AT THE GROCERY STORE ON HER WAY home to pick up a few things. It was hard to cook for one, but she'd come up with several single-serving recipes over the years. Nice not to rely on what she called freezer fodder—things like stacks of frozen dinners, personal pizzas, and burritos.

She pushed the cart up and down the aisles. Peanut butter, eggs, spinach wraps, mustard. She randomly selected items from her mental list. She probably should have written one but didn't think about it before she left the house to meet with this client. A man who found her on Facebook and messaged her about editing his book of memoirs. Different and intriguing from her normal genre, but it didn't really matter what the material was. Grammar was still grammar, and spelling was still spelling. The man had been delighted to find out she was local and insisted he meet her face-to-face. Most of her clients came from the internet, and even though friendships developed, she'd never laid eyes on them.

Too bad the guy had to cancel.

She picked up a bag of ground coffee. Sumatra. She paused as she ran her finger over the colorful package. Did Railroad drink coffee? She bet he did. Black and strong enough to stand a spoon up in it. Railroad. The man had popped up daily in her thoughts from the moment she first saw him. The woman he called Grams had no familial relation to him, but something about the way he treated the old woman touched her. The man was a mystery. He was a biker in an MC with a wild and criminal reputation, yet he made time to spend with the elderly Flora. He signed with fairly coherent ASL. He was single, handsome with a nice body... and scarred. She could sense there was more bubbling under the surface with this man. A depth that very few knew about and had the desire to plumb. She was curious as hell, but asking Penny about him would get her friend started on Gretchen's singlehood, and that was a road she did not want to travel.

Gretchen raised two fingers and traced the area on her face that paralleled Rail's scars. *I wonder how he got them.*

CHAPTER
SIX

"TRY IT NOW," PIGLET YELLED FROM HIS CROUCHED position next to a green John Deere tractor. It was a big one with back wheels as high as his head. There were ten more of these monsters lined up for him to fix.

The engine sputtered and then caught with a dull *lug-lug-lug*.

"Yes!" Nathaniel pumped his fist in the air. The yellow-haired giant grinned at him from the open cab of the vehicle. "Victory at last."

Piglet grinned back at the man's enthusiasm. Nathaniel wasn't the smartest guy on the farm, but he was the most fun. He loved to clean the tools at the end of the day and sweep the debris from the garage. His happiness and pride in those small tasks made him seem childlike, and he basked in the praise he got for finishing those jobs. Nothing made him happier than watching Piglet successfully fix a piece of equipment. The tractors were his favorite.

"Let's take it out for a spin. Brother David said they needed another tractor in the west field. We should take this to them."

Piglet slammed the cover on the running engine. "We could, but how will we get back if we drive it out that far?"

Nathaniel's face fell, and his big eyes jiggled back and forth like they did when he was thinking hard. "I don't know."

Piglet cleaned his greasy hands on a shop towel. "It's getting close to supper. Maybe we can test drive it partway and come back. I'll let you tell Brother David he can start it up in the morning before the brothers head to the fields."

Nathaniel's eyes lit up. "Yeah! Great idea! You're the best, Ezra."

Piglet smiled at the man's renewed joy. At one time in his life, Piglet would want nothing to do with anyone that slow in the brain, but Nathaniel was fun to be around. Always happy, and that shit was nice to see.

They climbed up into the cab. "Let's go."

"Let's go!" repeated Nathaniel.

The tractor lurched as the simple man put it into gear and moved it out into the bright sunlight.

Rain clouds were gathering on the horizon, and Piglet hoped they would stay away until the men got back to their quarters for the night. Nathaniel beamed as the tractor bounced along the worn dirt road between fields. Green met their eyes everywhere, the bright color of growing plants, and the smell of farm life hovered in the air.

Piglet noticed a group of workers in the far end working the long rows of sugar beets. He'd not seen a lot of people who actually did the field work. Most of the brothers drove the tractors and combines but didn't do a lot of the hands-on stuff.

He pointed them out to Nathaniel. "Itinerants?"

"What's a itnerant?"

"Field hands that move from place to place for work."

The tractor slowed as Nathaniel donned his thinking face. "No, they live here. Just not with us."

Piglet couldn't see much of the workers, only their small bent forms as they tended the green plants. "It's a big farm, but I haven't seen them before. They got a tent city or something?"

"What's a tent city?"

Piglet refrained from rolling his eyes. "Don't worry about it." He wondered sometimes about the big man. Nathaniel was somewhere in his twenties, but his mind was stuck in elementary school. He had some rudimentary education, but anything beyond simple math and early reading skills was beyond him. Piglet had put the lack of skills down to him being mentally challenged, but then again, perhaps the isolation of the farm played a factor. No TV, internet, radio, newspapers, or books other than tech manuals existed here. Piglet's cell phone had been cut off since he never paid the bill, and it had lost its charge a long time ago. There was a big world beyond the borders of this farm, and not many people ventured beyond them. This bugged him a lot, but in truth, Nathaniel did better here in this private little world. If he were to ever walk into a place like the Tiger Clan compound, or even just an average biker bar, he'd get eaten alive.

They passed another field, this one dotted with stubble. A work truck sat in the middle of the flat, bare ground, surrounded by a number of men doing something to it. Nathaniel made a noise in his throat and fell quiet, his normal happy chatter subdued.

"What's going on over there?"

Nathaniel shook his head and refused to answer.

Piglet kept his eyes trained on the sight, out of curiosity more than anything else. Heavy sacks were pulled from the back of the truck, and it looked like the men were burying them.

"Holy fuck, are those bodies?" He shouted the question before he thought about it.

"No, it's just chaff. That's all." Nathaniel sped by the sight as if eager to put it behind him. "Just chaff."

CHAPTER
SEVEN

"SIXTEEN-YEAR-OLD HAILEY CREST HAS BEEN MISSING since late Sunday evening. She was last seen leaving Randy's Burgers in Red Wing, Minnesota, where she works at the counter and didn't arrive home last night. Police are investigating this as a kidnapping. If anyone has any information, please contact..."

Rail stood up from a boat engine and felt the muscles in his back protest from his prolonged bent-over position. He wiped his hands on a clean micro towel that smeared the oil residue more than cleaned it off. The old radio was on for background noise more than anything else as he tried to distract himself with work. Twin spots of pain pulsed in either of his temples as his brain sifted and re-sifted thoughts that wouldn't resolve.

Even after chapel yesterday, the Dutchmen remained torn. Half wanted to go back to the way they made money when Iceman was in charge, and the other half wanted to go legit and give up any more illegal business.

Duke had spoken his mind during the meeting. He'd finally decided Rail was right, that chasing Piglet for revenge was a waste of time and resources. "Too damn risky anymore," he said. "We've lost people this past year. Xman and Blaze got killed ugly and in pain, and for what? So someone else can line their pockets with our blood? Fuck, no. We have the bar. We have the marina. We can expand and do other things." He pierced the other members around the table with his gaze. "It's time for the Dutchmen to evolve."

Rebel argued to go back to smuggling prescription medications over the Canadian border. "We're a fucking biker club. We don't do that office crap or nine-to-five bullshit. Find your fucking sack and quit being a fucking pussy. Let's do what we know."

Camo was for going legit. Desktop backed up Rebel. Spider tended toward the legit side but was teetering. Nutter was on the fence but leaning to staying out of the drug trade.

Only Rebel and Desktop were still dead set on

finding Piglet and making him pay for betraying his club brothers. Rail could understand Desktop more, as the man Piglet helped kill had been his club president. Rebel was a wild card.

Then there was Gretchen. She constantly hovered in his mind, but not in an annoying way. Thoughts such as *What is she doing now?* and *What is her favorite food?* and *What does she taste like?* were interspersed between *How do I keep Rebel from causing another war?* and *How do I convince Desktop to drop this insane vendetta?* and *I wish Nutter would make a fucking decision about his women.*

He put the cover over the engine and fired it up. The *vroom* it made gave him some satisfaction. At least one task had been completed successfully today.

He spotted Camo pulling into the dirt parking lot, and his gut fell. By the expression on the man's face, it was not good news.

"You remember Barker, the hangaround Musicman was considering for the Dark Horses before he was killed? I got a call from him this morning. Says he saw someone who looked a lot like Piglet working at the docks some weeks ago. Couldn't say for sure, but it makes sense as that was the same place we did a lot of business. Barker said some other bunch has taken over the trade there, but it's not an MC. I don't care who it is. I want us to stay out of it, but it could be he's right, and that guy is Piglet. He has knowledge of the river and might have some leftover contacts with the Canadians. What do you want to do?"

What did he want to do? That was the million-dollar question. Should he send men to Hastings or let it go? If Piglet turned out to be setting up shop with another group of men to resume small-time drug smuggling on the river, what would that mean for the Dutchmen and their plans for the Harbor Marina? What would Gretchen think if she found out the depth of his criminal past?

Rail cursed and shut off the boat's idling engine. Iceman had always processed whatever information he was given with precision and made his decisions with a cold, hard manner. What would he have done in in this situation?

"Tell Duke to make a run to Hastings to check it out. Keep this from Rebel. We don't need his ass going off half-cocked up there and shooting some-one. The Dutchmen still need to stay low. If Duke confirms it's Piglet, we'll talk about plans in chapel."

Camo nodded and seemed satisfied with Rail's answer. He turned back to the lot, mounted his bike, and left in a spray of gravel. Rail watched the dust cloud from the back tire float away in the air. Iceman had led the Dutchmen through some of its toughest times, and now it was up to Rail. It was a heavy weight to bear from a legacy he never wanted.

Rail's mouth twitched as he recalled one of the many lessons his Grams taught him that he still remembered. *"Being a good leader is more about being a good servant. A king takes care of his people, and they in turn take care of the kingdom. Says so in the good book, right there in Matthew chapter twenty, verse twenty-six."* She quoted the Bible often all through his years with her, even though he never followed her into her staunch faith. Her heavy Bible stayed on her nightstand and was there still at the retirement home. His memories were full of her reading in that huge book nightly and using it as the basis of her life. There were very few times he could argue with her about it or the wisdom in her words.

Rail had heard many tidbits of knowledge from the woman who raised him, and many of them stuck with him over the years.

"Can't go praising God on Sunday and preaching hate on Monday. It doesn't work like that."

"God doesn't care what you're wearing when you're praying."

"What would Jesus do? Instead of pointing a finger, he'd be reaching out a helping hand."

"People are hungry for more than just food, child. One little act of kindness is sometimes all it takes."

Rail looked at the boat engine. Kindness had fed him for many years, and right now, he was starving.

An impulse hit him. He needed to test it in the water, right?

CHAPTER
EIGHT

"The red velvet curtains hung like a rich velour steak, flowing lightly in the breeze."

Gretchen shook her head at the word choice. This was the second round for this book, and so far this author had ignored almost every piece of advice. The grammar and punctuation had been updated, but the line edits hadn't.

Velour steak? Flowing lightly? What the hell is a velour steak? Sounds more like a slaughterhouse than a bedroom. Her original comment still sat in the margin: "This is not good imagery. Try red lacy curtains or just lacy curtains. No need to add the steak description."

The author left a snarky comment of her own. "I like steak."

This was not the first time Gretchen had worked

with this author, but it may be the last. Her books were good with solid plots and story arcs, but sometimes she over-detailed or had scenes that would be major turnoffs to readers. This author didn't like criticism and argued incessantly before giving in and making changes. Gretchen wondered why she bothered with this client when she had many others who she could work with so much easier.

She pulled up her Google calendar to check the dates. She had a few more days to complete this manuscript, but the publication date was coming up fast. Gretchen had three more manuscripts to finish by the weekend, and she didn't have time to coddle this author. Her fingers flew as she typed her notes and saved the file.

The sun had started its downward path, and the river turned more gold than its normal muddy brown. Gretchen loved working outside. She sat at a glass-topped patio table and dug her bare toes into the cool thick grass of her backyard overlooking the Mississippi. Peaceful, easy, tranquil, still—she could find at least a dozen adjectives to describe her mood. Despite the random break-in with the bikers, she felt less stressed, less pushed, less jittery here. She noticed that even at the slower pace of life, she still got the work done and deadlines met. Maybe Penny had a point about coming here to live. Coming home. Sounded kinda nice.

The only real disturbance in her life was close by in Red Wing. After the extemporaneous lunch encounter, he popped into her thoughts with a frequency that bordered on obsession. *What was he doing? Did he behave like book bikers and have a small harem of women? Was he a criminal or just a bad boy?* The hard face he wore when she first saw him floated in her mind. Then she recalled the gentle look on his face when he signed to his Grams. There was more to him, and she found herself wanting to discover what it was.

The silhouette of a small pilot boat chugged lazily on the water and, to Gretchen's surprise, pulled up to the end of her pier. The man in the boat tied off and climbed out, lifting a small cooler and bag with him. She didn't need field glasses to recognize Railroad's tall figure coming toward her.

"I had to test out an engine rebuild. Brought you food at the same time."

She closed her laptop and leaned back in the bouncy chair. "How did you know I was hungry?"

"Because it's suppertime, and I'm hungry."

Her mouth twitched. "So, I suppose if you're hungry, that's supposed to make me hungry too?"

He plopped the bag on the table and bent to open

the cooler. "You're getting it. Brought a few beers and the best brisket sandwiches on the river."

"Why are these the best?"

He sat down and handed her a can of Jack Pine's Duck Pond ale. "Because I said so."

She popped the top and took a long sip of the nutty dark brew before freeing her hands to answer. "Are you being a smartass, or are you flirting with me?"

"I don't flirt." He handed her a paper-wrapped sandwich with a long pickle spear tucked in the side and a bag of plain potato chips.

The smell of tangy brisket barbecue reached her nose, and she inhaled deeply. "Whatever, dude."

He stopped. "Did you just call me dude?"

She grinned at him. "Yes. Need me to spell it for you?"

He blinked once, then opened his mouth to laugh. "Now who's the smartass?"

She lifted one shoulder and took a bite of her sandwich. Rich flavor burst on her tongue, and she had to agree with him: it was the best brisket sandwich she'd ever had.

They sat side by side, eating without signing, and just watched the movement of the river. He ended up with both pickle spears, as she didn't particularly like them, and she went into the house once to bring out some bakery cookies she'd picked up the last time she was in town. Washing down chocolate chip cookies with beer was a strange taste combination, but that didn't stop him from having three of the sweet treats.

The sun moved lower in the sky. The light grew dimmer as the temperature cooled with the river breezes.

"Why are you really here?" she finally asked him.

He watched her signs and answered back while facing the river. "There's a lot of shit I've had to deal with lately, and I needed to get away from it for a while. Had to test the engine anyway. Figured this was a good place to do it."

"Why me?"

He didn't answer for a few moments. His expression was unreadable as he concealed whatever churned behind his eyes. "I don't know. I just needed to see you."

No witty comebacks came to her. She wished she could hug him and tell him everything would be okay. It wasn't hard to figure out that he had a lot of responsibilities on his shoulders, and sometimes they got heavy. She rested back in her chair and sipped the last of her beer. The alcohol made her mellow, and the day's toils were catching up to her. "No other reason to come to Wabasha other than to test a boat and bring me supper?"

He cracked open a second beer for himself. "It used to be just my Grams. If she lived somewhere else, I'd never come here. Piglet provided a second temporary reason, but once the club business with him is finished, I didn't plan on coming back. But now you're here."

That bit of knowledge brought warm fuzzies to her belly. Or maybe it was just the beer. "Your grandmother is very sweet."

He sipped at the beer foam at the mouth of the can before continuing. "Yeah, she's my Grams. Obviously not biologically. We get weird looks sometimes when I take her out to lunch or something, but I don't care. She's still my Grams."

"She had some interesting things to say about your childhood. I noticed you didn't say much about your mom."

Rail's eyes stayed on the river, but his mind was clearly somewhere else. "My memories of my mother are blurred. There was a woman who fed me sometimes and gave me basic care, but I recall she wasn't my birth mother. I can't remember her face, but I remember being hungry. Cold. Dirty. Alone. That's a part of my past I'd prefer to stay there. Flora reached me when no one else could. She and Iceman. Gave me purpose to live by and people to live for. I wouldn't be here if it wasn't for my Grams."

Gretchen's breath caught at his words. "She said you were ten?"

"Around that age. I don't know exactly when my birthday is, so that's the best guess. She celebrates my 'gotcha' day as a birthday."

"That's nice. She's a special lady."

Rail's eyes wrinkled at the corners as the sides of his mouth turned up.

She turned her own eyes to the river. Her heart bled for the boy he had been. What kind of life did he have that made him keep himself in silence for nearly two years? Kids who went through some sort of extreme trauma would sometimes fold into themselves as a defense mechanism. Rail had obviously lived something like that in the course of his life. His facial scars proved it.

She shifted to face him again. "Is that how...?" She ran two fingers down her cheek.

His eyes followed the movement, but his hands stayed still. She could see him shutting down. Shutting her out. He stood abruptly. "I need to get the boat back to the marina." He stuffed their sandwich wrappers in the paper bag and crumpled it up.

"Thanks for the food," she signed lamely, not knowing what else to say.

He nodded and picked up the cooler to dump the ice cubes on the ground. He turned to face her, his dark eyes piercing her with a strange expression, as if there was something he wanted to say but didn't have the words or wouldn't speak them. "I enjoyed hanging with you today. I needed the break, so thank you for that."

She breathed out in relief. She had stepped over a line with her offhand question, but it didn't bother him as much as she thought. "No problem. I spend a lot of my days out here working on the computer. You're welcome to come by anytime, but you should text before you come, in case I do go out for some reason. Want my number?"

"I have it from your business card."

She smiled. "That's the one for the editing world. I have another for my personal world. Would you like it?"

He nodded and handed her his phone. Her fingers flew across the wide screen as she entered it, then hit Send. Her phone lit up and vibrated hard enough to move on the surface of the table where it sat.

"There. I have yours too. Text me anytime."

He took the oblong device from her hand and slipped it into his back pocket. She stared into those beautiful eyes of his, and her heart tripped. He was looking at her lips, and the bottom fell out of her belly. Would he kiss her?

She found herself wanting that touch. To feel that hard mouth on hers. He wouldn't be gentle. She bet he'd be rough, demanding, dominating. A shiver trickled down her spine at the thought.

She started swaying toward him when he abruptly pulled back.

"I'll come see you again sometime," he signed and turned to go, leaving her standing alone in the yard.

Gretchen pressed her lips together. Her belly fluttered at the near encounter, and she noticed he didn't ask if he *could* come back. He said he *would*.

Her gaze stayed on the logo on the back of his cut as he walked away. One long leg swung into the boat before he reached for the tie off. Half a second later, the engine fired up, and he pulled away from the pier. He didn't turn around or wave as he pointed the watercraft upriver to Red Wing.

Frustration mixed with irritation and a touch of desire in her lower body. She'd wanted that kiss, that brief taste of him, to give her some little answer of the mystery that was Railroad. That was probably the biggest reason for this attraction to him. Yes, he was incredibly handsome with a great body, and she was willing to bet he knew how to use it. She'd learned a few random bits from the chance lunch encounter, and more today. Still, she knew there was even more to the man, and she found herself wanting to discover it.

The boat had disappeared in the distance, and she woke up from her trance with a shake of her head. She rolled her eyes and shook herself to clear her mind. *Gretchen, get your head outta your ass and stop making the man into a book character.*

She made short work of collecting her computer and going inside her house. It was too early for bed, but her mind and body were too jumbled to work. She locked up and found a mindless Netflix series to watch to numb her brain so she might be able to fall asleep in a few hours.

THE NOISE STARTED TO BOTHER HIM THE MOMENT HE SET foot in the clubhouse. After the silence of the river with only the chugging boat motor making any sound, Rail found the wildness of the Dutchmen compound overwhelming. He wanted to go back to the little house on the river, but he doubted Gretchen would let him in after the way he left her this afternoon. He wanted to go to his room and shut everything and everyone out, but as the president, he had to stay visible for a little while. Iceman always made his presence known by sitting on the seat that served as his throne and letting people talk to him. Now that throne was Railroad's, and he had no desire to sit on it.

A club girl with pink hair and a nose ring brought him a beer and a Fireball shot. He downed the whisky, enjoying its burn, and told her to bring him another. She smiled at him and hurried to serve him. Four shots later, his mood began to relax. Duke wasn't back from Hastings yet, but Nutter sat with him across from Camo. Rebel had a woman over the back of a couch and was rapidly drilling into her.

Nutter yelled at him. "Goddammit, Rebel! Take it to a goddamn room, you fucking asshole!"

Rebel ignored him and kept going.

"Stupid motherfucker. He keeps that shit up, Peebles will leave his ass high and dry." Nutter swallowed half a bottle of beer in one go and burped out loud.

"You know all about that shit firsthand, eh? I heard Mimi froze you out too." Camo picked up a shot and threw it back.

"Goddamn women. I love 'em, but I hate 'em too. Mama J sent me papers today. Wants me to give her full custody and child support too. Mimi said I gotta be with her when she pops out the new kid, but after that, she's moving to Eau Claire with some new guy she has, and I have to pay her too."

"You make children, bro, you have to support them. Shit gets expensive."

"I got eight kids! How'm I supposed to pay for all of them?"

Rail nearly spewed his beer. "Eight? You have four by Mama J and three by Mimi once she has this one. That's seven."

Nutter sniffed drunkenly. "Kay came by to see me. She's got one in the oven and says it's mine."

Some people might have found it funny to hear the big man bemoan his paternal status with three women. Rail didn't. "For fuck's sake, you stupid asswipe. Either wrap it up, or better yet, stop sticking your dick into any female willing who'll take it."

Nutter's face registered shock that anyone would dare call him out. "But... she... I...."

"He's right," Camo chimed in. "You're old enough to know how babies are made. Get a vasectomy if you want to keep fucking your way through the women of this town. Three baby mamas? You *are* a stupid asswipe."

Nutter found his voice. "You've done your share of fucking. Both of you."

"We haven't made eight babies."

"Fuck this. Nutter, get it together, brother," Rail

said, then stood up abruptly and swayed as the alcohol hit his brain. He was suddenly exhausted and needed to be alone.

He made his way to his room and opened the door. It took a moment for his eyes to adjust to the dim light. In his bed was the pink-haired girl. She sat up straight with the gray comforter in her lap and her naked breasts displaying silver nipple rings.

Rail's irritation from earlier ratcheted up another notch. "What the fuck are you doing here?"

She chewed her lower lip. "You seemed really on edge, and I thought maybe I could help you out. Make you happy, you know?"

It would be so easy. To lose himself in her body, pound away some of the frustrations in her willing pussy, maybe have her suck him off, and then do it again. He could make her get on all fours and work out his ire by taking her ass. Hell, any woman in that club would spread at his command if he told them to. Two women in his bed at the same time. Three. Whoever he wanted.

He'd be no better than Nutter.

"What's your name?"

She smiled at him and lay back on the bed, opening her thighs in preparation. "Kimmie."

"How old are you?"

"I just turned nineteen."

He believed it. She had the naïve air of a girl playing at being a seductress, not the mature confidence of an experienced woman. "Get out."

Confusion showed on her face. "Um... aren't you going to...?"

"No, I'm not fucking a kid. Get the fuck out of my room and do not come back."

She seemed to crumple in front of him as she slipped out of the bed and pulled on her clothes. "I'm sorry. I just thought.... I'm.... I'll go."

He caught her arm as she tried to flee. He saw the tears in her eyes along with her quivering lip. "Listen to me, Kimmie. You're cute, and you have a lot of years left in your life. You want to be a whore to an old man, that's your choice, but there's better out there and better ways of getting it than spreading your legs. You want to make me happy? Go find it."

She sniffed and nodded.

Rail closed his door and flopped on his bed. Kimmie's fruity perfume lingered, but he couldn't picture her anymore. There was only one woman he wanted in his bed. He lay on his back and closed his eyes. Gretchen's face floated in his mind. The sensation of that near kiss still burned inside his gut. It took every ounce of control he had in that moment to walk away. One minute more and he would have taken her mouth. Hell, he'd wanted to strip her bare and fuck her right there in her yard. A vision of what that would look like came into his mind. Her soft breasts resting naked on her chest, slightly shifted outward. Her arms open to him as he eased between her legs. Her eyes going wide as his dick found her opening and he slowly pressed into her body.

Fuck, he was ready to explode just by thinking about sinking deep into her heat. He yanked at his jeans and fisted his rigid dick. It only took a few minutes before he came, shooting hard enough to cover his stomach. Iceman would laugh his ass off if he could see Railroad jacking off like a teenager.

Rail lay on the bed and contemplated staying there and not getting up, but he hated the sticky drying mess and went to clean himself up. He stared at his reflection as he finished stripping and wiped his stomach and chest. *You need to get this shit under control,* he told himself. *She's beautiful, but no fucking way is there a future with her and you. Keep your head in the game. It's not possible for saints to love sinners in the real world.*

CHAPTER
NINE

PIGLET GRUNTED AS HE CAME AND COLLAPSED ON TOP of the woman's body. He didn't remember this one's name, but she was available, and that was all that mattered.

His days had begun to blend together in one long string of monotony. Up at dawn, repairs on farm equipment with Nathaniel, eat, shower, and go see a comfort woman before going back to his bunk. Now that he'd become a working member of the farm, he no longer had the private guest cabin but rather a spot in the barracks held for the single men. He actually liked it more as he'd long been missing the comradery of being in a group. The men would talk about work, laugh at something stupid, brag about women they fucked and how many.

The woman closed her legs as he peeled off the

condom and threw it into the nearby trash can. As far as fucks went, this one sucked. When he walked down the row of shacks that housed the comfort women, she had been the only one sitting outside waiting. She silently watched him approach, then put down the basket of peas she'd been shelling and got up to enter her one-room place. Didn't even bother to strip, just lay on the bed, hiked up her long skirt, and spread her legs. As he tucked himself back in his pants, she left the bed to go back to her task.

The first few times he came to the row of shacks, it reminded him of the Tiger Clan's stable of prostitutes. Free pussy anytime a club member wanted it, but at least they made a show like they enjoyed the sex. With the comfort women, it was duty rather than pleasure. Fucking one of them was like fucking a zombie. Hell, his right hand was more exciting. He wasn't sure why he bothered to come here.

Matthias came up to him all smiles and clapped him on the shoulder. There was both something appealing about him, but still a part that creeped him out. "Nice to see you fitting in. Brother David tells me you fixed three of the big tractors so far. It's helped him a lot with scheduling. That's fantastic."

Piglet felt the need to please Matthias and earn the praises from his mouth, but he somehow feared them as well. "Glad to help."

"So, you've been here quite a while now and proven yourself very useful." Matthias's hand stayed on Piglet's shoulder, and its weight captured his attention.

He was used to getting money for working a job, but here there was no need for it. Food was served. It was plain but plentiful. He was given clothes, and somehow they got washed and stacked weekly on his bed along with clean sheets. He had as much pussy as he wanted, although that started to get boring. No one seemed to want to go anywhere different. No nights out at the bar drinking or watching strippers. No movies. No music. Everyone seemed to be content in this isolated little world, or at least no one complained. Nathaniel was content and happy. Perhaps Piglet should try harder to like it.

Matthias continued talking in a calm, friendly voice. "We need more men like you to be a part of our community. There's a meeting tonight at the main house, and I think it's time you see what we're all about here."

Piglet's heart sped up. Curiosity and fear mingled in his gut, and he gave a nervous laugh. "You gonna make me eat a live chicken or kiss a snake?"

Matthias's fingers tightened on his shoulder in a firm grip. Instead of providing reassurance, Piglet got the impression it was to keep him from running.

Matthias's mouth smiled and laughed, too, but it was more like a pause before pouncing. "No, we don't do that kind of crap. At least not to first-timers."

More nervous laughter came from Piglet as he felt a trap closing around him. "I guess I'll be there."

Matthias's white teeth gleamed. "Excellent. Starts at nine o'clock. See you then."

CHAPTER
TEN

FLORA SLAPPED HER HANDFUL OF CARDS ON THE TABLE. "Gin!" she crowed, then cackled at her victory.

Rail groaned and gave the old woman a baleful glance. "Shit. You're cheating again."

"I never cheat. I got mad card skills."

He'd come for a visit, but the van was being used, so no trip to Slippery's. Flora invited him to play cards with her on the wide veranda, and he obliged. She was wearing a long-sleeved sweater and had one blanket around her thin shoulders and another across her lap. Despite the warmth of the day, she said she felt a chill.

"What you got is another deck up your sleeve." He gathered the pile of thin rectangles and expertly shuffled them as his gaze rose to take in the approaching storm clouds. Once upon a time, he would watch Flora's nimble fingers as she fluttered cards between them. She taught him how to play a lot of card games as a child. Gin rummy, war, crazy eights, slapjack, and poker.

It had been raining the night she told him she loved him.

He stood in the doorway of her small bedroom that sat at the end of the hall. He wasn't ready to go back to his bed yet. He had the top bunk in a room he shared with three other boys. A new kid came today. A few years his senior, but much older in his eyes. This boy had seen some real shit in his life. He had a name, but the other kids dubbed him Iceman. He was in another room with boys his age.

Flora was playing solitaire when she noticed Railroad's presence. The other kids named him Railroad because of the scars left behind on his face. A few of them tried to bully him about it, but they learned to leave the smaller boy alone. He fought back. Hard, fast, and wouldn't stop. One kid tried to call him Trainwreck, but Railroad was the one that stuck.

"What's the matter, child? Can't sleep?" She put the cards down and signed the words to him in addition to saying them. Her soft voice reflected the gentleness in her eyes.

Flora had been the only adult here able to reach him. He could talk, but the words didn't come. She picked up on his rudimentary signs and taught him better ones. Because of her care, he started to come out of his shell. He still didn't want to answer the questions that he was peppered with daily, but he could communicate with Flora. The older black woman became his window to the world, and he clung to her kindness.

He lifted his hands. "Tim is farting like crazy. There's a cloud of his stink over my bed."

She chuckled and gathered up the cards in a neat stack. "Come on over, precious. I'll teach you a game, and we can listen to the storm together."

She patiently explained rummy to him, and they played a few hands. He got the hang of it quickly.

A flash of lightning lit the night sky outside her window followed by a boom of thunder that shook the old house. Rail jumped in panic, but Flora placed a calming hand on his arm.

"It's all right, child. That's just God talking to His angels, telling them where to put the good rain we need. He's got a loud voice, doesn't He?"

"He's scary."

Flora pursed her lips. "Some people are scared of Him, but they don't have to be."

"God punishes us when we're bad."

Flora put down her handful of cards and took both of Rail's small hands in hers. "You know what I think? I think God doesn't have to punish anyone. We do a good job of that ourselves. There's evil in this world, but it doesn't come from God."

Rail shrugged. He pulled his hands away and signed. "I thought God only likes high people. He hates low people."

"No, child. God doesn't hate anyone. Look at my skin and yours." She held up her forearm and pointed for him to do the same. "Some people think because I'm dark, that makes me less. In God's eyes, we're all His children, no matter what color we are, or what gender, or what age."

He switched subjects. "How come you don't have kids?"

She smiled. "My insides are messed up, and I can't have any. But that doesn't matter, 'cause I got lots of children. All these young boys under this roof in my care are mine. You know something else? I'm yours too. God knew these young men needed a grandma, and he chose me for that purpose. You have white skin and I have black skin, but that doesn't matter either. I'm going to love you and take care of you and be your grandma for the rest of your life. Understand me, precious?"

Rivulets of water ran down the window as the rain kept coming down. Rail listened to the patter against the glass and stared at the floor, pondering Flora's words. He wasn't sure he believed everything she said, but he liked the idea of having a grandma. Someone to love him for life. A tightness he didn't know was there broke free in his *chest, and suddenly he could breathe as he never could before. His lip quivered and he nodded, tears starting to fall from his eyes. He brushed them away as he wasn't supposed to cry, but Flora reached out her arms to him.*

"Come here, precious. I have no doubts God loves you, 'cause he brought you to me and me to you."

He choked off a sob and snuggled into her large lap as she wrapped her arms around him, cocooning him in her full embrace. "There, there, child. My beautiful boy. I got you. Let me set my Polaroid. I like having pictures of my boys around me."

She put the camera on the card table and set the timer. The flash went off as she rocked him back and forth.

Something foreign bubbled up in Rail's stomach. It was hot and burning. More tears fell, and his throat convulsed. He tried to swallow it down, but it came anyway. "Grammie."

"I love you, precious."

Grammie became Grams and remained that way ever since. They'd played hours of rummy and poker. She patiently tutored him in his schoolwork, getting him caught up to the grade level he was supposed to be. He never did follow her religious beliefs, but he respected them. She also respected his disbeliefs and still loved him. When he left the home and joined Iceman in the Dutchmen MC, she didn't turn him away but said she'd pray for him every day.

He had no doubts she probably still did.

"Looks like a nice soaking storm heading our way," she remarked from her nest of blankets. "Makes me sleepy just looking at those big black clouds of water. You think you should go before it starts? Riding your motorcycle in the rain isn't very nice, is it?"

Rail slapped the deck of cards on the table. "It's not a lot of fun, but I can handle it."

"You been over to see that pretty editor woman?"

Rail raised an eyebrow at his Grams. "Playing matchmaker, or looking for gossip to share?"

"Both."

He gave a quick laugh. "Yeah, I go by her place when I'm out testing boat engines. She's got a nice sturdy pier. I text her to see if she's home. If she is, I stop by and sometimes bring brisket sandwiches from the Harbor with me."

"Does she like the *lefse* you brought her?"

"How do you know I brought her *lefse*?"

"I guessed. So did she?"

Rail's face broke into a grin at Flora's nosiness. "Yes. Happy now?"

"I'd be happier if you brought her by to see me."

"I don't think so, Grams. She's a busy lady."

"Not too busy for brisket sandwiches."

Rail tucked the cards in their box. "You're the stubbornest woman I know."

"Also the oldest." She yawned and covered her mouth with one shaky hand. "And the tiredest. I think I'm gonna go take me a little nap before supper. You get on back home before the rain catches you."

He wheeled her to her room and helped transfer her to the motorized bed. She gazed at him with her faded eyes. "Thank you, precious. Love you coming to see me."

"Me too, Grams."

He paused when he got to his bike and peered at the sky. The storm moved faster than he thought. He wouldn't make it back to Red Wing before it hit. He pulled out his phone on impulse.

Rail: I'm in Wabasha on my bike. Mind if I come by, maybe wait out the rain?

The dots took a minute to start bouncing around.

Gretchen: Sure. I suppose no brisket today, then?
  Rail: Nope. Just me.
Gretchen: I've got food here. I'm not a great cook, but you're welcome to join me for dinner.
  Rail: On my way. Need me to pick up anything?

Gretchen: Ice cream. Butter pecan or cookie dough. If you bring plain vanilla, I'm not letting you in.

Rail barked a short laugh.

Rail: What if I like vanilla?
Gretchen: Allow me to expand your horizons.

This time he laughed out loud. Three drops of rain hit the pavement in front of him. Shit, he had to hurry.

GRETCHEN STARTED WATCHING FOR HIM THE MOMENT the heavens let loose and soaked the earth. This was a simple rain shower, no thunder and lightning or harsh winds. Just the kind of rain that pleased the agricultural folks around the area. A thrill zapped up her spine when the single headlight appeared in the foggy gray.

He drove into the car cover in the space next to her Accord and got off the bike. His clothes were soaked through, though his hair was mostly dry under the helmet. She held the door open for him and handed him a thick pink towel as he entered. He handed her the plastic grocery bag.

"I got all three kinds, plus spray whipped cream, sprinkles, and cherries for the top," he signed before briskly rubbing as much wet off himself as he could.

"We're risking a major carb load. I made spaghetti and meatballs, plus salad. And before you ask, my sauce comes from a jar. I don't cook a lot for other people."

"Spaghetti is good." He draped the towel over the back of one chair.

"I have some of Dad's old sweats and T-shirts I knock around in for yard work. If you want to wear them for a bit, I can put your stuff in the dryer. Probably take about twenty minutes to dry."

"Yeah, that'd be good. Wet boxers chafe like hell."

We wouldn't want that now, would we? she thought but didn't sign. She ran up the stairs to get the ancient sweatpants and a shirt. Both pieces were holey and stained, but they were the only articles of clothing she had that would fit him. Her normal daily attire tended to be stretchy patterned leggings and long T-shirts. She could offer him something of hers, but she doubted he would be interested in yellow-and-pink lollipops, or blue-and-green octopi. Nor would they fit.

He slipped into the laundry room just off the

kitchen to change and dump his clothes into the dryer. Gretchen stirred the simmering sauce and checked the noodles. She flicked her eyes in his direction, then stopped for a full stare.

The slatted door to the room didn't close quite all the way. She couldn't see Rail's entire form, but what she did see was exceptional. He faced away from her, and she got a sliver view of his broad back. It was covered with a black tattoo. Clean muscle lines traveled from his rounded shoulders to his tapered waist. She held her breath as he unsnapped his jeans and peeled them down his sturdy thighs, taking his boxers off in the same motion. Holy mother of all, what an ass! Tight, high, round cheeks with side indentations. There should be sonnets written in praise of that perfect rear.

The noodles chose that moment to boil over, and she wrenched her attention away from the sight of that luscious bottom.

"You okay? You look flushed." He came toward her, pulling the shirt down over a smattering of dark hair on his chest.

"Hot stove," she signed with a tepid smile. "Food's ready. Sit down and I'll bring it."

The spaghetti wasn't anything special, and the salad came from a premade bag, but the food was filling.

"Sorry, no garlic bread. I figured there are enough carbs in the pasta without adding more."

Rail forked more of the salad. "Doesn't bother me. Why are you so concerned about carbs?"

Gretchen leaned back in her chair. "I'm sure you've noticed I'm not exactly petite. I don't obsess over my weight, but I don't particularly want to put on any more."

"You're beautiful just like you are."

His remark was signed in an offhand, flippant way, but she enjoyed seeing it.

"You're flirting with me."

His dark eyes met hers. "I don't flirt."

She turned thoughtful as she got up to clear the table. She deposited the dishes in the sink before signing to him again. "The rain is still falling some. Ice cream?"

"I'll get it."

Gretchen watched as he scooped ice cream into two bowls, sprayed a mound of whipped cream on top, added chocolate sprinkles, and topped them off with two cherries each. This was the first time he'd come to see her at night. The other impromptu visits were during the day. He texted her ahead of time, brought food, and sat with her outside while they ate. Their conversations were mostly casual. He talked about the business at the marina, and she talked about a bothersome client or snag she had in the manuscript she currently had open. He mentioned a friend of his, Mama J, and brought the sweet Swedish treat the woman baked regularly. He complained about some of the drama going on between her and her ol' man, another club member. She regaled him about her life back in Connecticut. Him being here in her dining alcove with the rain pattering on the roof made this encounter more intimate. More personal. She took a brave breath and also took a chance, partially because of curiosity, and partially because she was starting to want more.

"You've come to see me a lot lately. Why? Just to hang out?"

Rail scooped up a spoonful of the cold sweet. "I like it here. I can think without too much distraction. You know there's shit going on at the club. I've already told you more than I should, but I don't think you're going to share it. Even with Penny. There are days I feel like I'm being torn apart in all directions. There are a lot of people in my life who have questions and look to me for answers I don't have."

He licked the spoon, and she followed the movement. Her stomach bloomed with heat, and she took her own bite of ice cream to hide her reaction. "If it's that bad, why don't you do what every parent does and just say no?"

He scraped the last bit from his bowl. "It's not that simple. I'm balancing like I'm on a seesaw between two sides. If I lean too far one way, this group gets mad. If I go the other way, others get mad." He leaned back in the chair. "I like that I can talk to you without judgment. It means a lot to me, and I need you to know how much I appreciate you giving me that."

Gretchen noticed his tired features. He really was under a lot of pressure. She didn't know the circumstances, but she understood his position and the heaviness of his decisions. "Being in charge sucks sometimes. I taught an adjunct course at the university for a while. It was tough being deaf and teaching at that level, but I made it work. I liked it, until other faculty started questioning everything I did or said. One woman tried to rewrite my curriculum for me. I think you know enough about me to know how well that went over."

He smiled at her.

She picked up the bowls and set them in the sink before continuing. "I'm deaf, not stupid. I don't really care about what other people think about me and what I do. I learned a long time ago that either someone cared about me, or they didn't. It's not worth my time to worry over it either. I get what you're saying, though. About the balancing act. The biggest difference is, I don't have people dependent on me regarding my decisions. You do."

She loaded the small dishwasher. Normally she didn't produce enough to fill it, but between tonight's dishes and tomorrow morning's breakfast, she'd have a full load.

Hmmm, breakfast. Would he be here to eat it with her? She hoped so.

"It might be simpler than you think. Again, I have no idea what you're debating, but if I were you, I think I'd look at the long-term implications. My work calendar is planned monthly, but my schedule is set roughly a year in advance. I have bookings all the way into next year for editing, appearances, lectures, and signing events. What direction I take in my life has an impact on that, and I need to think about the effect it will have. Maybe you should think about that for your club. What will happen next year based on your choices now?"

"Good question. I don't know. I've lived by the seat of my pants so long, not knowing if I would live to see the future, I'm not sure I can think in those terms."

She smiled at him. "I dare you to try."

He stayed silent for a moment, staring at the table without seeming to see it. Then he abruptly stood up. "Rain stopped. I need to go."

Gretchen didn't have to hear to figure out he'd just slammed a door shut. He all but ran to the laundry room to change into his dry clothes. She resisted the urge to spy on him this time and concentrated on wiping off the counters and table. When she took a quick peek, she saw him sit on his abandoned chair long enough to don his socks and his still-wet riding boots. She popped a tab in the dishwasher and started it. No breakfast plans happening.

He walked heavily to the door leading to the carport. Gretchen held her breath as he paused with his hand on the knob. Then he turned, and his charcoal eyes met hers.

His long strides started across the floor toward her, and for a moment, she simply watched. Then on impulse she met him halfway.

He seized her shoulders and brought her into his embrace. His mouth slammed down on hers, and her senses went wild.

The entire world contracted so nothing was in it but him. A nuclear bomb could have exploded and she wouldn't have noticed. Heat from his body surrounded her, and the intensity of his kiss flamed higher. One of his hands shot to the back of her head and slanted it so he could take their kiss deeper. His tongue pressed against her lips, and she opened to him. He explored, plundered, took with a thoroughness she'd never experienced, making every other kiss in her life pale in comparison. For the first time, she understood what the books she edited were trying to describe, and they all fell short.

Gradually, she became aware of other parts of him surrounding her. The firmness of his body, the strength in his arms, and the unmistakable hardness pressing into her stomach. Fire ignited low in her belly as his need poured into her. She was ready to let him strip and take her right there on the counter of her kitchen. *Breakfast is back on!* She moved her hand to cup his crotch, and the promise of what lay behind that zipper had her squirming. She needed this. She needed him.

She pulled at the button, trying to bare him to her hand, but he released her and stepped back. "I have to go."

He left without another word. Gretchen followed outside and watched in disbelief as Rail hopped on his bike, fired it up, and pulled out to head back up to Red Wing under the dark sky. He never looked back. Her body hummed with unfulfilled tension, anger taking the place of her confusion.

"Asshole!" she signed at his retreating back.

He didn't see it, of course.

She stomped back into her house.

What the hell is wrong with him? He had a golden

opportunity for some action here and he turned it down? Her thoughts were fierce as she locked the house and readied herself for bed.

She put on her standard tank top nighttime attire but noticed her panties were damp. *Son of a bitch!* She changed into loose boxer shorts and climbed into bed.

The ceiling had no answers, and neither her body nor mind could relax. His presence still lingered. She imagined his lips on hers, arm around her waist, hand in her hair, tongue driving in, his glowing eyes on hers as his hard length pressed against her opening, resisting and then finally entering.

Gah! She flung the comforter off and reached into her nightstand drawer for her vibrator. *An angry orgasm is better than nothing, and I need to get to sleep.*

THE BIKE ROARED ON THE HIGHWAY, RAIL PUSHING IT faster than was safe on the wet roads. Every fiber of his body screamed for him to go back to Gretchen's place, take her upstairs, and fuck her in the first bed he found. He wanted to bury himself in her more than he wanted to breathe.

The problem? It wasn't just fucking. There was a connection there—one that started the first time he laid eyes on her. He'd shared personal thoughts that no one, not even his brothers, had ever heard. These were pieces of himself that had always stayed private. Never did he have that level of trust with any other woman he'd taken to his bed.

Her invitation was there. He sensed it and realized if he didn't get out of there, he would take her up on it. It terrified him so much, he had to leave. He was afraid that if he took her to bed, he'd never leave it. Kissing her was a big mistake, as now he wanted her more than ever.

In his experience, wanting something didn't mean you got to have it.

CHAPTER
ELEVEN

PIGLET STOOD AT THE BOTTOM OF THE SHORT STAIRS AND regarded the large building in front of him. He was sure it had a more formal name, but everyone on the farm referred to the structure as the Main House. Night had fallen and with it a heavy, tangible darkness. Very few of the other buildings had electricity, and only a small scattering of pale glows was visible from those places fortunate enough to have oil lamps and candles. This was one of the few structures that did have power, but tonight the place was lit up by flaming lanterns.

Several men with rifles slung over their shoulders passed him on their way into the house. Their boots clomped loudly in the sticky humid air. Piglet swallowed. Just about every man on the farm carried some sort of firearm at all times, but these were heavy assault weapons. He'd been around plenty of guns and violent men from his time in the MCs, but something about these men was different. Almost deadlier.

"Ezra, I'm glad you made it." Matthias's hand came down on his shoulder once again, and the sense of being trapped came down around Piglet's heart. "Let me walk you in."

Sweat broke out across Piglet's back, and he hoped Matthias didn't notice.

Directly inside the house sat a straight staircase that led to the upper floors. Next to it was a long hallway leading back to a set of closed double doors. The farm men had placed their rifles in gun racks that lined the hall. Apparently, no one was allowed to have arms during a meeting. Piglet thought that was a good idea, as he remembered Grizzly randomly shooting during some Tiger Clan gatherings. More than one MC member ended up with holes in them.

Matthias stayed by Piglet's side as they approached the double doors. A pedestal basin was stationed near them, and Matthias rinsed his hands. "It's symbolic to show cleanliness before entering the sanctum. You're not a brother, but you should still wash yourself."

A tingling started at the base of Piglet's spine. This was weird. Almost like being in church. He had already figured out there was a religious component to this group, but he hadn't realized its extent. He dabbled his hands in the water and dried them on the towel hanging from the basin's side. It was damp from use and didn't do a lot to remove any moisture from between his fingers.

The doors opened into what looked much like a chapel. Angled, hard benches lined up in military straightness, and on a raised dais, an ancient man sat in a wheelchair. His sparsely haired gray head nodded as if its weight was too much to hold up, and his eyes didn't seem to focus on anything. Several other men stood with him. The rest of them filed in ranks and chatted as they waited for everyone to find their spot.

Piglet felt Matthias's hand release from his shoulder as he joined a row about midway down the aisle. "That's the head of the family and my father, High Brother Zachariah. He was a key member in getting the farm to where it is. Unfortunately, he had a stroke last year and can't speak as he used to. The man standing behind him is Brother Thomas, who does the job of caretaker. It's up to me to run these meetings, so I'll leave you here for now. Just stay and observe. When the chalice and bounty are passed, you can abstain if you want to, but if you have any desire to be one of us and perhaps join in the future, I suggest you partake."

Piglet nodded and gave Matthias a thumbs-up, but his mind churned with confusion. Chalice? What kind of meeting was this? Fuck, this whole scene was creeping him out.

Matthias walked to the dais and took his place on the other side of his father. The room fell silent. Not even a creak from the wood floor was heard. Piglet bit his lip as the urge to laugh rose in his throat. He choked it down.

"Call to order. We, the people, have formed our perfect union." Matthias's voice rang out with authority, and everyone in the room came to attention and repeated his words.

"We, the people, have formed our perfect union."

The room filled with shuffling noise as the assembly sat on the benches.

"Pass the chalice and the bounty in order for us to become one."

Piglet saw several men pick up heavy cups and platters. A man in the first row took a piece of whatever was on the plate and put it in his mouth before handing the platter to the next man. He sipped from the cup as well. Piglet remembered communion from when his parents made him go to church as a child. He never understood what it meant and didn't understand it now, but as uncomfortable as he was, he still picked up a piece when the stuff came around to him.

The dried-up black nugget looked like an old mushroom and tasted like sour dirt. Piglet chewed the tough lump and tried not to make a face of revulsion. When the cup came to him, he took a large sip to wash the nasty mess down his throat. He discovered too late that this was no fake wine but hardcore alcohol that scorched a pathway of lava to his stomach. No one else seemed to be affected by the potent brew, so Piglet forced himself not to choke and cough. He sat in misery as man after man droned on about the businesses of running the farm. He didn't really care about the levels in the store-houses, or underground cellars, or the status of the harvest.

Gradually, the fire in his belly calmed and his senses lifted. He took on an awareness of everything around him as if he was viewing it from the inside of a bubble. His head floated, and he swayed back and forth, noticing that his movements matched those of the man in front of him. When that man leaned to the right, Piglet leaned to the right. When the man moved back to the left, Piglet moved back to the left.

I'm high as a fucking kite. Piglet's euphoria increased when he heard his name announced.

"A big thanks to lay-brother Ezra for his work to keep our farm tools in good working order."

Piglet grinned. Brother Matthias was such a great man. It was nice to be appreciated for a change. Nice to get recognized for his vital contribution. Murmured words of thanks came to his ears. They sounded like voices from a deep well, but he still understood them. Why the fuck did he ever think this place was strange? Everyone had welcomed him with open arms. Leaving should have never crossed his mind.

The man behind Brother Zachariah stood and picked up a long staff with elaborate carvings on it. He began thumping the butt of it against the floor. The men followed suit by stomping their right feet in time. Matthias opened his mouth and started a chant.

"We of the wheat have become one man, one body, one spirit."

Everyone repeated the lines.

"We of the wheat have become one man, one body, one spirit."

"We have separated from the inferior chaff in pursuance of life and liberty."

"We have separated from the inferior chaff in pursuance of life and liberty."

"Our bodies are clean from the impurities that make us weak."

"Our bodies are clean from the impurities that make us weak."

"Our right is to protect the family from all threats, foreign and domestic."

"Our right is to protect the family from all threats, foreign and domestic."

"Our purpose is to propagate and lead the way to a better life and better world."

"Our purpose is to propagate and lead the way to a better life and better world."

Piglet didn't understand some of the words, but he said them aloud with everyone else. Joy filled his heart, and he stomped and shouted with great enthusiasm. He belonged here. He needed to be a part of this brotherhood. He needed… he needed…

He needed to get laid. He sported a boner in his pants that stood straight up, hard and aching in need of relief.

"Go forth and take what is yours by right."

Some of the men stumbled as they made their way from the house. Piglet saw every one of them had tented pants. A large group of the senior brothers headed toward a gated area of the farm, one Piglet had not been allowed to see. Yet.

He and a few of the lower brothers staggered their way to the comfort shacks. One of the men opened a random door and entered. A moment later, two small children came out and curled up on the ground next to the shack. The unmistakable sound of fucking followed them.

Piglet was so far in his own head, he barely acknowledged that he was seeing children for the first time. He got to one of the shacks and pulled at the door. The woman on the bed startled awake and peered at him with fearful eyes. The moonlight did almost nothing to pierce the darkness, and he couldn't see her face, but it didn't matter. She was a comfort woman. He watched with bleary eyes as she lay back and spread her legs open. She reached for a white jar on the small table next to the bed, and she smeared a thick oil over her sex. Her pussy glistened in the low light. Piglet's dick pulsed with need.

She beckoned to him, and he opened his pants, only pushing down enough to free himself. He crawled between her legs and plunged over and over into her body with relief. He came hard with a long cry. It was the longest and deepest orgasm he'd ever experienced. He pulled out of the woman and collapsed by her side on the narrow bed, breathing heavy as if he just ran a marathon. She didn't move but lay there with her legs still open and waiting. A beam of moonlight shone across her dusky breasts, and Piglet reached out a hand to pluck and play with one. His dick hadn't softened much and was starting to throb again.

What the fuck were those mushrooms, and how can I get more? Piglet rolled on top of the woman, sliding into her again. The vague thought came to him that he didn't wear a condom.

CHAPTER
TWELVE

"THIS TOP WILL LOOK SOOOO GOOD ON YOU! GO TRY IT on." Penny pushed a mint-green top with asymmetric cutouts into Gretchen's hands. "They have it in mauve and yellow too."

Gretchen sighed and walked into the dressing room to comply. She hated shopping in general. However, it was a necessary evil. The few times she tried to order clothing online had been more trouble than not. With her round curves, items often didn't fit. She would have to take the time to fill out forms, print return labels, pack the rejects to be shipped back, and then wait for a refund. It was easier to just go and let Penny play dress-up with her at the mall.

"Ooooh! That color makes your eyes pop. Go try the others."

"Why? If this one fits, then the others will fit too. Besides, why do I need three of the same top?"

Penny rolled her eyes. "Because next week you'll be kicking yourself for not getting them. Trust me."

She was right, in a way. The style accentuated Gretchen's classic hourglass figure beautifully. Gretchen turned in front of the three-way mirror to get a good look at the garment. The top clung to one shoulder and had a single strap on the other. The cutout at the front showed just enough cleavage to enhance her heavy breasts, and the draping bottom half minimized the slight pooch of her stomach. "It does look nice, but I don't go out often enough to need three new tops."

"Don't you need business casual stuff for when you meet new clients?"

"Most of my clients communicate through email or Zoom. The guy from last week that canceled last minute was the exception. I'm supposed to meet him Thursday afternoon at some swanky place in Lake City. We'll see if he shows up this time."

"What about dates?"

Gretchen blew out her lips. "Dates? As in men, or the fruit? I'd probably get more dates at the grocery store than in Wabasha."

"What about Railroad?"

Gretchen stiffened a little when Penny spelled his name. "What about him?"

Penny raised an eyebrow as she slapped three more tops into Gretchen's hands. "I saw the way he tried not to look at you and you tried not to look at him when we went out to lunch that time. There was practically a cloud of pheromones floating between you two."

Yes, there had been. The whole time she sat next to the man, she'd been aware of his presence. Aura, power, atmosphere, body heat—whatever term applied, she'd been attuned to his every movement and gesture. She admitted she was attracted to him but saw no need to tell Penny of his random boat trips and the recent nighttime visit. Or the kiss that still made her lips tingle when she thought of it. It had been four days since that encounter, and she hadn't heard or seen Rail since. Not even a text. She lifted a shoulder. "So what? He's good-looking and a biker. I can be attracted to that without the hassle of dating. Besides, I bet he's not the dating type."

Penny screwed up her mouth. "You're right about that. As far as I know, he's never had a girlfriend or significant other in his life. Just one or two nights and he's done."

Gretchen peered quizzically at Penny. "Just how well do you know him?"

Penny's raised eyebrows and pointed look told the story without words. Gretchen's mouth opened in a perfect O as understanding dawned. "You've fucked him!"

Penny shushed her even though the likelihood of anyone understanding the sign Gretchen made was low. "Yes, I did. Twice, a long time ago. I used to go up to Red Wing to party with the Dutchmen MC on weekends when I didn't have to work. I met Railroad there and recognized him from visiting Flora. We were a lot younger, and yes, we hooked up a couple times. There were a lot of women at the club who wanted to be his old lady, and every one of them got disappointed. He's like the mountain no one can climb or the apple no one can reach."

Gretchen held one of the new tops in front of her and wrinkled her brow. "I don't like the orange color of this one. So, why do you think he's someone for me?"

Penny took the rejected garment and pulled another one from the rack. "You're into bikers."

"MC romance books. That doesn't mean I'm into him."

"True, but there was something between you. I could see it clearly, and Flora could too. She keeps asking when you're going to come see her."

Gretchen blew out her lips again. Admitting she

liked him would be a mistake. Penny would latch onto that like a dog with a bone and become a mini version of Rail's Grams. "Flora is very nice, and I like her, but she's doing what every grandmother does from time to time. Classic character trope of the mother figure wishing her son had a woman in his life for happy couplehood with future babies. I've read it hundreds of times in the books I've edited."

Penny gave in. "Maybe, but I have a sense for these things." She flipped her hands up to frame her face. "Call me clairvoyant, but I can see you and Rail together."

Her stomach fluttered. "How?"

Penny shook her head. "I don't know. You just fit."

Gretchen rolled her eyes as she entered the dressing room. "You're blind."

"We should go up and party with them sometime. You wear that top and I bet he'd go a little crazy with you there. Added plus is you get to see that part of his life."

"I changed my mind. You're not blind. You're insane."

"Oh, come on, Gretchen. You spend most of your time holed up in that house with your computer and only go out the few nights a week I can get you to go bowling. When was the last time you went out with a flesh-and-blood man instead of a book character?"

She held up a hand and began ticking off points as she signed. "Rail is hot, even with those scars on his face. He likes boats. He likes the river. He's clearly into you, and, the big one, he can sign. I saw him treat you like a person, not like a person with a disability. Now that you have all these out-on-the-town clothes, let's not waste them at River Lanes Bowling. Let's go live a little wild."

"Won't it be weird for you?"

Penny wrinkled her nose and pulled out a shimmering pink blouse to hold against herself. "Not really. Don't get me wrong, I like Rail a lot, and he was fantastic in bed, but we just didn't connect. We work better as friends."

Gretchen couldn't help the sense of relief that flowed through her chest. Love triangles weren't her thing. *Wait. Stop it, Gretch. There is no love triangle. There is no love. Yet. Gah!* "That color is burning my eyes. What else do you know about him?"

Penny put the blazing pink top back on the rack. "Fishing for a character profile? You should write your own book someday. I don't know everything about him. How he makes a living, what his favorite foods are, what he likes and dislikes. The club is rough, and it's not a good idea to cross them, but from what I understand from the rumor mill, they're going through some changes. A lot of them stem from Rail, who's the new president."

"What happened to the old one?"

"Honestly, I'm not sure. I met Iceman years ago, but I'm not that involved. Since they're up in Red Wing, I don't have a lot of contact anymore other than when Rail comes to visit Flora. You wanna know more? That's another reason we need to go to their bar and party. Now, are you gonna buy those tops or not?"

Gretchen rolled her eyes. "Yes, I'll buy the tops. Happy now?"

"Nope. Now you need some kickass jean shorts and some heels to go with them."

The eye roll got bigger. "I am not... repeat... *not* wearing heels and shorts. In fact, I don't do shorts. Not with my ass and thigh spread."

"Oh, come on. There are women across the world who go under the knife to get an ass like yours. All round and juicy and—"

"I'm going to throw something at you."

Penny set off in peals of laughter, and Gretchen added her own version.

An hour later, both women left the stores loaded with bags. Any attempt at conversation was impossible with full hands. Gretchen's back was sending sore messages when Penny stopped short and her face lost its happy vibe. She jerked her head several times toward the opposite sidewalk. Gretchen trusted her friend to know what was best and hurried after her. A glance up told her why.

Three men with large rifles slung across their backs were loading piles of boxes into the bed of a truck. They wore camouflage T-shirts and pants along with mirrored aviator sunglasses and ball caps.

At first, Gretchen thought military, but there was no base anywhere close to Lake City. Hunters? Odd that any hunter would carry an assault rifle plus handguns on their hips. She felt the bump from Penny's hip signaling her to hurry up, and she turned away from the sight. Once they got to the car, Penny put down a handful of bags and pressed her car remote to unlock the doors. "Sorry to push you, but it's best not to be around those guys very long."

"Who are they?"

Penny opened the trunk and placed the bags inside before answering. "There's some sort of weird survivalist group out by one of the big farms. I met one of them on Tinder. Nice enough guy, but he had some strange ideas. Talked about too much government control and how his family is almost completely self-sufficient and lives off the grid. Kept repeating something about how separation of wheat and chaff is the only way to stay pure in this world. His picture looked just like one of those men. I ended up deleting my profile. Not much to choose from on there, anyway. So, are we going to Red Wing or not?"

"I'm trying to decide."

"Decide what? It's a simple yes or no."

Gretchen shook her head. "Not about Red Wing. That's a yes. It's what to say about you and Tinder and GI Joe back there."

Penny slammed the trunk lid down and rolled her eyes upward as she turned to face Gretchen. "Yeah, yeah, I tried the internet dating thing. I started it mainly to entertain Flora. She had a blast picking out my profile photo and then seeing all the responses. I did meet some really nice men, and a few weird ones too, but no chemistry. When I find it, I'm in, but right now I'm having fun watching you." Her lips curled into a big happy grin. "Now I get why Flora loved the dating app so much. It's fun setting someone else up. Like I'm a fairy godmother or something like that."

Gretchen pointed a finger at her friend before signing, "You can be a fairy godmother all you want, but I'm still not wearing heels and shorts to the ball."

CHAPTER
THIRTEEN

PIGLET STRETCHED HIS ARMS OVER HIS HEAD AND HIS back popped. He spent hours every day fixing farm machinery, but despite the long physical work, he felt better than he ever had in his life. Being forced not to smoke had opened his lungs, and breathing was easier. The fresh farm produce and healthy meals had made a difference in his overall well-being. He had more energy, and he appeared more vibrant. Other men knew his name, and when they spoke to him, there was a respectful tone in their voices, thanking him for his hard work.

"You coming tonight?" one of the other mechanics shouted to him across the garage.

Piglet grinned and nodded. "Yeah, I'll be there." The first meeting had been strange and uncomfortable, but the night had been incredible. After eating that nasty mushroom piece, his dick stayed hard for hours. He fucked and fucked and fucked all night long, so much that he lost count of how many times he came in the woman. She never protested or asked him to stop. She just let him take her over and over again, only reaching over to oil herself before he stuck his dick in her. Instead of being tired and wrung out, he was buzzing with energy the next day, and he hoped he could go to another meeting soon. He could listen to and repeat the crazy words if he got another mushroom.

"Some of us are gonna go train this afternoon. Brother Matthias wanted to know if you wanted to come to that?"

Piglet closed the hood on the work truck. There were places on the property he hadn't been allowed to see yet, and the mysterious training field was one of them. His grin got bigger and happier. If Matthias wanted him to join in, that meant he, Piglet, had earned deeper trust and acceptance into the brotherhood. The more Matthias liked Piglet, the more brotherhood privileges he received. Piglet found himself thinking daily as he worked, not about doing a good job but how happy Matthias would be.

After lunch, Piglet and a dozen or so farm workers scrambled into the bed of a massive work truck to go "train." Piglet had only a vague idea of what it was and imagined a line of men working out like martial artists in those old Blackbelt Theatre movies he watched as a kid. He loved the idea of playing with nunchucks and learning how to fight like Bruce Lee.

"So, do we partner up for this training or what? Is it like karate or something?" he asked one of the other men.

The truck bounced violently over several ruts before an answer came. "Not that kind of training, brother. We don't do that foreign shit here."

Piglet sensed the man's irritation and kept quiet for the rest of the ride. They came to a small area with a large locked shed. One of the men opened it while the others started stripping. Piglet looked on with his mouth open in confusion.

"What the f—" He bit off the curse word before it left his mouth. The first time he said the word fuck in front of Matthias, the man frowned so hard, Piglet felt shame. He'd been censoring himself ever since.

"Grab a suit, brother. You don't want to be the first one down."

Camouflage coveralls with hoods, chest protectors, and pairs of safety goggles were handed out. Piglet followed along with everyone and took off his outer clothing to don the heavy hunting gear.

Guns followed. Piglet's heart jumped into overdrive. These weren't paintball or air pistols. These were the real deal. A variety of automatic rifles that Piglet had seen only in military movies or shows. Expensive and not used for hunting.

A smiling man handed him a rifle. "Don't look so scared, brother. This is just training. We use simunition so no one gets killed. Hurts like a mother if you get hit, but there's a simple solution for that: don't get hit."

Peals of laughter erupted around him, but Piglet didn't feel reassured.

The training game was simple: shoot the opposing team until none were standing. The two teams were identifiable only by the way their camo ball caps were turned. Red and blue armbands were too obvious and easy to spot—therefore, no colors were used.

They scattered into the woods, and Piglet was left alone to figure out for himself what he was supposed to do. Move around? Stay in one place and wait to see who passed him? Build a hunting blind to hide behind?

Sweat dripped down his brow, making his pale hair cling to his scalp. He didn't dare wipe it away as that would make him let go of his tight grip on the gun. Time passed. How much, he didn't know. He strained his eyes looking for any kind of movement, and his ears rang as he listened for any scrap of sound. It wasn't as if he'd never been around guns or held one. All the MCs he'd been involved with had arsenals of different firearms and weapons. He'd participated in target shooting and had openly carried his own 9mm. If he didn't, the other bikers would have called him a pussy.

Only once had he ever fired at someone, and that was when he escaped from the fiery hell of the burning Tiger Clan compound. Half the man's face had blown off, and Piglet was still haunted by that memory.

Here in this wooded area, he felt out of place and outclassed by everyone else. He wanted to be accepted here and thought he'd made some headway with the meeting and the funny mushroom communion deal. Now, he shook in his boots like some scared little girl. He wondered what Matthias would say if he saw the fear in Piglet's eyes at this moment.

A sharp crack sounded, followed by a scream of pain. Piglet almost dropped his rifle. Fuck, what the hell was he thinking by staying here so long? He should have stolen a boat months ago and gone to Canada. He should have run far and fast at the first hint of trouble. He should have never joined up with the Tiger Clan in the first place.

Time moved on, punctuated by random shots and

screams. Tension rose in Piglet's body, and his head pounded with it. How many of his team were down? What about the other team? What kind of training was this supposed to be?

Bile rose at the back of his throat, choking him.

A flicker caught his eye, and he crouched low, keeping as quiet as he could. He could barely make out a figure creeping around a tree some yards away. The man's cap identified him as being on the other team. He stopped, leaned his rifle against the tree, and reached to unzip his fly. A stream of urine splattered against the ground near the base. Another shot reverberated through the woods.

Piglet's heart rate doubled, and his ears filled with white noise. His vision grayed until his only focus was the man still peeing despite the noise. Was it wrong to shoot a man with his dick hanging out? Was it wrong to shoot a man in the back? Was it wrong to shoot a man, period? What would Matthias do? What would Matthias want him to do?

Piglet lifted his rifle and took aim.

The man finished and tucked himself away. He picked up his gun and looked around. Piglet froze, hoping not to be spotted, and the man left quickly.

No such luck. Piglet saw exactly when the man found him. He watched through the sight as the guy's face changed and his mouth made a perfect O. He jerked his rifle up.

It was now or never. Shoot or be shot.

Piglet squeezed the trigger.

Piglet got him square in the chest protector. The man yelled and went down. He rolled on the ground in obvious great pain. Piglet scampered over to him from behind so the fallen man wouldn't see his face or the tears running down.

"I'm sorry," he whispered as he collected the man's cap. What was he supposed to do now? Help him? Leave him there writhing on the ground? When would this fucking game be over?

Piglet hurried away. The gunshot would surely bring someone to check, right?

More time. More shots. More screams. Piglet was ready to scream himself when he heard a bull-horned voice through the air.

"Return to the clearing, brothers. We have a winner."

Piglet sighed with relief, and he brushed away the traces of tear tracks. No way he wanted anyone to think him a pussy instead of a badass biker. He carefully made his way back to the staging area and saw many of the men had already returned. Some of them were limping and being helped by others, and some were rubbing their chests and backs. Only three were standing upright with no injuries: Matthias, Thomas, and himself.

Matthias greeted him with a wide smile. "Impressive, Ezra. Not many survive their first training. Maybe you have some pointers to give to the rest of the men."

Piglet stood up and preened a little at Matthias's praise. "This wasn't hard. I used to do a lot worse in the Dark Horses."

Matthias nodded. "I bet you did. I can't tell you how much of an asset you've become to the farm. The elders and I have been talking a lot, and… well…." The man took a big breath to impart the importance of his next words. "We'd like to invite you to become a full brother in our group with all the privileges of the title. It's a big decision to make, but I think you fit in here, and we need a man like you in our ranks. Take your time, but I'd like to get you initiated at the next meeting on Friday night. What do you say?"

Happiness welled up in Piglet's chest. Matthias's praise and the invitation to be a part of this brotherhood excited him. Gone were the fears and concerns he'd had during this so-called training. "I don't have to think about it. I'm in."

CHAPTER
FOURTEEN

Dusk had settled in over the Harbor Bar in a gray overcast mess. Rail leaned on a bare fence post and stared out over the water. Behind him, music bled into the parking lot from the crowded dance floor. This time last year, he'd have been in the middle of it, prowling for a woman and watching his brothers do the same. Now, he just wasn't interested.

His focus remained on the survival of the club and what form that would take. The in-fighting had grown worse over the past week. Rebel was banging every woman who would let him and spending most of his time in a drug-induced stupor. He claimed it was impending fatherhood, but at the rate he inhaled the fine white powder he'd somehow found a source for, it wouldn't be long until he left his kid an orphan. Peebles had already kicked him out permanently.

Rail lifted the bottle to his lips and took a long draft of the warm beer. The bar, the marina, and the new grill expansion were all doing well, bringing in a decent profit. Liquor sales were up, and people had no problem coming to spend money. Why in the hell did the club need to start transporting again?

He shook his head, not understanding the logic behind wanting to live on that razor's edge. One misstep and that was it. Over. The good news would be that someone only got hurt. The bad news would be that someone died.

He couldn't deal with it tonight. Chapel tomorrow would be soon enough. Tonight he wanted to drink himself to oblivion.

He turned to face the parking lot as a pair of headlights brushed across the area. Two women got out. Even in the dim lighting, it wasn't hard for Rail to recognize them. Penny had on a short silky dress and skyscraper heels that were way over-the-top for this locale. Gretchen's outfit of boot-cut jeans, a shiny top, and short boots was more appropriate, but Rail's attention still zeroed in on her like a magnet. The shimmering green fabric had cutouts showing off her shoulders and a deep plunge between the cleft of her breasts. Both women wore heavier-than-daytime makeup and appeared to be ready for a party. Or on the prowl.

Rail frowned. Gretchen looked good. Too good. The men would swarm around her in a heartbeat once she entered the bar. Jealousy along with a bit of anger surfaced in him. The kiss they shared had rocked his world, but they hadn't had any communication since. He hadn't texted her, but she'd been obsessively on his mind anyway.

How the fuck was he supposed to handle her? Never in his life had he done the dating thing or considered having an old lady. Take a woman for dinner, movie, dancing, or whatever the fuck couples did together. Women came to him for sex, and he showed them a good time, but none of them had ever made him want more. Gretchen was smart, beautiful, and so out of his league he'd never catch up. She was a classy, educated businesswoman and had a confidence in herself few people achieved. Her deafness didn't stop her from having a great life. He was a biker who fixed boat engines and used to make a living by running illegal drugs up and down the Mississippi River. In what world would they ever work together? He'd thought he might be able to just fuck her and get it out of his system, but after that kiss, that fucking fantastic kiss, he knew it would never be enough. She hadn't texted him either, so she clearly didn't feel anything toward him like he did her.

Yet here she was, all dressed up and sexy as fucking hell. If he had an ounce of pride, he'd leave and go directly to the clubhouse.

He cursed, poured the rest of the beer on the ground, and entered the bar.

———

GRETCHEN FELT THE THUMPING BASS FROM THE MOMENT they entered the bar. A DJ was set up in one corner, working his system to the delight of the happy crowd. She didn't have to hear to pick up on the vibe of the room. If loud had a meaning for her, it was the excited atmosphere of the place.

Penny signed that they should go to the bar, and they both wound a path to the square counter. Heavy resin coated the flat wood, and Gretchen's eyes lit up when she spotted the tiny metal figures of turtles scattered in the hardened clear filler.

"Very cute and creative," she signed.

Penny grinned and handed her a bottle from a local microbrewery. "Cheers, girlfriend."

They clinked the necks and took long swallows.

"The music is really loud. No one will be able to tell that you're deaf unless they see me sign to you.

It's nice not to have to shout, so score for knowing ASL." Penny bobbed to the music, and Gretchen saw the rhythm as well as felt it.

Deaf people could dance, contrary to popular belief. Gretchen liked dancing and, frankly, had stopped caring a long time ago what people thought of her. She was curious about Rail's opinion, even though he'd left her hanging on the pier. She hadn't seen him yet. Perhaps he wasn't here tonight.

Her disappointment didn't last long. A cute, lanky man with a nose full of freckles and a ginger mullet pulled at her arm. His mouth formed the word "dance." The rest of his question was lost, of course, but his big smile and shining eyes told her all she needed to know. She chugged the beer and left it on the bar as he tugged her into the gyrating crowd.

There wasn't a lot of room, but she moved with the surrounding bodies. The man said something she didn't catch. She laughed, pointed to her ears, and shrugged. He shrugged back and gave her a big grin. Apparently, whatever he said wasn't that big a deal. No reason to let him know she was deaf from birth and not from the music.

Penny danced by with a burly brunet fellow. She hip-checked Gretchen with a big grin, and they danced side by side. Somehow they switched partners, and she found herself in front of the big brown-haired man. His front teeth overlapped a bit, and he had a small gut, but so did she. In her book world, people were perfect. Women always thin, beautiful, and fragile, and the men tall, virile, dominant, and cut with muscle. She'd rather have the small imperfections of the real world that made people human.

Rail came to her mind with his scars and secrets.

The dancing shifted again, and she found a new man in front of her. Sandy-blond hair and light blue eyes. It seemed all she had to do was stay in one place and the world danced around her. Heat built up from the bodies, and she started to sweat. Another beer bottle found its way into her hand, and she gulped the cold liquid, not caring about the mild burn in her throat. More dancing and several beers later, she needed to take a break. Her head was getting buzzed from the alcohol, and it wouldn't be long before she had to go break the seal and pee. Penny waved off another admirer and motioned that she was heading to the bar. Gretchen nodded and made to follow, but a pair of hands grabbed her hips and pulled her back. A hard body started grinding itself against her butt, and she managed to turn her head long enough to see ginger-mullet man pumping away.

Nope. Big turnoff, fella. She tried to dislodge his hands and shake him off, but he gripped her harder.

The glare she pitched over her shoulder had no effect. In fact, his face showed his determination that she was going to stay right where she was. A frisson of fear trickled down her spine. She was being assaulted right there on the dance floor, and no one noticed or was stepping in. Should she stomp his foot? Claw his hands? Elbow him in the gut?

The grinding stopped, and she lurched forward into another set of hands as she was freed. She looked up into the face of one of the Dutchmen who broke into her house. His attention wasn't on her but on what was happening behind her. She glanced back to see Rail's back as he stood over her aggressor. Mullet man was on the floor, holding his nose. Blood dripped between his fingers. The faces of the other patrons showed varied expressions of shock, fear, and, oddly, satisfaction.

Penny came up to Gretchen. "Are you okay? I saw that asshole dry-humping you and tried to get to you, but Rail took him out first." She shook her head in disbelief. "This is Duke, another Dutchmen member. He said a big bunch of traveling oil workers came down from the refinery tonight to blow off some steam. Not the first time these guys have gone overboard here, but it might be the last."

Mullet man slowly got to his feet and yelled something at Rail. He made the mistake of pointing a finger in his face, and Rail punched him again, sending the man to his knees. Oil workers started squaring up against Rail, and several Dutchmen appeared as Duke slipped past the women to cover his MC brother's back. Gretchen held her breath as she was sure an all-out brawl was about to happen. Then the room collectively looked over at the bar. Gretchen saw the bartender clanging a giant nautical bell hanging on the wall. Whatever he shouted diffused the situation, and the tension in the room dissipated.

Penny let out a whoosh. "Thank God someone had some sense. Better to lose some money on free booze than have to pay for repairs and hospital bills."

Gretchen agreed and took a shaky breath. For all her bravado, she'd been scared. But just like on the night she met the Dutchmen for the first time, Rail protected her. She remembered the one they called Rebel had been rabid in his anger, and both the other men stood by, but Rail promised her no harm. Here he was again, keeping her safe. Emotions swirled in her mind. Gratefulness to him for his rescue, guilt because he had to rescue her in the first place, and angry at the man who started it all.

Rail's head turned, and his eyes burned straight into hers. Rage. Pure rage. At what exactly, she didn't know. *Hmph, it better not be at me. I didn't do this. I didn't—*

With three long strides, he came to her and grabbed her arm in his iron grip. No chance of falsely interpreting his message that, though wordless, clearly said, "Come with me now." She thought briefly of resisting but decided against it. He wouldn't save her just to hurt her, and if he wanted to yell at her, she had plenty to say back. She kept up as he pulled her behind him out to one of the long piers where the boats bobbed in the river.

"What the fuck were you thinking?" His movements and words were jerky with his anger.

She got pissed. "What do you mean, what I was thinking? I wasn't thinking anything other than someone get that asshole off me. Thank you for that, by the way."

He ignored her gratitude and kept up his tirade. "What did you think would happen, dressed like that?"

Oh fuck no. "Are you saying because I'm not wearing a nun's habit, it's okay for a man to hump my ass? I didn't realize my clothing choices had anything to do with issuing an invitation for assault."

"You should have figured out men were going to hit on you. These guys are the types that see a little cleavage as a neon fuck-me sign."

Gretchen lost it. "How is that my problem? You're telling me that men turn into slavering idiots if they see a sliver of female flesh, and the only way to control that is for women to assume the responsibility for their bad behavior? That's fucking bullshit, and you know it."

"Don't be stupid. You're a beautiful woman who came to a biker bar. Fucking trouble started the moment you stepped inside."

Her face flushed at his *beautiful* comment, but she was still angry at the way he blamed her for the fight. "Still not my problem. If men can't control their dicks, that's not on me or any other woman. Besides, why should you care? It's not like we're involved."

His face grew darker.

She raged on, ignoring the storm clouds in his eyes. "I know you had ample opportunity to be with me at my house. You were the one who walked away. As far as I'm concerned, you have no say in my life. Who the fuck do you think you are?"

His mouth opened, and she was sure he let out a long angry yell. He picked up a long piece of two-by-four that had been left in a scrap heap on the pier and hurled it powerfully into the water.

Time stopped. Gretchen's lungs gulped air, and her rage trickled away into fear. No, not fear, exactly. There was no doubt in her mind that he wouldn't lose his temper and strike her. Curiosity might be the better word. What the hell was going on in this man's brain?

He finally faced her, and his eyes glittered with something. She didn't see anger. She didn't see remorse. She didn't see distress.

He looked at her fully, and her breath caught. Pain. There was pain in his eyes.

She pulled her shoulders back and stood tall, wrapping composure around herself as a shield. "Railroad, you've sat by me a number of times. We've talked. You've told me some about your club. A little about your past. I think you've shared more with me than you have with anyone in a long time. Am I wrong?"

His hands clenched into fists before he raised them to sign to her. "From the first night we met in that fucked-up house raid, all I can think about is you. I'd rather be sitting next to you watching the river flow than hanging with my brothers. I've never sat at a table, eating dinner a woman cooked for me. Had a real conversation where I could unload and be safe when I did. No one except for Flora gave me that. The only other person who ever came close was Iceman, but even with him, he was my president first, friend second."

He raised his face to the night sky, and Gretchen

waited for him to gather his thoughts. "I want you," he finally signed. "Not once have I ever burned for someone like I do for you. It makes no sense. We're from two different worlds, and I still want you more than any other woman I know. I don't know why, and it's killing me."

He paused again, breathing hard. Gretchen breathed with him. His words brought a thrill to her, but she saw he struggled against these feelings he'd not experienced before.

"What you don't get is that at the clubhouse, people fuck all over the place. I've seen the girl who gave me a blow job one night bent over the pool table and getting herself drilled by another man the next. Never bothered me. I saw that man touch you, rub himself on you, and all I could see was red. I wanted to kill him. Put that motherfucker in the river and watch him sink to the bottom for daring to put his hands on what's mine."

He gave a rough laugh. "Problem is, I don't know if it's mine. I want it. I want you, but I have no fucking idea what I'm doing, and I'm scared shitless I'm gonna fuck it all up. How's that for a badass biker?"

Gretchen didn't say how his words affected her. She showed him. Two steps brought her to him, and she reached for his head with both hands to bring his mouth to hers. His groan vibrated against her lips, and his impregnable wall crumbled as his arms claimed her.

She met him halfway, clutching and clawing to get closer. His tongue invaded her mouth, and she dueled with him for dominance. Fire erupted in between her legs, and she pressed them together to ease the ache. Any residual argument evaporated as pure lust took over. She fisted her hands in his thick hair as he fed from her, drawing her closer. He reached down and lifted her onto a wooden pier table, spreading her thighs by pushing between them. She gasped into his mouth as his rigid dick rubbed against her pussy.

God, she wanted him. She wanted to feel his mouth at her breasts. She wanted the promise that strained behind his jeans to be inside her. She wanted to see his body over hers as he thrust into her over and over. Damnit, she should have worn a skirt tonight. If she had, he would only need to open his fly, pull aside the crotch of her panties, and....

Fuck me, I'm gonna come!

She tore her mouth from his and ground herself against him as the first spasm hit her body. An utterance of satisfaction left her throat, and she didn't care if he heard or not. Waves of pleasure ran through her body, and she slid her hands to his ass to grind herself to him. He took her hands and pulled them behind her, taking control as the last of her orgasm washed over her. He bent his head and sank his teeth into the bare skin showing through the cutout at her shoulder. His body shook, taut as a bowstring before letting loose an arrow. He fought for control, and she realized that even though she came, he didn't.

Breath sawed in and out of his mouth that was still clenched on her shoulder. She remained motionless, partly because of the iron grip he had on her and partly because she didn't want to make things worse on him. He finally let her go and stepped back.

She awkwardly hopped off the table. This shit only happened between the pages of the romance books she edited, and they gave no clue as to what to do now. She watched as he turned away from her and continued to suck in huge breaths. He raised his hands to the back of his head as he faced the river.

She had no idea if she was supposed to walk away, stay and wait, or grab his ass. Duke's appearance took care of that.

He got Rail's attention, and Gretchen only caught a few words by reading his lips in the dark night. Something about "Nutter" and "gun." She saw Rail curse and jerk his hands to his sides. He nodded to Duke and reached for her hand.

"Shitty timing, but I have to go. I'll explain later.

Right now, I need you on the back of my bike so I can take you to my compound where I know you'll be safe."

"What's going on?"

"Trouble, and not the good kind. Will you please trust me and go to the compound? I'll come as soon as I can."

Half a dozen responses ran through her brain, none of them appropriate. "Yes, I'll wait for you. Where's Penny?"

"Duke's got her."

He took her to his bike in the back of the lot and showed her where to put her feet. As many MC books as she edited, it was much different seeing the big machine in real life.

"No helmets?" she signed as she moved to mount up behind him.

He took time to answer her. "Usually, yes, but we're not going far, and I didn't bring them. I'll grab mine from my room once I get you settled. Promise me you won't leave."

The fervency of his request pierced her heart. "I promise."

The ride was short, over almost before it started, but even in that little bit of time, Gretchen learned something about the man in front of her. No jerking jackrabbit starts as he pulled out. No show-off revs or weaves. Just careful driving until they reached a gated gravel lot. Rail drove in and parked, letting her dismount first before kicking down the stand and getting off himself. He took her hand and strode quickly through the clubhouse, not giving her much time to form an impression. She saw a wide-open space, a topless woman dancing around a pole, and several astonished faces. Perhaps seeing Rail with a woman in tow was a rare sight. She liked that idea.

He led her down a hall to a room in the back. It was plain with little decoration but held a neatly made queen-sized bed. Rail picked up a helmet from the top of the dresser and gestured to the drawers. "I have extra T-shirts if you want to change. Bathroom is through there. Mini fridge has waters in it. You hungry?"

She shook her head.

He stared at her for a long moment, then crossed the room. She was back in his arms, and this time his mouth was gentle as he covered hers. He kissed her thoroughly and released her lips with reluctance. Without another word or glance, he left.

CHAPTER
FIFTEEN

MAMA J HAD MOVED INTO A HOUSE THAT USED TO belong to Gabriella's uncle Roger. He was now deceased, one of the victims of the war between the Tiger Clan and the Dutchmen. Gabby had no need of the house and Mama J did. Therefore, Gabby generously gave it to her before moving to the Outer Banks of North Carolina.

Rail rode up to the house and joined Camo and Spider. He switched off his bike, and the *lug-lug-lug* of the engine died away, letting him hear the wild yelling coming from the front lawn of the house.

Nutter staggered around the neatly trimmed grass, a half-empty liquor bottle in one hand and a 9mm pistol in the other. Nutter was a dangerous person in a fight. His sturdy build wasn't gym quality, but he was strong, and his punches had some serious power behind them. A sober Nutter could hurt someone bad. A drunk Nutter could be lethal. A drunk Nutter with a gun removed all doubt that someone was going to die.

Rail watched as Nutter lifted the vodka and took a healthy swallow. He gestured with the gun and shouted at the house. "Yoo can't keep mah kidz frum meh!"

Yes, she could, and Rail wouldn't blame her. No woman in her right mind would let her children hang out with a drunken and armed father. It got worse.

"Ah know yoo gotta man in ther. Send 'im out here to face meh like a man shud. Thinkz he'z man enuff to take mah woman? Fuck that shit!"

Camo filled Rail in as the situation escalated. "Nutter thinks Mama J's got a friend. A male friend. Nutter saw him cutting the grass earlier today and went ballistic. He claims this guy is inside the house with her and the kids, and Nutter's been calling for him to come out so he can shoot him."

"Ged oud here, muthafucka!"

Rail kept his eyes on Nutter's weaving body. Maybe the vodka would make him pass out soon? Fat chance of that happening. He'd seen Nutter put away booze in such quantities that other men would die from alcohol poisoning.

"Why didn't Mama J call the police?"

Camo rolled his eyes and scoffed. "She should have but called us instead. They are definitely over, but she still has feelings for him. Despite all the shit Nutter's piled on her over the years, I don't think she wants to see him jailed."

Rail wasn't sure he agreed with that sentiment, but he would roll with it. "Any chance the neighbor called them?"

Camo shrugged. "Maybe, but I haven't seen any blue flashing lights yet. Might be afraid of retaliation from the club if they do. Nutter's got his colors on, and people know enough to be afraid of us."

Rail's conflicted mind and heart ran in circles. If Iceman were here, he'd end this shit by taking out his own gun and shooting Nutter in the shoulder to drop the big man. Then he'd stand over the fallen biker and drill rounds in each leg for pissing him off. But Iceman wasn't here, and Rail found it distasteful to put a bullet in a brother no matter how bad he fucked up.

All bets were off, though, if Nutter pointed that gun at the house or any of the bikers watching. "Rebel know about this? I don't see him."

"Not that I know of," Camo answered. "The last thing we need is his ass here making it worse. He's been egging Nutter on for weeks about Mama J and getting his bitch back in line. The shit with him and Peebles has gotten extreme, and I expect she'll be calling us soon to get him off her front lawn too."

"Gawdamn prick! Yoo bedder not be fuckin' mah woman!"

Rail wished Iceman would appear and lead, but that was like wishing for the moon to step down from the heavens. He himself had to take charge. Now.

"Hey, Nutter. What's going on, brother?" he started, keeping his tone friendly, as if he was just joining the group.

Nutter swung around in surprise, but the gun stayed pointed to the ground. His bleary eyes finally focused on Rail and the men behind him as if seeing them for the first time.

"Ther'z an asshole in there fuckin' mah ol'lady. I'm gonna shoot 'iz ballz off."

"Maybe you should think about that. What are your kids going to think if you fire that gun at someone?"

"Leaf mah kidz oudovit."

"Hard to do that when they can see what you're doing right now."

Nutter paused to take another big swallow. Rail imagined he was too drunk to notice the burn. A flutter of movement in one of the windows confirmed that someone occupied the house, but he had no way of knowing who and how many.

"Ah fucked up."

Rail wanted to roll his eyes. He'd seen this pattern from the big man before. When Nutter got drunk, he would get blustery and bold at first, full of righteous indignation over whatever subject hit his head. Then a switch flipped in his sodden brain, and he descended into teary-eyed self-pity. Most of the time, he was ignored by the other members and left to sleep it off. If they were back at the clubhouse, it would be an easy task to convince the drunk man to go to his room and pass out. Not an option in this situation. A slobbery depressed Nutter with a gun was still a danger. "Yeah, you did. You fucked up, brother. Maybe so bad, you can't make it right. What you can do right now is not make it worse. You want to help me with that?"

"Luv my brotherz. Luv the Dussshmen." Nutter's face crumpled, and he sat heavily on the ground. "Luv my Mama J too."

The gun dropped to the man's side in his loose grip, but Rail wouldn't feel safe until the firearm was in his own hand. "You and Mama J need a talk. A long one. She's not going to do that with you waving a pistol in her face. The fastest way for you to say your piece is to give me the gun and go sleep off the vodka."

Nutter sniffed and wiped under his nose with the hand holding the vodka. A splash of the clear liquid landed on his cut. "Think she still luvs meh?"

Rail sighed. He couldn't lie to Nutter. "I don't know. What I do know is, if you keep this shit up, she won't want anything to do with you."

Nutter slumped down in a picture of absolute defeat. He raised his red eyes to the house and gave a huge sigh. With a grunt, he gracelessly lifted himself from his seated position on the ground. An explosive fart came from him as he heaved upward. Rail heard a bark of laughter behind him, and he turned with a scowl on his face. "Shut the fuck up. It's not helping to kick a brother when he's down."

Nutter gained his feet and took a big, labored breath at the effort. "Here. Yoo can hav-it." He handed the gun to Rail.

Rail took the piece with gratitude. "Thanks, Nutter. Camo and Spider will get you back to the clubhouse so you can sleep off the booze. We'll talk tomorrow and get a game plan going, yeah?"

Nutter wailed and stumbled as he moved to hug Rail. "Yoor the best bruther ever."

The weight of the staggering man almost took

him down. "Ease up, Nutter. Spider, you got your truck?"

"Parked down the street."

"Get it and get him out of here."

It took all three men to load Nutter into the truck bed. The drunken biker flopped down onto the hard bed and immediately started snoring.

Rail checked the chamber and removed the clip from the handle. He gave both pieces to Camo. "If you can't wake him up at the clubhouse, just throw a tarp over him and leave him there. I'm going to see if Mama J will talk to me."

The biker nodded, slightly out of breath from having to help the heavy man now lying asleep. "You bet."

Rail waited until the taillights disappeared before he approached the door. Mama J opened it as he raised his knuckles to knock. "Thank you for coming to get him."

Her voice was tired and worn. She looked thinner under the long, flowered robe she had belted around her waist. The woman was usually boisterous and happy in all things. He'd never seen her this low. Doubts if he was equipped to handle this arose in his mind, but he was the only one left. "You okay? Where are the kids?"

She sighed. "Come on in. Want a drink? I don't

have any beer. Just water, milk, and some Capri Suns for the kids. They're in bed and didn't wake up to see their father's fit. I think they're so used to hearing such noise, they can sleep through a tornado."

"I'm good." He sat in her living room on the sofa.

She followed and sat in a side chair. She didn't wait for him to ask her anything. "I'm not seeing anyone. Nutter decided I was when Carson Knilling came over to move a refrigerator for me and put in some new appliances. He was kind enough to cut my grass without charging me for it." She shook her head as tears began to flow down her cheeks. "I can't believe the man I committed myself to treats me this way. I ignored his cheating for years and told myself it didn't matter because he still loved me. He gave me his patch and called me his old lady, right? That's supposed to mean something. But he gives himself to other women while I stay here and take care of his house and children. Even the ones he made with another woman."

Rail watched Mama J pull a tissue from a box on a side table and wipe her nose. The room contained an old box TV that had toys scattered around it. Rail had been here to fix some house problems with the sink and other small jobs, but there was always something else that needed work. "He ever come by to help you?"

She shook her head and sighed. "No. I've asked him to, but he always has an excuse. Club business. Something with Mimi and her place. I'm always last on his list of priorities, and I'll always be last." She gestured to the front of the house. "That show he put on out there? I don't think he'd ever hurt me deliberately, but I can't have that again. What if he shot me by accident? What would happen to my kids? He'll never step up, and anyone who thinks he will is a fool. If you're going to ask me to take him back, the answer is no."

Rail leaned forward and placed his elbows on his knees. "I'm not asking you to do that. If you took him back, it would be the dumbest move you've ever made."

Mama J gawked a bit in surprise. "I thought for sure you would. I bet there are other Dutchmen who think I should shut up and deal."

"If there are, they need to shut up themselves. We have enough problems already, but that's not your concern. Club business is club business. If anyone gives you a hard time, including Nutter, you call me, and I'll take care of it."

She worried the tissue in her hands as she stared into her lap. "He has another child on the way. Some woman named Kay."

Rail could feel the woman's pain. He heard it in her voice, saw it in her defeated posture. "I'm sorry."

Mama J shrugged. "Not every story has a happy ending. Those are for romance books and Hallmark movies. I'll grieve my so-called club marriage, strap on my boots, and make a new life. I watched the hell Gabriella went through with Iceman, and she got herself together. I can do the same."

"What are you going to do?"

The woman smiled. "Gabriella had the best *lefse* recipe, dont'cha know. I made some for the school bazaar, and they sold out real quick. Marta Matthews asked me to make some for a party she was having. Someone from her house called me to place an order. I decided to take a chance and set up a booth at the River Walk Festival. My neighbor kept the kids for me so I could do it. I ran out of ingredients before the first day was over and had to buy more for the second day."

Her eyes got big, and she smiled. "I made a little over two thousand dollars selling *lefse* that weekend. Just me and my griddle."

Rail was impressed. "That's great."

She sat up straighter. "I was able to catch up on the bills and still have some money left over. I have an idea for a business, but I'm scared to try."

Rail leaned back. "Tell me."

She took a breath. "There are so many weekend festivals, craft shows, outdoor concerts and such events that I can go to and sell my *lefse*. That way, I'm home during the week to take care of my children and be a mom, and I can earn the money we need on the weekend. I've already booked three more venues, and I have a list of others this summer that are looking for vendors. My neighbor is willing to come be with the kids when I'm out. I'll make *lefse* on demand, of course, but it will be easier if I have some boxes already made up to buy. I don't have a lot of equipment, and that's what Carson was putting in for me. A large flattop grill and a big commercial mixer to make *lefse* ahead of time. Maybe I'll put up a website and sell online."

Rail smiled at the woman's enthusiasm. "Congratulations. I can see your sign. 'Mama J's Old-World Treats.' How about one of those food trucks instead of a booth?"

She shook her head. "*Uff da*, no. I don't have that kind of money, and the bank isn't going to loan to an out-of-work housewife."

Rail grunted an agreement. "Yeah, I guess not. That's a lot of work you've made for yourself. I'm sure you can handle it. You need something, you call me directly. You and Nutter might be over, but you're still a part of the Dutchmen family. I'll make it right."

She dropped her eyes. "Thank you, Rail."

The chances of her actually calling the MC for help were slim, unless she was desperate. Rail made mental plans to check on her and help her with whatever she would accept. "Best of luck, Mama J. I mean it. You need something, call me. I'll have your back."

"Even with Nutter?"

That was a huge question. Brothers didn't side against brothers, but with the club transforming into something new, there was no telling what the future held. Alliances were changing, and if Nutter was half the man he claimed to be, he'd never deny Mama J what she needed. "Even with Nutter," he said firmly.

He rose to his feet and came over to where the woman sat in her chair to lean down and kiss her temple. "I mean it. You need something, you call me."

He left Mama J sitting in her living room. The warm night air hit his face as he mounted his bike and donned his helmet. Nutter would be good until the morning, when he awakened with a serious hangover. Mama J would be all right in time. There were other club worries to deal with but not now. He had something waiting for him in his room at the compound. He started his bike and drove off.

CHAPTER
SIXTEEN

IT WAS QUIETER THAN USUAL BACK AT THE COMPOUND. The Harbor Bar had closed, and the few hangarounds who lingered weren't invited to the clubhouse for more partying. Rail met a tired Camo in the main room.

"Nutter managed to drag his ass to his room. A couple girls wanted to join him, but based on tonight's events, I kept them back." He jammed a hand over his face. "Christ, what a mess."

Rail grunted an agreement. "Rebel ever make an appearance?"

"Nobody has seen him in a couple days. Hasn't answered his phone either. Spider saw Desktop at the Marina earlier, but he hasn't been around tonight either."

What the hell was Rebel up to now? Rail's brain

fog increased as worried thoughts whirled in his head. The merry-go-round of concerns made his head hurt, but at least he could put them away for the night. He jerked his chin toward the back hallway. "My woman is back there. I'm crashing for the night. Deal with this shit tomorrow."

Camo gave a brief nod before he headed to his own room.

Rail closed the door softly. There were no windows to provide light, so the pale glow of his cell phone guided him to the bed. Gretchen lay smack in the middle of the mattress, sleeping soundly. Her blonde hair formed a wavy halo around her head, and he noticed she'd commandeered both pillows. His lips twitched upward. Beautiful.

He'd never slept all night with a woman. His past encounters had consisted of him fucking his choice for the evening, sometimes more than once, but ultimately kicking her out when he was done. He would make sure his partners were satisfied, but he didn't allow them to stay any longer than necessary. Sent the wrong message that there might be more than sex on offer. Gretchen would be the first woman in his life that he'd wake up to, and he hadn't touched her more than with a stolen kiss or two.

He stripped in the bathroom down to his black-and-gray briefs. His toothbrush was damp as he loaded it with paste and popped it in his mouth. She probably used it, as he didn't have a spare. He didn't mind.

When he returned to the bedroom, she was in the same position as before. He sat on the bed and shook her awake to get her to move over. She startled but didn't bolt.

"It's only me." He hoped the cell phone light was enough for her to see the signs.

She relaxed and signed back. "Everything okay?"

"It is now. Move over."

She shifted and gave him one of the pillows as he slipped into the bed beside her. He lay on his back, and she snuggled under his arm, giving him no choice but to hold her to his side. He put one arm around her and the other behind his head. She curled in tight, her soft breast pressing against him. His dick twitched with interest, but he ignored it.

She sighed, and he felt the moment she fell asleep with her hand across his chest. He hadn't been inside her body yet, but at this moment he was more satisfied than if he'd just come. Twice. He closed his eyes and let sleep take him.

CHAPTER
SEVENTEEN

PIGLET SHIVERED IN ANTICIPATION AS HE WALKED UP TO the big house. This was not an ordinary weekly meeting. Tonight was his acceptance into the brotherhood. When he became a Dark Horses member, there was booze, weed, and as much pussy as he wanted. He didn't know what to expect at this initiation. He hoped he didn't have to eat a live chicken or anything like that. If he did, he'd choke it down to be a part of this group. He wanted it that bad.

Matthias stood at the dais in his usual spot with High Brother Zachariah and his caregiver opposite him. Instead of the throne, a weird table with straps centered the platform. Piglet looked at it and swallowed, hoping they weren't going to tie him down and circumcise him or something equally disturbing.

Matthias motioned him to the front as the assembled men recited the opening litany. Piglet felt a frisson of fear trickle down his spine at the satisfied smile on the man's face. It was predatory.

"Ezra Davonsky, you have lived with us these past months. Eaten our bread, drunk our wine, slept under our roof. You've shared your skills and partaken of the brothers' rites. You've proven yourself to be a good and faithful follower of our creed. A man of superior blood and bone. Do you wish to become one in our brotherhood? To dedicate your life to the farm and all who live here?"

Piglet's heart swelled with pride and happiness. "I do."

"Then swear allegiance to the Brotherhood of the First Order, forsaking all in the past, giving your whole being to the cause until your last breath. Swearing to uphold all that is asked of you, and if you stumble or fall into chaos, to relieve yourself of this life by the blade."

What? Did that mean he'd have to kill himself or die if he decided he wanted out? Fear sparked in Piglet's gut, but looking around at the rabid men, it was too late to change his mind. He swallowed before he spoke. "I swear it."

"Brothers, tonight we bring into our fold one who has been found worthy. A brother of superior blood and bone. One who promises to dedicate his life to our cause and bring to the table his body, mind, spirit, and issue. What say you?"

A voice rang out from the back of the room. "Accept!"

Another one sounded. "Accept!"

One by one, they added their voices to a reverberating chorus of acceptance, and Piglet fought to keep his eyes from tearing up.

"Rise, Brother Ezra. Become one of us and take your rightful place as a member of the First Order."

Piglet stood up and willed the water in his eyes not to spill over. Applause surrounded him as a plate holding a dried mushroom and a small glass of liquor appeared in front of him.

"Take and eat, Brother Ezra."

Brother Ezra. Fuck, he liked the sound of that! He didn't mind chewing the dirt-flavored piece and washing it down with the acidic shot. The men around him started chanting as the effects of the mushroom hit his head. Fog filled his brain, and the noise became muted. Reality became surreal, and his last coherent thought was to wonder when he could take his rising boner and get to the comfort women.

"Bring forth the wife."

Wife? What the fuck?

Piglet's bleary eyes spotted two men escorting a pale robed figure into the room. He could tell it was a woman with white-blonde hair wearing a gossamer thin robe that hid none of her naked body. His dick hardened instantly at the sight of her rosy nipples and the shadow of her pussy. She seemed to be staggering a bit as if unable to hold herself up or walk straight. Drunk was the word that crossed his mind. Or she got a mushroom herself. Damnit, he needed to get out and go fuck....

Holy shit! He figured out what the table was for.

The two men brought the woman to the dais and stripped her bare. Piglet's dick pulsed painfully as they lifted the woman onto the table and strapped her legs open. Her carefully trimmed pubic hair glistened with the same oils he'd seen the comfort women use.

"Take what is rightfully yours, Brother Ezra."

The woman turned her head to the side as if resigned or falling asleep. Piglet felt as if he too was an observer and not a participant. It was someone else, not him, who removed his clothing. It was someone else who stepped up to the woman's pale body. It was someone else who thrust his straining dick inside her. It was someone else who pumped so hard her breasts bobbed violently. It was someone else who cried out in great pleasure and relief when he came.

The triumphant cries around him swelled.

He had the vague realization that he wasn't wearing a condom, and no one offered one. The mushroom worked its magic, and his dick rose again as if he hadn't just come. His new brothers shouted their encouragement. He looked down, and through the hazy fog in his brain, he saw the woman turn her face back to regard him. Her cornflower eyes were unfocused as they met his. She smiled. Fucking smiled.

He started thrusting again.

CHAPTER
EIGHTEEN

GRETCHEN WOKE TO DARKNESS, BUT SHE DIDN'T HAVE TO have any light to recognize Rail's body next to her. She barely recalled him getting in bed with her last night, or rather, early this morning. The room was not air-conditioned, and the stuffiness had caused them to toss the blankets off. Extricating herself from him was difficult since their bodies had tangled together in the night, but she had to pee. Once freed, she got up and fumbled for her cell phone, then used the screen's light to find the bathroom. After taking care of business, she leaned over the sink and looked in the mirror.

"You're an idiot," she silently told the reflection. If she'd had any sense at all, she would have gone home last night before letting Rail get under her skin. But he was there already. His bold confession, the kisses from last night on the pier, the fierce desire she felt for him, and her surprise orgasm just from feeling him through his jeans all told her she was in big danger of losing her heart.

Hell, if she was honest with herself, it was already lost.

She delayed in the bathroom by brushing her teeth with his toothbrush again. She also picked up his hairbrush and ran it through her long locks. "You have to face him sometime. Just go out there and demand he take you to Penny or home."

The bedroom was still dark when she reentered it. The light from her phone screen glowed across his bare chest. Damn! He was fine. He didn't have carefully sculpted lines from working out at a gym, but he had a nice wide chest and defined pecs. She let the light drift lower over his flat stomach and navel. She could see the outline of a nice six-pack under his skin. Muscles from daily physical work that kept him toned and fit. She moved the light lower to illuminate his black boxer briefs and the outline under them. A long ridge tented the front.

Her mouth filled with saliva. This was what she had rubbed against last night until she came. Her pussy had ached for it and wanted it inside, filling that void. She drew on the vivid memory, reliving the experience. His mouth on hers. His driving tongue and taste. The fierceness of his desire. The orgasm he pulled from her body with just his touch. Her lower stomach clenched and relaxed as her pussy heated.

The sudden glare of light from the nightstand lamp had her blinking in surprise. Rail was awake and watching her. Neither of them moved. The expression in his eyes was unreadable.

Gretchen had several thoughts at once. In a book this would be a scene that could go in several directions. She could see him lift his hand to stroke himself to completion as she stood there and watched. She imagined him jackknifing up to grab her, flinging her across the bed and passionately ravaging her body. Maybe it would go in another direction. Perhaps he would tell her the party was over, that she'd had her eyeful, and now it was time to go. Nope, that wouldn't be it. The setup was too good to be anything other than a sex scene. A turning point perhaps in the relationship. *Was* there a relationship?

His chest rose and fell as he breathed deeply while staring at her. The ridge in his briefs rose higher as he waited.

Gretchen felt the moisture gathering between her legs. She didn't need an author to write this scene. She'd do it herself. The phone dropped from her fingers to the floor as she reached for the hem of the shirt she wore and pulled it up and over her head. She hooked her fingers in the sides of her panties, and she pulled them down and stepped out of them in one motion. She didn't hesitate, as she was sure of her welcome when she lifted a leg to slip over and straddle Rail's hips. This brought her pussy directly on top of his dick, leaving only that single thin layer of cloth between them. She lowered her head to take his mouth, letting the tips of her breasts graze his chest as she did.

That was the last act she controlled. He took over, his hand going to the back of her head to control the angle of the kiss. He pulled her to the side and over so she was on her back. She gladly shifted, even though she lost the contact with his penis. He speared his tongue into her mouth, mimicking the act of penetration, and she hoped they would get there soon. He brought his hand up to cup her breast, and his thumb twirled over her nipple, shooting sparks straight to her clitoris. She arched her back, asking for more. He obliged by moving from her mouth to her breast, drawing the turgid point between his lips. She clutched at his hair as he laved at her, alternately licking and sucking until she writhed against him in one big ball of want.

He fumbled for something at the nightstand and went back to kissing her with his body over hers and resting between her thighs. She wanted more. She wanted him inside her.

Then he was. She gasped and tore her mouth from his as he filled her. To the brim. Hard. Full. Pulsing. Every nerve ending firing. Every muscle straining. She arched to take more and clutched at his ass to pull him in tighter. He set his teeth against her shoulder and then began to move. She clawed his back in pleasure. His thrusts were slow, pressing, thorough as if he sought to savor every stroke. She made a frustrated sound in her throat as she wanted him to move faster, pound hard and drive her up into a fast orgasm.

He kept his pace, even with her writhing under him, grabbing him, and trying to increase his speed. He seized her hands and pushed them over her head as he stroked in and out of her body, his head raised and his eyes locked with hers. The intensity of those dark depths made her even more ready to come. Climax was just beyond her reach. He held it back from her. Drawing it out. Teasing her. Making it last much longer than she wanted. She twisted to free her hands, wanted to shove one to her pussy and finish with her swollen clit. He seemed to read her mind and wouldn't release her wrists. It was driving her mad.

Then she tipped. With a soundless cry, she came

with a rush of pleasure she'd never experienced before. Sure, she'd had orgasms. Some with partners and some self-produced, but never anything that had her come apart so completely. This one radiated from her middle and fired through every nerve in her body, sending sheer bliss to her toes, but her awareness focused only on Rail and the sensation of him inside and around her. Another orgasm followed the first, and she arched, going mad from the pleasure. He finally let loose and pounded into her through her second climax until he came himself, his body bow tight as he emptied into her.

He collapsed on top of her still hard and buried in her body. His grip on her wrists loosened, and she lowered her arms to wrap them around his back. Euphoria filled her mind and body. This was what authors tried to describe in words. This feeling of contentment. An intangible connection between people when they found the ultimate belonging in each other's arms.

It didn't last.

Three heartbeats later, Rail slipped out of her and walked into the bathroom without a word. She watched through the cracked door as he stripped off the condom he had somehow donned without her noticing it and leaned over the sink, his head too low for her to be able to see his reflection. He stood there long enough that she closed her legs and sat up in bed. She didn't bother to lift the blankets to cover herself, hoping perhaps he might gear up for another round. Her body hummed pleasantly, and she really hoped for more of the same. She closed her eyes and savored the moment he slid inside her, his hardness penetrating her. Oh yeah, she was ready to go again.

She opened her eyes to find him dressed and looking down on her. His frowning face was closed. Unreadable. Dark. He dropped the tangle of her own clothes on the bed, a silent invitation for her to get dressed herself.

Worry and fear wiggled into her brain. She wrinkled her nose as she snapped on her bra and pulled the shirt over her head.

"What's wrong?" she finally asked.

"Nothing."

The one-word reply didn't match his demeanor. Frustrated, she tried again. "Something is wrong. Please tell me."

"I said nothing. Finish up, and I'll take you home."

"What about Penny?"

"Duke took care of her last night."

He turned away, sending a clear message that his participation in any conversation was over. Anger replaced her fear, and she jerked on her panties and jeans. She'd take a long hot shower when she got to her house. A few minutes ago, she felt great. Now, she felt dirty.

The main room was void of activity, but she still didn't get to look around much as he hurried her out the door. Wordlessly, he handed her a helmet and put another on his own head. Both had shaded visors, so she couldn't see his face. He waved for her to mount up, and he took off as soon as she settled behind him.

This ride was longer. The sun was still rising in the early morning as they zipped down the highway to Wabasha. She had her arms around his waist out of necessity, but as close as they were sandwiched together, she perceived a chasm had opened up between them. The bike vibrated between her legs, and her lady parts reminded her of the pleasure she experienced this morning. The man in front of her might as well have been stone.

He stopped in front of her house and paused only long enough to take back and secure the helmet. Then he was gone.

"Fuck you, asshole!" she signed furiously at his back.

He didn't see it, nor did he see the tears tracking down her face.

RAIL HELD HIMSELF RIGID UNTIL GRETCHEN'S HOUSE disappeared in his rearview mirror. She was pissed, and he couldn't blame her. It was a dick move for him to say all that shit to her, fuck her, and then dump her as fast as possible. A dick was exactly what he needed to be.

She couldn't find out how she'd just shattered his world. God, he should not have slept with her, should not have talked to her, should not have let her into his fucked-up life.

His heart beat faster when she was around. His body craved her. His eyes lit up when he saw her. His hands longed to touch her. Sliding into her warmth was the best and worst moment of his life. The culmination of a lifetime of looking for a place and finding it at last. Homecoming. Game point. Match and done.

And he couldn't have it. He couldn't have her.

Why not?

She deserved someone higher than him.

CHAPTER
NINETEEN

GRETCHEN SENT THE BALL SPINNING DOWN THE LANE. At the last second, it curved to the left and only caught a few pins. The spare wasn't much better. Two pins were left to be cleared by the machine as the automatic setter did its job. Her lip curled in disgust, and she flumped down with irritation on the plastic chair.

"You're off your game tonight. Like *bad*," Penny signed after adding the dismal score to the total. "We're normally neck and neck, but the way you're going, you'll be lucky to break a hundred. What's going on?"

Gretchen picked up her warm beer and set it back down. How was she supposed to tell her best friend that she'd had the best sex of her life, and then the man promptly rejected her? That man being Railroad. "I'm just having a bad day. That's all."

"Hmmm… so nothing to do with our trip to Red Wing this past weekend?"

"Not at all."

Penny gave her a dubious look, but she changed the subject. "I'm sorry again for abandoning you. Duke hustled me out before I could stop him and told me Rail would take care of you. He's a nice guy."

Gretchen scowled. "I'm guessing you're talking about Duke and not Rail?"

Penny blinked. "Rail's a nice guy too, but I was referring to Duke. I didn't want to go to the club-house, and instead of arguing about it, he followed me all the way home. I'd call that nice."

Gretchen relaxed her face. "Yes, that is a nice thing to do."

Penny smiled. "Did I tell you he wouldn't let me go in my house alone? He opened my door and made sure I was safe before taking off." She stood to pick up her ball. "I expected him to make a move on me, but he didn't. The perfect gentleman."

Gretchen wanted to throw up. Her ass had barely cleared the seat of the bike before Rail had taken off, leaving her standing in front of her house. The bastard! "I'm glad he was good to you."

"So, nothing?"

Gretchen didn't have to read minds to figure out where Penny was heading with that. "Nope. Nothing. Zero."

Penny sighed. "That's too bad. I really thought you two would hit it off."

We did, Gretchen thought but didn't share. *He blew my mind and then turned into the asshole of the year.* She shrugged as if it didn't mean anything and watched as Penny took her turn. The ball rolled and took out all ten pins.

The problem was that it did mean something. He meant something. Up until she'd met him, she'd been perfectly content with her life. She had friends to hang out with in Connecticut and here. Work was steady and successful. She made her own money and lived very comfortably. She could travel when she wanted to and had made more than one solo trip. Being deaf did not stop her from enjoying her life. Sure, there were challenges, but she'd done the work to overcome them and had grown into a confident woman with a prosperous business. A month ago, she was fine being single for the rest of her life.

Then Rail blasted into it and took her heart when she wasn't looking. She hadn't expected to fall for a man. Certainly not like this one. A fucking biker in

Minnesota with more baggage than Samsonite could carry.

Tears burned her eyes, and she fought them back. *No. I'm not crying over that bastard. He can go pound sand as far as I'm concerned.*

"Flora is asking about you again. I know you don't have any real connection with her, but would you consider visiting? You don't have to see Rail. He always calls ahead to get the van, so I know when he'll be there."

Gretchen looked at Penny as she stood to take her turn. Maybe she wasn't doing that good a job of hiding her feelings from her friend after all.

"Gretch, I love you. You're my best friend, no matter if you're on the East Coast or here, and I know you're shit at relationships."

Gretchen blinked and got angry. "How does that shit make you my best friend?"

"Because I'm not afraid to tell you like it is. You had Gary for a while. Before him, it was Marvin. Before him, it was Ronnie. All of them adored you, and I know you cared for them, but I never saw any of them take your breath away. Rail does that. I saw you two out on the pier before Duke took me home. That man is so in love with you, he has no clue how to handle it."

"Rail is an ass. He dumped me, Penny. Right after

he got what he wanted from me. In no way, shape, or form is that love."

"Duke told me a little of what's going on in the club. It's not the pretty world you see in those books you edit. It's dirty, gritty, filled with violence. Rail is in charge of it, and he's floundering, but Duke said he's never seen Rail scared shitless. He is when it comes to you. I think that's why he's running. The man is terrified of what he's feeling."

"Rail is not scared of me. He's an asshat and a user."

"That asshat and user is the only person to come spend time with a dying woman. I'm telling you, there is more to him, Gretch. That man has so much love to give, it's mind-blowing. You don't have to forgive him, but I don't think he fucked you over because he's a jerk. I think he's protecting himself."

Gretchen turned away and readied herself for her next throw. She misjudged the distance, and her aim was off. The ball guttered, and she gave it the single-finger salute with both hands. "How the hell do you know him so well?"

Penny ignored the irate tone to the gestures and pinned Gretchen with a firm look reserved for her recalcitrant patients. "Who do I talk to every single day at work? Think about it. There's no one who knows Rail better than Flora. He was ten, Gretchen.

Ten when he was dumped into that boys' home. No speech. No schooling. No ID. Nothing. He has no memory of his life before that, and the doctors said something happened to him. Something so damn bad he erased it from his mind. It took years for Flora to break through that thick wall around him. She's the first person he's ever let in. You're the second. Don't you think that's telling?"

Gretchen raised her hands to retort back and let them fall to her sides for a moment. Penny did have a point. "He *hurt* me, Penny. Gary, Marvin, and Ronnie, not so much, but Rail…. He gutted me."

"Yes, he did. Now, what are you going to do about it? The Gretchen Davonsky I know would fight back. She would grab that man by the balls, twist those suckers upside down, and not let him get away with treating her like shit."

Gretchen's mouth twitched. "I like the way you think."

The next ball she threw cleared all ten pins.

CHAPTER
TWENTY

RAIL WAS IN A BAD MOOD. THE RIDE FROM RED WING to Lake City should have put him in a better one, but it almost made it worse.

The morning started with the discovery that the repair shop was out of some key parts needed to complete several pending jobs. Nutter was supposed to keep a running inventory, but apparently that was too much on top of his personal life struggles. Getting some of the parts would take more than a week, and three of them were backordered. Rail was ready to explode by the time Camo located a few of them in Lake City.

"At least we can get one job done" was his answer before he and Duke took off to go get what they could with the intent of returning quickly. The trip was short, but when they arrived, the small parts store had a sign on it that read "Closed until 1:00." Rail cursed and had the urge to throw something through the window.

"Ease up, Rail. You need to calm down. There's nothing we can do about it except wait a couple hours. Let's go grab some food down at the waterfront."

Duke's Zen attitude helped. They cruised along the waterfront road until they found a café with an open patio. The day was clear and bright with vivid colors popping out. The blue of the sky, the red table-cloths, the green of the trees along the riverbanks, and the gleam of white sails on the water. Rail sat down and picked up a folded paper menu. The tension in his back and shoulders relaxed as he perused the items. He was aware of the looks he and Duke received. Their dark clothing, jeans, and cuts singled them out, but he ignored the curious glances.

"Camo's been talking to Nutter. Thinks he'll be agreeing with our side soon." Duke closed his menu and leaned back in the metal chair, making it creak.

"I'm not sure how reliable that is. Nutter's head is focused on all the shit he's in with his women. Fucker can't keep his dick in his pants long enough to concentrate on making any decisions."

"Um…. Are you ready to order, gentlemen?" The perky redhead appeared out of nowhere with a pad in her hand.

Duke smiled at her as Rail cursed under his breath. "Cheeseburger with the works, sweetheart, and a Red Oak on tap."

"We only have bottles."

"That's cool."

Rail handed her the menu. "Same, but set me up with a Jack Pine. Whatever you have on tap."

The waitress nodded and left. Duke watched her ass as she walked away, and Rail reached out to punch his shoulder. "What the fuck? You're perving on a kid."

Duke shrugged and turned to face Rail. "Old enough to serve beer."

"Christ. You're just as bad as Nutter."

Duke huffed a laugh. "At least I'm not making any kids. There're no laws against looking, right? Maybe you need to get some. Might improve your mood."

There was only one person who could do that. Rail changed the subject. "Nothing up in Hastings?"

Duke's face changed from teasing to businesslike. "Nope. No sign of Piglet. I asked about Ezra in case he used his real name. No luck there either. The guys at the docks mentioned a man who resembled him, but he hasn't been seen in almost two months. If it was him, he's long gone from there."

The waitress came back to plunk their beer orders in front of them. Her face was flushed, and she gave Duke a long side-eye. Whether it was from nervousness or awareness, Rail couldn't tell. Frankly, he didn't care. He had other business to think about. "Piglet has no allies, no club, no friends, and no family. Where the hell is he hiding?"

Duke tipped his bottle back and took a long swallow. "No clue, but you're wrong about the family. He still has his sister in Wabasha."

Condensation ran down the sides of the tulip-shaped glass in front of Railroad. "Gretchen said she hasn't seen him for years. Didn't sound to me like they were close."

Duke let out a soft burp. "Family is family. I think he'll come here soon since he's out of options everywhere else. They may not be all huggy-great-to-see-you siblings, but when the chips are down, family sticks together."

Rail watched a long drop slowly travel downward to add to the pool on the red plastic tablecloth. "That's not always true. Blood doesn't mean much to some people. Look at what happened to Iceman's woman, Gabriella. Turned out okay for her, but the only reason she ended up getting involved with him was her piece-of-shit uncle set her up. I've seen a lot of betrayals in my life. Brother against brother, family against family, and it doesn't matter if they share blood or not. The oaths men take are forgotten just as quickly as they're recited. Vows of allegiance and fidelity don't mean squat anymore." He raised his hand. "I can count on one hand the people I trust to have my back, and I'm sorry to say I'd have fingers left over."

Duke grunted. "Fuck, Rail. You don't trust the Dutchmen?"

Rail sighed and poked at another drop gathering on the glass. "Would you trust Rebel? Desktop? Hell, even Nutter right now?"

Duke went silent. He didn't need to say anything as he got Rail's point.

The waitress approached with two heavy plates of food. "Here ya go, gentlemen. Can I get you anything else?"

"Another beer, sweetheart." Duke grinned at the girl.

Rail was biting into a seasoned fry when the back of his neck pricked up. A few tables over, the hostess was seating a man and a woman. With his khaki pants, pastel golf shirt, short sandy hair, and mirrored aviator sunglasses, the guy's appearance was so stereotypically yuppie hipster, Rail paid only peripheral attention to him. It was the woman with him who caught his eye.

He almost didn't recognize Gretchen. She looked like she'd just stepped out of a Hollywood fashion magazine. Her blonde hair was loose and held back with a pair of sunglasses, framing her face in a cloud of gold. Whatever makeup she wore accentuated her blue-gray eyes, making them smoky. Her maroon dress was short and showed off her luscious curves. Rail watched her smile at the waitress as she smoothed the skirt, sat down, and crossed her legs. She even wore heels with an ankle strap. Fucking heels!

Gretchen set up an iPad and portable keyboard in front of her, and Rail guessed this was how she planned to communicate with her (goddammit!) date.

Much of Rail's world came in black and white. In this moment, his colors turned green and red. Anger filled his chest, and his heart sped up. He wanted to stomp over to their table and punch the smiling preppie in his perfect white teeth. Then put Gretchen on his bike, take her somewhere, and remind her who she belonged to.

But she didn't belong to him, did she? He set

what they had on fire, threw it away, and watched it burn.

"What's up your ass now, Rail?" Duke had scarfed down half the giant burger.

Rail glanced at the plate in front of him. His appetite had dried up, but he forced himself to pick up his own burger and take a bite. "Nothing."

As he ate, he made no attempt to hide the direction of his attention. He stared as Gretchen typed her half of the conversation. Her smiles and gentle looks contrasted with the fire he'd seen in her eyes when he kissed her on the pier and the fierce desire on her face the next morning when his dick slid into her slick pussy. She seemed coolly detached and professional, so maybe this wasn't a date. When their food arrived, he saw she had a burger and fries placed in front of her, while the guy had ordered a big chef salad. Rail took some sense of satisfaction from her food choice. It didn't look like she was trying to impress her companion and felt comfortable ordering what she wanted. A smirk lifted his mouth, and she raised her eyes to meet his dead-on.

If she wasn't aware of his presence before, she was now. Her eyes widened, and her mouth dropped open. The world faded to white noise until only the two of them existed in it. A wave of lust hit him so hard he lost his breath. His heart pounded until he thought it would jump out of his chest, and his dick swelled.

Then she shut down, cutting him off before turning back to her date, and smiled as if nothing had occurred. Her fingers flew over the keyboard, and she nodded at the man before standing up. Her movements were sure and steady, but her eyes met his once again. Rail watched as she walked to the small building on the other side of the café that housed its outdoor restrooms.

"Be back in a minute," he gruffly told Duke.

The man didn't look up from dousing his fries in a lake of ketchup.

Rail didn't hesitate when he entered the ladies' side of the restroom. Three stalls lined up in the blue-and-white facility, and only one was occupied. The bolt clicked as he slid the lock closed. A moment later, he heard the toilet flush, and Gretchen came out. She didn't show any surprise to see him there. She washed her hands before facing him.

"What do you want?" Her stance was rigid. Her face was flushed, and her pupils dilated slightly. She kept her mouth tightly closed, but she breathed deeply and rapidly through flared nostrils. There was a defiance to her stance, and she tilted her head back as if daring him to answer.

"I'm sorry."

Two words. That's all he had, but there was a wealth of meaning behind them.

"You're sorry. For what? Meeting me or fucking me?"

"I'll never be sorry for meeting you."

"So, you're sorry for fucking me. Glad we cleared that up. Have a nice life, Rail."

She moved toward the door, her eyes shiny with tears, and it tore into him that he put them there.

"No, Gretchen. I'm not sorry for... for...." He shook his head. "I can't call it fucking. What we did wasn't me getting my rocks off in some random club pussy. No other woman has been in my bed since I met you. There's this... this... power you have over me. You can bring me to my knees, and it makes me vulnerable in a way I've not been in a very long time. Being with you scares the shit out of me, and I do not know how to handle it. The problem is being without you fucking scares me worse."

He paused and noticed she had relaxed her stance. Gladness darted through his middle that she was seeing him and getting it, but fear followed. The rawness he'd felt in the last few days lay on the surface of his mind. He took a deep breath and continued.

"My head is fucked-up. My heart is fucked-up. Hell, even my body is fucked-up." He placed two fingers on his face and traced the scars. "I've been this way for a long time. I don't think you know this about me yet, but I don't have a separate place from the club. I live in my room there. Lots of members have apartments or houses. I don't. A friend willed me his cabin, but it's not really mine. I lived in a room with three other boys for years. After I left there, I slept in a back room at the marina garage until I was accepted into the Dutchmen. Closest thing to family I've had in my life outside of Grams."

He stopped again. His stomach flipped, and he had to swallow several times to keep from embarrassing himself by throwing up.

"When I slid inside you, I found home. I wasn't looking for it. Never thought I'd find it. But there it was like it was just waiting for me, and I fucking blew it. I ran from it. From you. All I can think about is the shit I did to you. It was wrong. So fucking wrong, and I'd take it all back if I could. I don't know what I'm doing or what I'm feeling, and I... I...."

He took a deep shaky breath, and his hands dropped to his sides as if the weight was more than he could hold up. "I'm sorry."

She waited for three long heartbeats. If she turned away, he would unlock the door and leave. Instead, she took two strides forward and grabbed his head to pull his mouth to hers. No playing around. No hesitation.

A tangled knot of gordian proportions suddenly released in his gut, and his head grew dizzy. He slanted his head and took her lips, pressing them apart and diving deep. Mint. She tasted of the complimentary butter mints the restaurant gave out with the bill. Blood sang through his veins, and he could feel it flow through to his fingertips. Awareness of the woman in his arms flooded his cells, every part of her imprinting in his mind and in his heart.

Her hand snaked down, and before he could move, she grabbed his crotch in a viselike grip. The pain made him jump back, but she kept her hold on him.

"You're not the only one."

His heart jumped as he heard her voice. He remembered she told him she didn't like speaking and preferred to use ASL only.

"I let you in too. Snuck in when I wasn't looking. No one has ever gotten this close to me. If I have this power over you, you have it over me too."

Her voice was low and the inflections somewhat monotone. She sounded like she had a heavy foreign accent. The whole time, she kept her hand tight around his balls. Not enough to be painful, but enough to be uncomfortable.

"I know you've had a shit life. Mine hasn't been roses and castles either. I had the loving parents you didn't, but growing up deaf in a small town is isolating no matter what kind of family you have. It took me a long time to get where I am, and the only reason I'm here is because I had that family to support me. You didn't find your support until Flora. I get it. I understand. People like you and me have a hard time with others. We feel weak if we let someone else have any kind of control. You say you found home when you slid into me. You need to know, I found it too."

Rail stared at her face, which was so close he could see the myriad of blues that made up her eye color.

"But you still hurt me. Bad. I think you're asking me to forgive you so we can move on. Maybe explore this thing between us. Perhaps I can, but I need to know: Do I only have this—" He hissed when her fingers tightened. "—or do I have this too?" She raised her other hand to his chest to lie flat over his pounding heart. "I'll forgive you when you can tell me for certain and I believe you."

She let go of him and stepped back, visibly shaking off the emotional roller coaster of the last few minutes and stepping into the cool professional businesswoman persona. Her hands came up, and she settled back into her signing.

"I'm going to go finish my meeting with this new client. You go back to Duke and whatever it is you have to do today. Give me a day or two, and then come see me. I haven't had a brisket sandwich lately, and I miss them."

"I will."

She gave a sharp nod and moved to unlock the door to the bathroom, turning to grin at him as she did so. "I can't believe we just had a major life-changing conversation in a public bathroom."

He smiled back at her. "Lucky there's no one dancing outside." His face dropped, and he reached for her hand. He traced the soft skin between her knuckles before bringing it to his lips. "Thank you for giving me a second chance. I swear you won't regret it."

Her eyes met his, and she pulled back the bolt. "Be sure to bring some of those *lefse* when you come, or *you* might."

Rail watched her saucy ass sway as she left. He had no illusions that he was there yet. She granted only an opportunity, and he had to work to get back in again. He swore to the God he didn't believe in that he wouldn't fuck it up.

Rail hurried out and strode back to the dining area with long steps. Gretchen sat across from the grinning yuppie as if nothing had happened. Her eyes briefly darted to his, and she gave a nod but kept her main focus on the client.

Duke sat waiting and playing a game on his phone.

"Paid the bill?"

Duke paused the bouncing balls and closed the app. "You bet. Let's get those fucking parts and get going."

"EVERYTHING OKAY?"

Gretchen shifted in her chair again and smiled as she typed on the keyboard. "Yes, everything is fine. Did you have enough time to read the sample I just did for you?"

The man sat back, slouching a bit in a relaxed, comfortable manner. He shifted his knees out from under the table and spread them slightly as if displaying himself to her. "Yes, I did. Very impressive. You're a talented woman."

She kept her eyes either on his sunglasses or the iPad screen. "I've learned to be fast and accurate. I don't like wasting time—mine or my client's. Your project, however, is a challenge from the standpoint of line editing."

The man shook his blond head, and Gretchen noticed that none of his hair moved. "I don't want any words changed. I only want the proofing and the formatting. Email a contract, and I'll pay an advance."

It was her turn to shake her head. "I don't require any payment upfront."

"I insist on paying you something. It ensures me you'll do the job."

She gritted her teeth at the man's doggedness. If he wasn't a new client with an intriguing project, she might have refused him. The memoir angle was what kept her on the line.

"Very well. Ten percent up front will do. I'll email a modified contract, and you can send me the raw manuscript any time after. After I take a good look at what the job entails, I'll send you a reasonable deadline. If that doesn't work, I have no problem with dissolving the contract so you can look elsewhere for an editor. Does that sound acceptable?"

The man nodded. "Perfectly fine."

"Excellent. I look forward to working with you and your father."

"That biker who passed by here a few minutes

ago. The one with the dark hair and beard. Do you know him?"

Gretchen wondered why he wanted to know. Biker prejudice? "Yes, he's a friend of mine who's based in Red Wing."

"What kind of friend is he?"

Good question. She didn't have the foggiest idea, but the fledging peace between her and Rail wasn't something she wanted to share. Especially with a new client. "Just a friend."

"Those scars." The client's hidden eyes bothered her. His speculative tone of voice did too.

Anger flared in Gretchen's middle, and she tamped it back. "Yes, he has some facial scars, but I don't know how he got them, and I really don't care. He's my friend, and that's all that matters to me."

The client backtracked immediately. "Yes, I understand. He just looked familiar to me for a minute. I've probably seen him around when I've visited Red Wing on business. The St. James Hotel is a lovely place to stay."

The subject switch was a good one, and they chatted for a few minutes about other local sites. Gretchen made a point of checking the time. "I need to get home and finish an editing deadline. It was very nice meeting you. I'll send the contract by this evening."

The man inclined his head as if giving permission for her to leave. Something about the guy bugged her, but after today, they'd be communicating through emails. No need to sit across from him again.

She wished like hell he'd taken off his sunglasses just once.

CHAPTER
TWENTY-ONE

CHAPEL RESEMBLED MORE OF A WAR ROOM THAN A CLUB meeting. Rail sat at the head of the table—at least for now. Duke sat on his right and Rebel to his left. The lanky biker had been fidgeting ever since the gathering was called to order. The main topic was the direction of the club. Rebel had shown up with a proposition from the Canadians about a new cargo load of oxy pills that were ready to ship. Rail was angry about it, as Rebel had gone and set up this deal without talking to him or any of the other club members about it.

"It's a fucking chance to get back in the game. We're the goddamn Dutchmen, for fuck's sake, and this is what we do."

Rail crossed his arms and leaned back in the chair.

Ice would have handed Rebel his ass already if he were here.

"You're right, Rebel. We are the Dutchmen, and going off half-cocked is not how we do business," Duke spat. He and Rebel had been at odds for a long time, and it was getting worse. "You don't get to make those kinds of decisions for the club."

Rebel sneered and rubbed his nose. "Bunch of fucking pussies! We can't waste this chance. We need to go back to making money and living the way we always have. Why the fuck can't you assholes see that?"

Camo spoke up. "Because there's a bigger picture. The distribution network has changed further south. Yeah, we can transport a couple boatloads of pills, but right now, we have no one to receive them or sell them to. Desktop is the last of the Dark Horses, and he's stated more than once that he can't find buyers who will do business with us. Too risky. It's only been around six months since the FBI raid on the Tiger Clan, and there's still an active investigation going on. You shits aren't keeping up with the back-page news, but they're still uncovering shit about the Galanos crime family and that huge network." He shook his head. "It's damn good we never got in bed with them, else we'd be under that same microscope. We don't need that shit."

Rebel rubbed his nose again. "Pussies! Who the fuck cares about a crime network over in Phil-adelphia? That's got nothing to do with getting some pills from the Canadians. We'll find buyers."

"You can't find your ass with your hands. You're jacked up so much, I'm surprised you still have a nose on your face," Duke stated with a sardonic grunt.

"Fuck you!"

Rail kept his place and silence as he listened to the two sides argue. Iceman conducted past meetings similarly, hearing everyone before making his deci-sion. He hadn't been diplomatic, exactly, but the members trusted him to make the best calls for the club. Hell, the man gave up his life to save the club and his woman.

He took in the Dutchmen motto embossed on the meeting table. The words were printed under the image of a ghostly ship. "Die Free." What about "Live Free"? Shouldn't that be their credo? Their goal? Living free meant riding, drinking, fucking, doing what they wanted without a sword hanging over their heads. No worries about any wars between MCs or the FBI, or the Galanos family coming after any of them. "Live Free" meant peace.

"The good book says, 'Blessed are the peacemakers, for they will be called the children of God.' Wanna know why,

precious? It's because it takes a tough man to keep it. Fighting is easy. Staying still is hard."

Flora's words washed over him. Ones he'd heard many times after he'd been in a fight at school. She would click her tongue, give him one of her looks, and then bandage up his cuts.

"Sometimes you gotta work to keep the peace. Maybe even fight for it, but I'll tell you, child, it's always worth it in the end."

Rail stood up and looked down the table at the divided membership. Their bickering stopped as he grabbed their attention. He placed his fists on the surface and leaned over, staring each one in the eye before speaking.

"Does anyone remember the last shipment the Dutchmen received? It was a box that was delivered and sat right here." He tapped a spot in front of him. "Remember what was in it? The heads of Xman and Blaze. Killed by Grizzly. There were pictures in that box too. Women in our club. Kids."

He looked at Nutter. "Mama J and your kids."

He looked at Duke. "Your son up in Duluth with your ex."

He looked at Camo. "Your sister."

He looked at Desktop. "Your kid brother at college."

He looked at Rebel. "Peebles, pregnant with your child. A girl, from what she told me."

He sat back down. "We've lost Xman, Blaze, Boots, Musicman. We have men rotting in prison. We lost Iceman. I'm done with losing people. I'm done watching over my shoulder for the next bullet. I'm done with my people bleeding over a fucking carton of pills. I'm done with it. I want true freedom. Freedom to ride without worry. Freedom to live life as I see fit. Freedom not to stare at every fucking shadow to see if it moves. The marina and bar expansion are making us plenty of money. We have to work at it, but so fucking what? We had to work the pill runs to make money too, so what's the difference? It's that we don't have to look at every fucking man as an enemy coming to kill us. I'm tired of watching my brothers bleed. Iceman talked about taking us legit. I say we quit fucking around and get it done. No more transporting shit. We're going to vote, and afterward, the subject is closed. I'll tell you now, if it's decided to open back up to running contraband again, I'll accept it, but I won't be a part of it."

Nutter spoke for the first time. "You mean you'll step down?"

Rail shook his head. "I mean I won't be a part of it."

By their expressions, everyone at the table understood the magnitude of Rail's statement.

"Rebel has a proposal on the table for resuming transport. Yea or nay?"

Duke started with a definite "Nay."

Rebel squirmed again in his seat and barked, "Yea."

All around the table, votes were spoken out loud.

"Nay."

"Nay."

"Yea."

"Yea."

It came to Nutter. The man's face was haggard. He had only half paid attention to meetings lately, so lost in his own world. He could go either way. He raised his eyes to meet Rail's and firmly said, "Nay."

Rail let out his breath. "I vote nay. We're done. No more transport. Our focus is on the marina."

Predictably, Rebel exploded. "Fuck you! Fuck all you pussies!" He jumped up with such force, his chair toppled over. Rage twisted his face into a mask full of hatred. "It's time we had a leader with some goddamn balls. I have another proposal. I propose me as president of the Dutchmen and not this pansy-assed shit who thinks we're so fucking weak!"

Duke erupted from his chair at the same time. "I

propose we excommunicate Rebel for insubordination and being such a goddam pain in the ass!"

Rail brought the gavel down with a crack. "Enough!" he roared. Fury ran through his veins, making his face red and his fists double up. "We will *not* fall apart. You're either a Dutchmen or you're not. Anyone who has a problem with the direction we're going in can leave. There's a tattoo machine in the corner. I'll fire it up and black out their club ink right here, right now. Choose!"

Utter silence hit the room at this ultimatum. Many of the faces showed discomfort, but no one raised their eyes or hands to be removed from the club. Rebel gaped, a bit taken aback, but recovered his bravado. He stomped out, slamming the meeting room door with a last "Fucking pussies!" over his shoulder. Desktop stayed put, as did the others who voted for Rebel's plan.

"Any more bullshit? Good. Adjourned."

The membership filed out, oddly subdued. Most meetings gave way to a day of drinking and a night of fucking. It didn't seem that would happen this time.

Rail sat back tiredly in the chair and pinched the bridge of his nose between a thumb and index finger. Fuck, he was drained. He had no energy or spirit left.

"You handled that well." Duke had hung around

after the room emptied. "Rebel is too shortsighted. His only concern is his next fix. He keeps it up, and he'll be dead. We can't go down that road." He sighed. "I don't get it. The marina is making a killer profit, and it's only going to get better. No one has to take any more risks on the river or on the roads." He spread his hands wide with a huge grin. "We can just ride."

Rail grinned back. "I hear you. Just riding sounds good to me. Maybe we're getting too old for this shit."

Duke snorted. "Speak for yourself, brother. These gray hairs are ones of experience, not age."

Rail huffed once and opened his mouth to tease Duke about his choice of young bedpartners when his phone buzzed with a call. He glanced down, and his blood iced over.

No. I don't want to answer this. I don't want to know.

He swiped the green icon. "Yeah," he answered, his hands starting to shake.

"Rail, it's Penny. You need to come. Now."

CHAPTER
TWENTY-TWO

"Walk with me, Brother Ezra. I have much to show you," Matthias said as he appeared at the garage door.

Piglet picked up a worn shop towel and did his best to wipe the grease from his hands. He had been initiated into the brotherhood three nights ago. The event was one huge blurry dream, and he only sort of remembered it. There had been a mushroom, a woman, and fucking, maybe? He woke up the next day in his bunk without a clue as to how he got there. The events bothered him, but he'd keep that to himself. Being accepted into this group was more important, and he'd do everything he could to stay in Matthias's good graces.

"What's up, brother?" Ha! He could call Matthias

"brother" now. If that wasn't a big kick, he didn't know what was.

"Now that you're a part of our family, you need to know all the work we're doing here and why. It's time for you to take your place in the bigger cause."

Cause? "I'm ready."

Matthias spoke leisurely as they strolled to the locked fenced area behind the big house that only full brothers had access to.

"Our world is getting overrun with inferior people. Mixing blood with the lower classes has diluted our intelligence and made us dependent. More and more government programs. More and more people who can't think for themselves, fend for themselves, or survive without some bureaucrat holding their hands and making decisions. It's disgusting and unworthy of true men."

Piglet wasn't sure if he understood what Matthias was getting at, but he nodded. They walked toward a barracks building similar to the one the men occupied. Piglet's senses buzzed. Something wasn't right.

"Think about when we harvest. Black, brown, yellow, red—these are the colors of dirt and chaff. We separate the good wheat from the chaff to keep it pure. To keep it white because, as we all know, the purist color is white. People are a lot like this, you see? We have to separate the wheat from the chaff.

Our founder, Highest Brother Jepthah, saw this and said enough was enough. He built this place based on the divine thoughts he received from our creator. His great mission was to purify the blood and bring us back into greatness again. This is why we live off the grid, off the books, and out of sight. The government doesn't need to know what we're doing here until we're ready to start the final holy war and at last take back our rightful place in the world. Do you understand, brother?"

Piglet swallowed. Despite his lack of education, he wasn't stupid. Personally, he didn't care about someone's skin color or background. The thought had never occurred to him that one man was better than another because of race. He couldn't see that it made a difference as it was what sat between the ears, between the legs, and in the heart that really mattered. Smarts, balls, and guts was what made a man a man. Everything else was variations.

Piglet's belly flipped. This might be dangerous for him. If he disagreed, there was no telling what could happen to him. He repeated in his head the part of his brotherhood vow that stated he would cut his own throat should he stumble. He looked at Matthias's inquiring expression and grunted, "Yes, I understand."

Matthias smiled, but it didn't reach his eyes.

Piglet got the feeling his response wasn't that believable but was acceptable for now.

"Jepthah's vision was to purify the blood of the wheat by keeping only the wheat and discarding the chaff, producing as much wheat as we can to build our army of pure men, all with the same goal. We've kept to that practice, and many of the brothers are the result. You've seen how physically superior they are. Tall. Proud. Perfect male specimens. Our founding father's brilliance shines in every one of them."

Piglet pondered this. He hadn't really paid attention, but Matthias was right. All the men who attended the meetings were big and powerful from hours spent working and training. But that didn't help his trepidations much.

They'd reached the doors to the barracks. Mathias produced a key and slipped it into the lock. "There was a problem that Jepthah, in all his wisdom, didn't see coming. His plan was unsustainable." He opened the door. "This is our breeding facility. Your wife lives here."

Wife? Fuck! Piglet broke out in a sweat as he stared at the opening. Every fiber of his being resisted walking through that door. His heart jumped in his chest, and he wanted to run away.

He stepped inside.

The interior was nicer than he expected it to be.

He found himself in a large room that was painted white with cartoons on the walls. The floor was carpeted with those colorful spongy gym squares. Child-size books, tables, and scattered toys made the place look like a preschool classroom.

The women in the room looked up, startled and a bit fearful. Two of them were heavily pregnant, and three more were on the floor with young children. Lots of white-blonde hair and pale skin.

"This place used to be full of children. Smart. Growing. Learning to love our life. Now we're getting fewer and fewer pregnancies. Those born now have come out with problems. Cleft palates, club feet, webbed hands, retardation—a whole host of issues. We've been so focused on purifying our lines, we've become too close in our gene pool."

Piglet gazed at a woman who had an infant in her lap. The child's head appeared to be squashed flat, and its jaw protruded in an exaggerated underbite. Drool dripped from its slack mouth.

"More and more of the girls born are sterile, and some of the boys never drop their testicles. We have perhaps one or two more generations before our cause dies. I can't let that happen. The only way to keep our way of life going is to add more people to our ranks. We look for men who can breed more men of the wheat. We identify them and bring them into our fold. You have the right build and hair and eye color, which is one reason we wanted you to be a brother. Your children are vital to our continued survival."

Children? He was fucking forty-six years old! Children had never been in his plans, let alone a wife.

Matthias moved toward a hallway and motioned for Piglet to follow. With a twisting stomach, he did.

"This is where we keep our newest breeders. We find them as runaways or fosters thrown out on the streets. Abused and neglected, we take them in, give them new names and a better life."

This is better? The hallway was filled with small cubicle partitions. Only seven were occupied. The girls all looked the same. Blonde-haired, blue-eyed, slim, and pretty. A closer look showed vacant expressions as if they were drugged. Black monitors were strapped to their ankles.

"Every once in a while, one of them is taken with the devil and tries to leave. They are brought back, of course, and reminded of the vital role they play in our cause."

Piglet didn't want to think about what that reminder might entail.

"Ah, here is Naomi. She's one who was born here and knows her place."

A young girl somewhere in her teenage years

skipped up to them. Her plain prairie dress was just like all the others, except it was pale yellow. The others in the nursery were pink. Piglet just stared at the girl. Her eyes were slightly bugged out and offset, and her lower jaw recessed to make her front teeth protrude. She wrapped her arms around his waist and snuggled into him with a big grin. He glanced up at Matthias, who frowned. "Aren't you going to greet your wife, Brother Ezra?"

Bile rose in Piglet's throat. His "wife" appeared to be in her teens. *A fucking kid!* It took every bit of control he had not to hurl right then and there. He coughed and swallowed hard. "Nice to meet you, Naomi." Fuck, what the hell else was he supposed to say?

"It's too soon from the time of the marriage ritual to be able to tell, but we're hoping for good news in a few weeks. Naomi was chosen for you as she was at the height of her fertile period, but just in case, you should visit her as often as you can. No more comfort women until she's pregnant. All your seed needs to go in your wife. After that you can go back to the shacks for your relief."

Piglet cleared his throat. "What if I get a comfort woman pregnant?"

Matthias shrugged. "It happens. The child is judged whether it's a wheat child or a chaff child.

The wheat children come here. The chaff children stay with their mothers until they're old enough to work the farm. If you impregnated a comfort woman, don't worry about it. They have so many different men in them, it's hard to tell who the father is anyway."

This is wrong, this is wrong, this is wrong, Piglet's brain repeated over and over as Naomi continued to cling to him all the while. Her hand drifted downward to stroke over his crotch. *Goddammit, I'm getting hard.*

"This is a lot for you to learn at one time, Brother Ezra. We usually don't bring in new brothers this fast, but we need your skills in other areas besides the farm machines. As you can see, we don't have enough wives, and sharing will cause the same inbreeding problems down the road. Our program is carefully crafted, but we have to have more women in order to get a bigger, more sustainable gene pool. When you were with that motorcycle club up in the cities, you had access to resources for getting things across the Canadian border, right?"

The girl unzipped his pants and got on her knees. He wanted to jerk away from her, but he was afraid of what Matthias would do or think. "Uh... yes, there were contacts on the Canada side."

His breath hissed as she slid his dick into her

warm mouth. Matthias placed a hand on her blonde head and stroked it as he would a favored pet. Piglet had never felt more uncomfortable in his life. Not even the violence he'd seen in the motorcycle clubs compared to this unnerving situation. His dick didn't agree and got harder under Naomi's stroking tongue.

Matthias continued as if having a normal conversation and not standing across from a man getting sucked off. "There are some new women we've collected. Prime breeding stock that we need transported down here quickly and quietly by boat. I'd like you to help with that. We also need a place for them to land that's close by and discreet. The council and I have decided that the perfect place is your old house over in Wabasha. It's isolated, has its own pier, and is large enough to hold the women until we can get them to our compound. Your sister is currently occupying the house, but that will be dealt with."

His fingers trailed over the blonde hair again. "It's a shame she's deaf. Even at her age, she could be a breeder for a few years."

Did he mean he would kill Gretchen? He hadn't even known Gretchen was back. Piglet had very little contact with his half sister and didn't particularly care if he saw her again or not, but he didn't want her dead.

"When you get your people in line for the transport, let me know. Money is not a problem, but don't go crazy. Yeah?"

Piglet felt the noose tightening around his neck as his balls gathered to come. Somehow Matthias knew what was happening, and he jerked Naomi back by her hair. "Take your husband to your bed and fuck him dry. His seed needs to be in your womb. Nowhere else."

"Yes, Daddy."

Oh, fuck no! Piglet wanted to run. Wanted to get out. Escape this place and somehow scrub it from his mind. But he couldn't. He had no vehicle, no money, no direction, and no resources. Worst of all, he had no doubt that if he did run, he'd be brought back. Brought back to face the wrath of betraying this brotherhood. Of betraying Matthias. Iceman would have had his head on a pike. Matthias would crush it flat.

Naomi tugged at his hand and skipped a little as she pulled him to her cubicle. He regarded it more as a walk to a guillotine rather than getting his rocks off.

Out of the corner of his eye, he saw Matthias smile.

CHAPTER
TWENTY-THREE

THE HOSPITAL BED OVERWHELMED THE TINY FIGURE lying on it. She had an army of machines and wires around her that were no longer hooked to her frail form. Not even an IV line was left. No need for anything anymore. Flora was dying.

She'd been asleep but awoke when Rail entered the room and sat next to her. She reached for his hand and weakly smiled. "My boy," she rasped. "My beautiful boy."

Rail's eyes burned as he grasped the fragile fingers. He'd spent the ride to the retirement center denying Penny's words, bargaining that it was a false alarm and they'd all have a good laugh at the scare Flora gave them. It was a joke, right? It had to be.

One look in the room told him different. This was

real and here at last. He had to face this loss, and it killed him.

He just sat there silently holding Flora's hand and listening to her labored breaths. Every few minutes she would tighten her fingers on his.

Penny came into the room and stood next to him. She put a hand on his shoulder and kept her voice low. "I'm glad you made it in time. I don't think it will be much longer. You need anything?"

Did he need anything? Fuck yeah, he needed God not to take away the woman who raised him. He wanted to curse at the deity that Flora believed in for letting her die. Rage welled up in his chest to fight with the pain of losing his beloved Grams. No, his *mom*. Why did God let this happen? It wasn't right. Goddammit it... it...

It hurt.

He shook his head and didn't say anything. He was afraid that if he did, he'd collapse on the floor in a quivering heap. Penny gave his shoulder a squeeze and padded softly out of the room.

Minutes ticked by. Then more. Flora suddenly opened her eyes and smiled. "There it is."

Her words were weak, but her eyes glowed. Rail's gut clenched in pain, as he knew she was leaving. Whatever she was seeing was not on this earth. The air in his lungs froze into a rock he couldn't shift. It was harder to breathe, and he opened his mouth and sucked in what sounded to him like a sob.

Flora's eyes focused on him, and he could see the questioning in them. "What is it, child?"

Her voice was stronger and her face radiant. Hot tears trailed down Rail's cheeks as his throat closed. He remembered the times when he was a young boy who used to crawl into this woman's lap for comfort. She would hold him in her arms as if she would never let him go. Many nights he cried himself to sleep, grieving for what he'd lost. She crooned and rocked his thin body for hours, singing old gospel songs. He couldn't bear it.

"Please don't leave me." His voice broke.

Concern wrinkled her brow. "Oh no, my precious boy. I'm not leaving you. I'll just be somewhere else watching over you. That's all." Her eyes lit up, and she smiled. "It's really nice here. I can see my place. It's just like I hoped it would be. There's grass so green and pretty. My favorite daisies all big and blooming. There's a river too. Flowing easy."

Rail took a shaky breath. Flora's face showed joy in its luminescence. The years fell away from her as she talked to him one last time.

"I got people waiting for me to show the way. Old friends looking real fine. Everyone is smiling and happy. It's good. All of it. Someday you'll see it yourself, and I'll be waiting to greet you right here in this wonderful place."

Rail let the tears flow, too afraid to let go of Flora's hand. Too afraid that if he did, these last few moments would disappear. "I hope you're right, Grams. I've not lived a very clean life. There's a lot of bad stuff I've done. God doesn't have a place for sinners like me."

Flora smiled at him. "My beautiful Rail, listen to me and remember: God doesn't hate anyone."

She gripped his hand. For a moment her face appeared younger, her hair fuller, and her eyes deeper. Her voice carried authority as she spoke to him. "My precious son, you've already been forgiven."

She closed her eyes, and her expression relaxed into long, weary lines. Her thin hair grayed and frazzled to match her ninety-eight years. She took two more shallow breaths. That was all.

Rail felt his heart split. There was no other way to describe it as the organ ripped in half. He choked as the air around him became unbreathable, and his eyes stopped seeing. Pain. All he knew was pain. In that pain, anger raged inside him. He wanted to hit something. He wanted to tear something apart so this pain would be felt by all. Hot. Bloody. He wanted... he wanted....

Two invisible arms came heavily onto his shoulders, hugging him from behind. Big. Warm. Secure. Cocooning him with a mother's love he knew only from one person. These arms held him through the worst times in his life. Flora was giving him one last gift. The rage left him, and he was able to take a full breath. The pain was still there, spilling through his chest, but he was able to accept something else. There was peace. His throat made a sound, and the arms tightened.

"My precious son, you've already been forgiven." Grams's last words echoed in his ear and his mind. His eyes focused at last on Flora's hand that lay limp and still in his. Even in death she held him. His Grams. His mom.

A click of the doorknob caught his attention, and he turned his tear-filled eyes to see who came in. Gretchen stood in the doorway. Her face crumpled when she realized Flora was gone.

"Penny texted me to come. I'm so sorry." Her hands shook a little as she signed. She came over to him and leaned over to hug him. It was awkward with her standing and him seated, but she made it work. Penny came in and waited, sniffling from time to time.

Rail finally let go of Flora's hand.

"She made all the arrangements already. There's

nothing for you to do, Rail, except set a time and date for her funeral. I have copies of everything right here. Stay as long as you need to, yeah?"

Rail cleared his throat and stood. "I'm good. Thanks for everything." He turned to Gretchen and her watering eyes that were full of concern. For him. "Will you come with me?" *I don't want to be alone.*

She nodded, and he threaded his fingers through hers. Tight. Comforting. Together. He led them from the room, straight down the hallway, and out the front door. His bike sat where he'd parked it. He never had removed the extra helmet from the saddle-bag, and he pulled it out to hand to Gretchen.

"Are you sure you can ride? Would you rather take my car?"

He shook his head. "I need to ride. I need you behind me while I do it."

They mounted up. When her arms came around his waist, she held him close, resting for a moment against his back. He started the bike and pulled out of the parking lot, heading north.

The sun was out, shining brightly, making the colors flashing by more brilliant. Wind buffeted his chest as he rode, muffled under the helmet. The bike rumbled its comforting power as the miles disappeared under its wheels. And Gretchen. Gretchen sat behind him. Warm. Present. Holding him close.

He drove to the turn off the bridge and past the marina. The entrance to the clubhouse also lay in that direction, and he passed it as well. A few miles later, he slowed down and turned onto a dirt road that opened to a log cabin. Iceman had willed the place to him. Rail didn't come here often. He owned the place now but spent most of his nights at the compound. He still believed it was more Iceman's house than his, but he didn't want to go to the clubhouse. He wasn't ready to face anyone. Not yet.

He parked and waited for Gretchen to dismount. It was warm and a little stuffy inside the cabin. Rail remembered Gabriella cooking all sorts of sweet treats in the kitchen, filling the open floor plan with the scents of vanilla and cinnamon and lingonberries. She turned this place into a home for her and Iceman. There was a lot of love that happened in this house. Maybe that's why he had to be here now.

Home. His throat worked as he felt sadness welling up in him. More tears gathered in his eyes. He turned to the woman standing beside him.

Her gentle hands took his, and she gazed into his eyes as if waiting.

He broke.

She held him as great sobs of grief poured from his mouth. He cried. He purged. He let loose agonized torrents of the pain in his heart. There was only one other time in his life when he had opened himself up like this with Flora. Memories he'd never shared with anyone but her bombarded him. Secrets he vowed to take to his grave. Abandoned. Rejected. Unwanted. Unloved. Ignored. Powerless. He'd found comfort in the broad arms of the only person who ever gave a damn about him. His beloved Grams.

Now he found it in the arms of his beloved Gretchen.

Somehow they'd made it to the couch. She cradled his head against her generous breasts as he lay half on top of her. She stroked his back, her fingers soothing with their gentle touch. He was drained. His eyes were swollen, and his head weighed a hundred pounds. He raised it with some difficulty and stared into her face, seeing in the blotchy skin around her eyes and reddened complexion the evidence that she'd cried with him.

He needed to tell her something but didn't want to let go. His lips moved. "Stay with me."

She mouthed back, "I'm not leaving you."

He settled back onto her firm bosom and slept.

CHAPTER
TWENTY-FOUR

PIGLET'S HANDS SHOOK AS HE DIALED ANOTHER number. All afternoon, he'd sat with Brother Matthias on the front porch of the Main House, searching for a way to get his... um... *cargo* across the Canadian border and down here to the farm. The first three people he dialed told him to fuck off and hung up. The fourth guy told him he no longer had a connection on the other side. The fifth one said the same thing.

He was running out of options, and Matthias was getting impatient. Every cut-off lead made Matthias's frown deepen. Piglet sweated bullets, hoping that by some miracle, he would find the line he needed. The situation sickened him, but what other choice did he have? He could do what Matthias asked, or....

"Yeah?" the rough voice grunted at the other end.

"Carver? It's Piglet."

Carver was a low-level drug dealer out of Hastings who spent as much time sampling as he did selling. He'd been a distribution point for the Dark Horses at one time, but Musicman cut him off when he'd proved to be unreliable.

"Piglet? What the fuck do you want?"

"I'm looking for a connection out of Canada to move some cargo downriver. You got a source?"

"Fuck no. I never got into that end of the deal. I just sell the stuff. Mostly meth now. Can't get my hands on any oxy or coke. Fenta's fucking gold."

Piglet's anxiety rose as Matthias's frown deepened. He was failing, and there would come a point when Matthias would take the phone back. Then what would happen? Would he make Piglet give up his "wife"? That would actually be a relief, as Piglet was exceedingly uncomfortable with that situation. Would he be made to leave the farm? Very few did.

A vision of the farm truck being unloaded into the field rose in front of him. Fuck, who else could he call? Who else?

"Rebel is your guy for getting stuff across the border."

Piglet jumped, his heart suddenly renewed with hope. "Rebel from the Dutchmen MC?"

"Yeah. He's been buying shit from me regular for

a while 'cause he can't get it anywhere else. Got some deal working with the Canadians for a load of oxy to come over. That fucking club doesn't deal anymore, so Rebel is going it alone. I've heard there's a lot of in-fighting, but I got nothing to do with that shit. You want something brought in, Rebel's your guy."

Piglet's head turned dizzy as the weight of judgment lifted off him. He wanted to jump and pump his fist in the air but held himself back. "Rebel, eh? I know of him. Got a way to contact him?"

"Fucker probably wants you dead. I heard about the shit that went down in the cities. The rumor is you played both sides. Not a good thing to be associated with you now."

"I'm willing to bet Rebel needs money or coke more than he needs me dead."

Carver sucked air through his teeth. "Could be. I don't get into that shit. I just sell and make my cut. That's it. I'm not getting involved in this either. Most I'll do is give Rebel your number. After that, I don't plan to hear from you again. Get me?"

Piglet pressed his lips together, slightly embarrassed but not surprised at the cool reception. Many avenues were closed to him now, and he was extremely lucky to have found anyone who would talk to him. Rebel was a wild man, loved to party, loved to fuck, was up for anything, and held very little fear. Piglet recalled one night when the Dark Horses and the Dutchmen were having a blowout get-together, a dare had been made for someone to go out on the new Eisenhower Bridge spanning the Mississippi River and jump off. Laughter rang out as no one took it seriously, but Rebel had climbed on a table and announced he would do it. Bets and money exchanged hands as the entire population of the club-house took themselves to the banks of the river and watched. Rebel rode up to the middle of the bridge, made a big show of tipping back and emptying a bottle of vodka, then, with a long whooping cry, leapt out into the air. The drop was a little over seventy feet and seemed to take forever. Cries of fear erupted from several women as he hit the water. When he surfaced, there were collective shouts of relief. Then the fucker got someone to take him back up to the bridge so he could do it again.

If Rebel was his only option, he'd either be all in or all out. At least he would have an answer. "Yeah, I get you," he told Carver before hanging up.

"Will this Rebel person help us?" Matthias's soft inquiry held a minor note of irritation. All the calls were on speaker, so Matthias heard every word. If this didn't work out, Piglet had no doubt he'd be in trouble.

He tapped the phone to the home screen and

handed it back to Matthias. "Rebel is a wild card for sure, but if he's on the outs with the Dutchmen, there's a good chance he will."

It was obvious Matthias didn't like it, but he would bide his time for now. "Have you seeded your bride today?"

Piglet cringed inwardly. He wanted to lie, but there were cameras all over the farm and the women's center. It would be a simple task to find out if Piglet had made a visit. "Not yet. I thought I'd wait a few—"

Matthias shook his head and spoke as if admonishing a child. "Now, now, Brother Ezra. This is an important part of your daily chores. If our mission is to be met, everyone must be diligent in their work. The men gifted with wives must seed them at least once a day until they become pregnant. Do you need a booster? I noticed you were able to come many times after eating one."

"No, I can manage. Thanks." *Christ, so that's what those damn things are for. Getting boners to fuck as much as possible. I can manage? Shit!* "I'll go over after supper—"

"You should go now."

Piglet felt the trap around him. The last thing he wanted to do was walk into the women's building and stick his dick in Naomi. His body would respond, but for the first time in his life, he hated the idea of fucking.

Matthias stared at him with his eyes narrowed, waiting for an answer.

Piglet only had one choice. "I'll go now."

He stood up when the phone in Matthias's hand chirped a new text. The other man tapped the screen and smiled. "It seems your friend is ready to talk a deal."

Piglet tried not to let the relief show in his face. If he played his cards right, perhaps he could get out of performing this particular duty today. He sat back down and assumed a businesslike demeanor. "Let's see what Rebel has to say."

CHAPTER
TWENTY-FIVE

"It was decided that only the strongest should propagate, keeping the blood of the first men pure."

Gretchen rubbed her gritty eyes. Whatever the hell this book was trying to be made no sense. If this was a memoir, it missed by a long shot. Hell, the thing read more like some sort of manifesto with a mixture of rules, political propaganda, and a bunch of different religious ideologies. In short, it was weird.

Strange or not, she still took the job. Thankfully, it was for proofing and not content. She could clean up tenses, grammar, and punctuation without examining and commenting on the words. She would treat this like any other job, even though the document was disturbing as hell.

Her phone lit up on her desk.

Railroad: Emergency repair just came in. I'll be late.

Gretchen: How late?

Railroad: At least an hour. Maybe more. Family took a day trip up from Lake Pepin. Stuck here until I get their boat fixed.

Gretchen: Too bad. I'm sitting on my back deck totally naked and waiting for you.

The screen stayed blank so long, she thought he'd left her. Then the device buzzed in her hand with a new text.

Railroad: You're an evil woman. How am I supposed to work on this motor while thinking about your tits?

Gretchen sent him a shrugging emoji. She thought about lifting her shirt and sending him a very personal selfie and debated if it was going too far. Then she grinned and did it.

Gretchen: Just to tide you over.
Railroad: You're killing me!

She saved her work and shut the computer down for the night.

For the past two weeks, she'd been living the dream. Rail was in her bed every night, whether it was here or at the cabin. After Flora's simple funeral, they were together as much as possible. Sometimes they slept, but most nights they'd spent exploring all the fantasies ever imagined in a romance book. Gretchen grinned. More like erotica than romance. So many positions, some of them not yet named. Her toys saw some creative uses. They made use of whatever area of the cabin or her house they happened to be in. Even outdoors. Nothing was taboo.

Just last night they'd been at her place. She'd been cutting up greens for a salad when flashing lights indicated his arrival. He'd come into the kitchen, carrying her mail. His dark eyes glowed at her when he saw she wore an apron and nothing else. He plucked the knife from her hand before he lifted her onto the counter, spread her thighs, and went down on her.

Gretchen felt a little shudder at the memory. Rail was a cunnilingus expert. No fumbling around. No teasing. He zeroed in on her clit every time, circling, licking, and sucking until she exploded. The cold granite counter under her ass had contrasted with the hot mouth between her legs, making the sensation more intense. After he made her come, he reached for the knife and cut open a small shipping box. He'd clearly been doing some internet shopping, as he pulled out a string of beads from the box and a small bottle of lube. His quirked eyebrow and cocky grin were the only signs she needed for her to understand him.

She'd cleaned the wilted greens off the counter this morning.

It wasn't just loads of sex. It was him and all his broody self. He slotted into her life like he was meant to be there. They shared whatever space they were in with precision, never getting in each other's way. She was able to relax and work either here or at his place. They cooked together, ate together, slept together. She rode on the back of his bike everywhere they went. He anticipated her wants and needs as she did his. Many of the books she edited had worked over the familiar trope of soul mates. That one perfect person for everyone who created a flawless world of love with a bright and happy future. Gretchen loved the concept but had always thought of it as fiction. Now she had started to believe it was true.

The only problem? He hadn't told her he loved her. At least not yet. No matter how long they were around each other or how comfortable she was with him, there was still a part he kept hidden. She'd shared everything he'd asked about, in great detail.

"So where did you go to school? I'm assuming you went to college to be an editor."

She got up from the bed and sat astride his hips so they had room to talk. "It didn't start that way. My degree is in creative writing with a minor in English literature. I was all set to be the next great American novelist while I supported myself by teaching at a high school. It turns out not many places will hire a deaf person for a hearing classroom. I tried for a year but didn't make a lot of headway. Mom and Dad were supportive, but they didn't quite get it. They never treated me as disabled growing up, and I guess I got used to people just accepting me as I am. College was a real eye-opener to the world. Most of my classmates were cool, but there were some who simply didn't know how to handle being around a deaf person. It bothered me, but there wasn't a damn thing I could do about it. Therefore, I decided it was their problem and not mine."

She shifted and felt his growing interest underneath her. Grinning, she deliberately rolled her pelvis and watched his eyes close. He brought one of his hands to her hip to stop the movement.

"You're going to kill me. I'm not a young man anymore, and it takes me a little while to recover. How did you end up in Connecticut?"

"Yale offered me a graduate fellowship for my master's."

His eyes widened. *"You have a master's degree? From Yale?"*

She winked at him and leaned back. "I figured out early enough that the professor thing wasn't for me. I liked the adjunct thing okay and would do that again, but not the full academic thing. I had a knack for proofreading and did a lot of it for my thesis supervisor. He got me into editing papers for the department as his graduate assistant. I found out I could make money at it and started taking outside gigs for hire. A romance author used my services and liked my work. She told others about me, and I got more romance books sent to me. I finished the degree, but I was making so much from the books, I decided to make it a formal business." She raised her arms palms up to frame her torso. "Now, here I am. A full-time editor with a fat queue of books and a half-finished novel of my own." She circled on him again, and his body jumped under hers.

"Keep that up, and I'll finish your book right here and now."

"I dare you." She smiled and made the movement again.

He didn't say anything but gave her a half smirk as he arched. She gasped as he filled her. "Challenge accepted."

She glanced outside at the late afternoon sun making its way to the horizon and continued to type.

Gretchen: I'll stop texting in a minute so you can get to work. Instead of you coming here, I can pack up a few things and drive up there. This new editing project is kicking my ass. All sorts of weirdness. Want food?

Railroad: That would help a lot. I might need to go to the clubhouse tonight though.

Gretchen: So?

Railroad: No old ladies allowed.

Gretchen read his answer several times, trying to decide between being thrilled and pissed.

Gretchen: So I'm your old lady?

She knew what the term meant from the countless books she'd had cross her computer. It was more than a girlfriend. Being a biker's old lady put her on the same level as wife. It was a true and complete commitment.

Railroad: Yes.

She waited for more than his single-word answer. He must not have felt a need to elaborate as nothing else showed up on her screen. She tried a different tactic.

Gretchen: I've already been there once. Remember?

Railroad: You weren't an old lady then.

Gretchen: Aren't you the president?

Railroad: Your point?

Gretchen: It seems if I'm the president's old lady, I should get a pass.

She waited for a moment. Three laughing emojis appeared.

Railroad: Good try. I don't remember a president who had an old lady. I suppose we can set a precedent.

Gretchen: Excellent. Now what do you want. Burgers, wings, or tacos?

Railroad: Whatever you get is fine with me.

She tapped the screen closed, deciding to take a shower and dress in one of those slinky tops Penny insisted she buy.

An hour later, she pulled into the marina parking lot near the garage. Rail raised his head from the boat he was working and gave her a big smile of welcome. His white teeth gleamed. With his hair pulled back in a ponytail and the glint of the gold stud he wore in his left ear, it wasn't the first time she'd likened him to a pirate worthy of any seafaring romance. His sleeveless T-shirt might have been white at one time but now was slick with sweat and grease. A family—husband, wife, and three kids—stood close by, watching him carefully. The oldest girl was somewhere in her teenage years and had stars in her eyes as she watched Rail work. Gretchen also noticed the wife's appreciative glances at the muscular arms working a set of wrenches.

"Try it now," Rail directed.

The husband started the motor, and Gretchen saw bubbles froth up from beneath the boat. Rail gave a thumbs-up and climbed off the boat and onto the deck.

"Stop," Gretchen ordered with one hand while holding bags from Fiesta Mexicana in the other. "Don't come near me."

Rail blinked. "Why?"

"You're not touching me with those hands or that shirt. Shower first."

He grinned. "What if I kiss you anyway?"

"I'll be pissed and take my tacos home with me."

"I know how to make you unpissed."

She stuck her tongue out at him, and he threw his head back in laughter. "I get it, baby. I won't mess up your shirt. At least not yet. Let's eat first and then get to the clubhouse, yeah?" He motioned to a set of covered picnic tables. She sat and arranged the food while he pulled two soft drinks from a cooler in the garage. "Thanks for doing this. I was getting hungry."

"No problem. How was the rest of your day?

They ate and chatted. She liked it. She liked it a lot. It was domestic and homey and just nice.

"You sure you're ready for the whole Dutchmen experience? It can get wild sometimes. There's a poker game tonight, and a lot of people will be there. You might see some stuff you'd rather not."

His warning didn't faze her. "You get what I do for a living, right? I've had rather intense clinical discussions with more than one author on the proper use of butt plugs. I've had to draw maps to figure out positions of threesomes and foursomes. One book I edited last year was about a space alien with three penises. I think I can handle your MC."

He laughed again. She loved watching him. "Mind if I get in your car? We can park it in the fenced area at the clubhouse where it will be safe."

She wrinkled her nose. "I suppose. Just put a towel down and don't touch anything."

THE CLUBHOUSE WAS FULL OF PEOPLE. MUSIC, VOICES, and laughter rang through the air. Railroad clasped her hand firmly as they made their way through the crowd. Several shouted greetings hailed him, and he waved or nodded. Gretchen admired the respect shown to him by the men and recognized the attraction in the women. More than one set of envious female eyes followed her across the room, and she wondered how many of them had been in Rail's bed. She had no illusions that he'd been a choirboy before he met her. It would just be nice to know how many knives were aimed at her back.

He stripped off the nasty shirt as she closed his bedroom door, and he tossed it into a laundry basket on the floor. "I'll be out in a few minutes. Help yourself to the fridge." The rest of his clothes came off, and he walked naked into the bathroom.

Gretchen's mouth watered after his finely sculpted ass. His magnificent body was proof there was a God. Defined shoulders, strong back that V-ed into his hips, a rounded butt that was high and tight, long sturdy legs, and high calves—all of it in one handsome package of a man. What the hell? She had extra makeup in her purse, and her hair didn't require a lot of complicated styling. *I can afford to get wet.* Her mouth curled up at the thought. *Pun intended!*

She stripped off her own clothes and entered the small bathroom.

The shower was a small inset one with little extra room. Rail's head was under the steamy spray, rinsing off the last of the shampoo, when she tapped him on the shoulder. He turned to face her fully and quirked an eyebrow at her. She smiled at him with the confidence of a woman who was sure of her welcome and reached for the bar of soap. He raised his arms and braced himself against the wall as if saying, *Have at it.*

She did.

Lather built between her fingers as she glided the soap over his shoulders. The shower water made the black hair on his forearms seem thicker and darker. It did the same for the patch on his chest. She stepped closer to slide her hands behind him and up his back, letting her pointed nipples graze his chest. He reached for her, and she moved back with a sharp "No."

"Keep your hands on the walls or I'll stop," Gretchen told him. She loved the power she had in this moment and planned on using it fully.

His jaw clenched, but he complied. She began to touch him again, running her slick palms over his body. His dick rose between them, hard and pulsing. She pinched his nipples between her fingers and rolled them. He jumped and closed his eyes. Yep, he was sensitive there. His arm muscles tensed as she put her mouth to one brown disk and sucked.

In teasing him, she also tortured herself. Her pussy grew heavy, and wetness gathered between her folds. She sank to her knees, nipping the skin just below his navel. His penis had lengthened even more and bobbed in front of her, a bead of moisture sparkling at the tip. She opened her mouth and licked the engorged head before taking him in completely. His taste was clean, musky, and slightly soapy. She sucked at him as she stroked him, controlling her movements and his depth by holding his hips. His thighs trembled, and his dick was solid rock.

Boldness rose in her as much as her own lust. She slid a hand between his legs to cup and play with his balls. He spread his legs and arched his back, telling her he liked what she did to him. She went even further, pressing into his perineum with two fingers. He shuddered, and she knew he was close.

Gretchen wondered again how many women out there had ever been kneeling in this position between Rail's legs with his dick in their mouths. She was willing to bet none of them did what she was about to do. She slipped a soapy finger between those perfect butt cheeks of his and pressed it against his anus. The muscle clenched in shock, and his entire body stiffened. She sucked him to the back of her throat, and his ring relaxed long enough to allow her finger to penetrate. His body trembled in imminent climax, and she pushed further.

His body shook, and she sensed his cry as he started to come. Her mouth filled with salty sweetness, and his ring pulsed around her finger as he crested over. It seemed to go on for a long time, and she reveled in her victory. After he was finished, she spat in the drain and rinsed her mouth as she rose to stand in front of him. He leaned against the tiles, his lungs heaving to take in as much air as possible.

"Has anyone ever done that to you before?" she asked.

He shook his head, his eyes still glazed.

She smiled at him in triumph. "Good. For the rest of the night, every time another woman looks at you, you'll be feeling me."

He huffed a laugh as she used his own words against him.

CHAPTER
TWENTY-SIX

HE'D BEEN DRUNK MORE THAN ONCE IN HIS LIFE. HE'D been high on weed. However, nothing, not a goddamned thing, could ever compare to the euphoria he felt tonight with Gretchen by his side. She could read lips well enough, but it was still better for her to stay with him for any kind of communication, as only he knew her first language. He had never liked clingy women, but with Gretchen, he found himself hanging on her, keeping her close with her hand in his or an arm draped around her body. Never had he kissed a woman in public, but he laid a long one on her when they stepped in the main room, staking his claim. Whoops and hollers filled the air loudly enough that he saw she felt the vibrations from the noise.

True to her words, he did feel her intimate invasion whenever he spotted a club girl watching them.

Bar food appeared from the Harbor Marina's restaurant in big aluminum-foil pans. Booze flowed freely. The poker players gave up on the games and just enjoyed the night.

Duke came up to them, beer in hand. "This is a fucking great night, eh? This is the life the Dutchmen should have."

Rail agreed. There were smiles, laughter, dancing, people having a good time everywhere he looked. Nowhere did he see anyone worried about shipments, cops, timetables, cleaning money, or anything else that a smuggling run would generate. All he saw was happiness.

Duke took a huge swallow of his beer and burped. "Hey... um... Gretchen." He overexaggerated his mouth movements. "Did Penny come with you tonight?"

She overexaggerated her signs back to him. "No, but I bet she'd make the drive if you invited her." Rail interpreted and tried not to laugh at her sweet expression while she signed "you big dumbass" at the clueless man.

"Yeah, thanks. I'll go do that." He wandered off.

Rail spotted Nutter sitting in his usual spot, oddly alone and wearing a morose expression. Rail motioned to the still man and lifted a brow in question to Gretchen. She nodded, and they walked to sit with him.

"What's up, brother?" Rail signed as he spoke to keep Gretchen in the conversation.

Nutter didn't bother to glance up. "I got a package today. Mama J sent me her property patch back. It's really happening. She's leaving me."

Rail frowned. "I'm sorry, Nutter. Mama J is a good woman."

"Mimi's left me too. After the baby is born, she's planning on leaving for Eau Claire with this new man she's found. Kay's not speaking to me either. She texted to tell me she's going to give up all her parental rights, and I can either take the kid or give it up for adoption. She doesn't care." The man's face crumbled. "I fucked up so goddamn bad, I don't know how to make it right. I miss my ol' lady! I miss my home! I miss my family!"

Before Nutter collapsed into a mass of blubbering hysteria, Gretchen reached forward and knocked sharply on the wood table to get their attention. She motioned for Rail to speak for her, but her words were directed at Nutter.

"Yes, you fucked up. I'm surprised your Mama J kept you around this long. If my man cheated on me, there wouldn't be a second time, as he'd be gone the first. Want to know why? Because I'm me, and I'm worth something. I may not have a fashion model's body, and I have a disability that turns away a lot of people, but that's their problem, not mine. My deafness does not make me less, and I refuse to let anyone treat me that way. I've never met Mama J, but Rail has told me about her. She's a hard worker. Takes good care of her kids. Kind. Giving. Worthy of love and fidelity. She doesn't have to earn it. She deserves it."

Nutter sniffed and wiped under his nose. "I know all that. I never appreciated it before. Never thought about what I had until I lost it. I want it back. I want it all back."

"Every book I edit, historical to paranormal, has one commonality. They all have happy endings. Real life doesn't always have happy endings. It may be too far gone for Mama J to trust you again. You may never get back together, but you can still love and respect her, and that will go a long way to heal this breach. How is simple: Be there for her. Show up when she needs you. Become a better father to your children. Give up banging other women and devote yourself to her and only her. You want her forgiveness? This is the price you pay."

Nutter stared at Gretchen and nodded. His face

grew serious, and he put down the beer bottle. "I understand."

Camo rushed up with a cell phone to his ear and a grim expression on his face. "We have a problem. Not life or death, but still a problem. Peebles is on the phone. She's in labor and can't find Rebel. Been texting him all day. Said she hasn't seen him in weeks. She needs help and doesn't have anyone else in her corner."

Rail pressed his lips. "Isn't this too soon?"

Camo shrugged. "I have no idea. All I know is she's at the hospital and in a lot of pain."

Just like that, the weight of responsibility crashed onto his shoulders. The difference now was someone had his back. He turned to Gretchen. "I need to go make sure she's okay."

"Need me to come with you?"

"Yeah."

"Okay."

It amazed him that she was so matter-of-fact.

The ride to the hospital took close to twenty minutes. By the time they got there, Peebles was in active labor and surrounded by a team of medical people. Rail and Gretchen ended up in the waiting room for several hours. Rail paced and made calls, trying to track down Rebel, but no one had seen or heard from him in days. Desktop had also been suspiciously absent as well. A bad premonition settled in Rail's gut. He should have known this good day wouldn't last.

Gretchen flipped pages in an outdated magazine and sipped at a plastic bottle of Diet Coke. She rolled her eyes a few times. "Too many word echoes in this article. The writer needs a thesaurus ASAP," she explained when Rail asked what was wrong.

"Always working, eh?"

She nodded. "Yes. So are you."

He heaved a tired sigh and sat down next to her. "Thanks for coming with me. Peebles hasn't been in the clubhouse in months, but she's been with the Dutchmen for a long time. No family around to help her. Rebel has checked out, and now she's about to become a mother. I need to be here, but you don't. I can call Duke or Camo to come take you home."

She stifled a yawn. "You feel better with me here?"

"I'm always better around you."

"Then I'll stay."

"Family for Opal Novak?"

It took Rail a minute to recognize Peebles's real name. "Here. How is she?"

"Mom and daughter are doing well. Six pounds two ounces and a head full of red hair. If you'll come this way."

Gretchen stood and followed Rail and the nurse to a private room. The hospital bed was cranked up to an acute reclining position. Peebles held a blue-and-pink bundle in her arms. This was the first time Rail had seen her without heavy makeup. She looked young and vulnerable on the white sheets. Her bleached hair had grown out into a pretty strawberry blonde shade. Her tired face showed the remnants of her labor with bags under her eyes and flushed cheeks. Even exhausted she met his eyes with a big smile.

"Hi, Rail. Thanks for coming. Isn't she beautiful?"

Rail looked at the rosebud mouth of the sleeping newborn. His heart tripped. "Yeah, she is."

"Who's this?"

"Gretchen, my old lady. She's deaf, so I'll have to sign for her to get in on the conversation. That okay with you?"

Peebles's eyes opened wide, and her mouth formed an O. "Old lady? Of all the Dutchmen, I never thought you'd get caught."

"Neither did I."

"Have you heard from Rebel? I've been trying to find him to tell him he has a daughter. I can't tell if he's not taking my calls or if something bad has happened to him." Two tears tracked down her face.

"We haven't been... um... getting along very well lately."

"He hasn't been at the clubhouse for a while."

She looked at her baby girl. "My mama told me a long time ago, the best way to find and keep a man was to learn how to suck cock and do it well." More tears flowed, and her lip quivered. "I've sucked a lot of cock, and it's gotten me nowhere. I'm still alone." She gave a little laugh. "I guess it was always going to end up this way. I thought Rebel loved me. Maybe he did a little, but he loves that white powder more. He liked the idea of being a father, but when he figured out what it would really be like, he bailed."

A tear dripped onto the baby's blanket.

The hookup between Rebel and Peebles had shocked a lot of people. She had been a regular club girl for years, which meant she'd slept with most if not all the Dutchmen at one time or another. Rail himself had been one of them, and she'd had her mouth around his dick more than once.

"We're about to be evicted. I don't have any money to pay the rent and no insurance either. Mama J said we can come to her place for a while. There's not a lot of room, but she said we'd manage."

Rail reached out a finger to touch the fiery hair of the sleeping baby. Her tiny face scrunched for a moment, then relaxed. "You don't have to move in with Mama J. The Dutchmen will cover your expenses. I'll make sure you're taken care of."

She made a sound in her throat. "No. I need to do this on my own. If I let someone take care of me like I have all these years, what will that teach my daughter?"

She raised her watery eyes and met Rail's dead-on. "I'm not helpless. The Vo Tech has a cosmetology program for learning to cut hair and do nails. They also have help for people like me."

Rail's heart skittered again, with a combination of pride and guilt. He'd been a willing participant in the few times Peebles had been in his bed, and he hadn't given a thought about her after. He couldn't change the past, but he could sure as hell do something about the future. "If that's what you want, you should go for it, but you'll still need help. The Dutchmen will cover the hospital bill and give you some money every month until you don't need it anymore. The baby is Rebel's, and you're entitled to child support. I'll make sure you get it."

She took a breath and let it out slowly. "Okay, I can live with that. I'm still moving in with Mama J. She could use some help with all she's got going on. It's going to be hard the next few years, but I'm ready for that." Her face filled with determination as her tears dried up and she sat up a little taller. "I'm not sucking cock again."

"Life sends us challenges every single day. Some are cracks in the sidewalk we only have to step over. Others are hills we have to climb. Then there are the mountains that are so big, it seems like they can't be crossed. Don't believe that, child. Nothing is impossible. It just takes a little time, a lot of effort, and good people at your back to help you up when you fall down."

Rail smiled at her as he remembered Flora's lessons. Other words came to him that had been signed by the woman who stood behind him.

"She doesn't have to earn it. She deserves it."

"You don't have to do a goddamn thing you don't want to, Peebles. If anyone tries to make you, let me know. I'll have your back."

"Opal. Peebles is the name I had as a club whore. I'm not Peebles anymore."

"Opal it is. What's the baby's name?"

Opal glowed as she looked at her daughter, and Rail was struck by the beauty of the love between mother and child. It shook him to his core. "I'm naming her Pearl. I like the sound of it. Opal and Pearl."

"It's beautiful. Get some rest. I'll check on you later."

He leaned down and kissed her head before

turning to Gretchen. The expression on her face was unreadable, but she smiled at him as he took her hand.

He decided on the ride back not to go to the club-house. He drove to the cabin instead, wanting to be alone, just him and his woman. A plethora of different and unfamiliar emotions swirled through his mind. Ones he'd never experienced and didn't know how to handle. He was feeling so much, he was brimming over with it.

They entered the cabin, and Rail immediately took Gretchen to the bedroom. She went into his arms as if already sensing what he needed. He didn't fall on her like a ravenous beast. He took his time, slowly undressing her and savoring every part. Her gentle kisses on his lips as she met him halfway. Her sharp breath as he nipped at the curve of her neck. The surface of her nipples as he teased them into tight little points.

There wasn't one part of her that he didn't relish. He fingered the tiny mole on her rib cage just below her left breast. Traced the scar on her forearm from a previous injury. Worshiped the softness of her lower belly under his mouth as he kissed it. Reveled in the taste of her sweet pussy on his tongue and loved the gasp of her breath as she came apart under him.

When he slid inside her body, she wrapped her

arms and legs around him to hold him close to her. Warm. Welcoming. That sense of home he wanted and needed so much. He felt an intimate connection with Gretchen that far exceeded anything he'd ever had before, and the beauty of it overwhelmed him. He'd fucked a lot of women, but this was the first time he ever made love. There was a difference, and he recognized it now. This was love. He loved Gretchen with every fiber and cell in him. It should have scared him and sent him running away. Instead, he jumped feet first into the emotion and craved more of it.

He couldn't contain all that welled up inside him, and he kissed her, trying to put everything he was feeling into it. She met him with equal measure, running her hands over his skin as if she couldn't get close enough.

A tingle at the base of his spine told him he was about to come and that this pleasure would be the most glorious experience of his life. It was too much. He had to tell her before he came. He had to give her the words he'd never uttered to any woman before. He raised himself up enough to look into her incredible eyes. Her face reflected the same ecstasy back to him. He had no doubt they shared the same feeling. Her body spasmed around his, and she dug her fingers into his shoulders as she found the pinnacle.

He reached his own crest and spilled over, crying out as he rushed headlong into this new world.

His mind formed the words *I love you,* but his mouth said something else.

"Marry me."

CHAPTER
TWENTY-SEVEN

PIGLET GLANCED AROUND THE DOCKS FOR THE FOUR hundredth time. Nervous didn't even begin to describe his thoughts as he and Matthias waited. Rebel was late. Very late, and Piglet wasn't sure the man would actually turn up. Matthias showed signs of anger, and that made Piglet more nervous. An angry Matthias was someone Piglet never wanted to see.

"Well, lookie here, Desktop. We're seeing something I never thought we'd get to," Rebel said as he sauntered onto the floating pier. "A goddamn fucking traitor."

The other man sneered at Piglet. "I ought to shoot you where you stand. Toss your ass in the water. No one would give a shit if I did."

"I would," Matthias countered.

"Who the fuck are you?" Rebel spat.

"I'm the man who's about to give you a lot of money."

Piglet could see the storm clouds gathering in Matthias's demeanor. He obviously didn't like Rebel, but he had few options other than dealing with the wild biker.

Rebel's appearance shocked Piglet. The man had always been thin and lanky, but now he appeared almost emaciated. His clothes were dirty and hung loosely on his gaunt frame. He smelled. His red eyes darted around, and Piglet noticed their dark, dilated pupils.

The Dutchmen daredevil had given up on coke and moved to cheaper meth.

Rebel picked at a spot on his arm. "Yeah, I get it. Me and Desktop got your little errand covered. Two more guys are meeting up with the Canadians in Duluth and transporting your cargo to the cities. Desk and I will pick it up from there. You got the money?"

A muscle ticked in Matthias's jaw. He paused before reaching in his blazer pocket for a thick yellow envelope. "This is a third of your payment, as agreed. You bring the cargo to me in good shape and you'll get the rest."

Rebel snatched the mailer from Matthias and stuffed it in his jeans pocket.

"Expect us sometime on Wednesday of next week," Desktop said with a growl. Piglet shuddered at the absolute hatred that shone in his eyes. Rebel might say he would shoot him, but Desktop would actually do it.

"I think we're done here. The cargo is virgin, and I expect it to be that way when they arrive. Well fed and well cared for. They have husbands waiting for them, and those men will not be happy if their future wives are harmed," Matthias warned.

"Whatever." Rebel grabbed his crotch. "We won't even make them suck us off. We'll deliver them all nice and tight and ready to fuck."

If the crudity bothered Matthias, he didn't show it. He turned away. "Good. One more thing. If you fuck me on this deal, there won't be enough pieces of you left to feed to the river."

Desktop spoke up again. "There won't be any problems."

The men separated and left. Piglet followed Matthias to the car, subdued and taken aback. He'd never heard the man cuss, let alone drop an F-bomb. He must be very displeased to let that emotion break through his usual magnetic charm. Piglet hoped and prayed this transport would run smoothly. There could be any number of complications along the way. Sickness, injury, police randomly stopping boats on the river. Piglet was so lost in his worries, he almost walked into Matthias when they reached the vehicle.

The man in front of him beeped the locks, then turned and coldcocked him across his jaw. Piglet went down in surprised pain and landed on the rough pavement. Blood filled his mouth, and he spat it on the ground. Yes, Matthias was angry, and it was his fault for not finding someone better to work with. If anything went wrong, Piglet would be paying for it alongside Rebel and Desktop.

"Get up," Matthias said in a cold voice from above.

Piglet spat again and wiped the mess from his mouth and face. He got in the car, and Matthias handed him a wad of tissues. "Don't bleed in my car. Naomi isn't pregnant yet. I expect you to double your daily visits until she is."

CHAPTER
TWENTY-EIGHT

RAIL RODE OVER THE BRIDGE AND INTO RED WING, guiding his big black bike through the small city and into a residential area. His destination was Mama J's house so he could check in on her and see how she and Peebles were working out.

Not Peebles. Opal.

He also needed to get away and clear his mind. After his blurted proposal, Gretchen had shut down on him. She'd gone to clean herself, then rejoined him in bed but rolled away from him to fall asleep without touching him. The sudden abandonment after such an intimate joining made him feel intensely alone.

He didn't get an answer.

It had been four days since Gretchen left to go

back to Wabasha. Her explanation was that she had an editing deadline for this crazy memoir job she needed to get through and needed to stay in her own place by herself. Rail figured it was as good an excuse as any to get away from him. Perhaps she didn't feel the deep connection he did. In her mind, this might be only a summer fling before she returned to her life in Connecticut. He hadn't thought about what the future would bring with it. He'd asked her to marry him and be a permanent part of his life. He'd forgotten she had a different life waiting for her somewhere else.

He'd had stuff to think about too these last four days. If she left for Connecticut, would he quit the club and follow her there? Was that what she wanted? Was that what *he* wanted?

Mama J's house came into view, and for a moment, Rail forgot his tangled situation with Gretchen. A ladder was propped up on the front of the house. Nutter was on the roof, installing new shingles. His shirt was off, and his back tattoo gleamed with sweat. It showed signs of sunburn, which told Rail the man had been there for a while already.

Nutter paused his work when he heard Rail pull up. He picked up the shirt he'd left on the roof and wiped his face. "You ever hear from Rebel? This roofing shit is his thing more than mine. Been calling and texting his ass for days and can't find him."

Rail clicked his teeth. This was good. Better to talk about club business than family business. "No. He hasn't called anyone. Desktop is missing too. I'm guessing they're together. I have a bad feeling they're up to something and we're not going to like it."

"We haven't liked much about Rebel lately. He snorts anything and everything he can get his hands on." Nutter shook his head. "He's gonna end up dead, and that cute little baby in there won't have a dad."

"Do you really think Rebel is good father material?"

The big man didn't take too long to ponder. "Based on what he's doing now, no. Peebles… excuse me… Opal is better off as a single mom."

Two kids burst from the house, chasing each other with water pistols. Mama J appeared in the doorway, wearing a flour-covered apron. She slung a dishtowel over her shoulder and yelled, "I said the backyard!"

The kids ignored her and started to wrestle. Nutter climbed down from the roof and stopped the squabble by lifting one kid in each hand. "Your mother said the backyard. Now."

The two children fell silent at the authoritative tone. "Yessir," they intoned before scampering behind the house.

Mama J's face closed down. She bit out a thank-you before turning to go back in the house.

"She won't let me in," Nutter observed. "I don't blame her. I showed my ass so bad last time I was here, I'm surprised she hasn't called the cops yet."

"I have no answers for you, brother. Truth is, I have nothing but questions of my own. All I can say is those two women in there are good women. They were handed a raw deal by the club, and it's up to us to make it right. Mama J might not let you in the house ever again, but there are four lives you made together. That's gonna connect you until you stop breathing. Gretchen was right. You want her back, you step up and be the man she needs you to be. She might not open that door again, but for the sake of your children, I'm willing to bet she'll forgive you."

Nutter humphed and picked up another stack of shingles. "It's changing. Life, the club, all of it."

"Yeah."

"I heard Gretchen drove down to Wabasha for a bit. She coming back?"

Rail made a decision and answered one of his own questions. "If she doesn't, I'm going there." He stuffed a roofing hammer in his back pocket and motioned for Nutter to climb up. "Now quit stalling, and let's get this shit done."

CHAPTER
TWENTY-NINE

"ONLY THE PUREST OF MEN HAVE THE POWER TO RULE, *whether the household or the kingdom. The true beginning was the great flood, ridding the world of inferior people, but for the blight of Noah's son, Ham, only the superior would have survived. Ham saw his father drunk and naked, and instead of covering him and turning away like his older brother had, he stared and laughed. This disrespect to Noah earned Ham the eternal curse of slavery to his brothers. Thus, the curse has extended throughout history, making some men pure wheat and others the lowest of chaff."*

Gretchen shifted back in her chair and rubbed her eyes in irritation. This memoir was getting harder and harder to take. She was not a biblical scholar, but she did remember the story of Noah's Ark. This memoir was turning out to be a mixture of different parts of the Old Testament, Nazi propaganda, conspiracy theories, and survivalist practices. In other words, it was a big fat mess.

"Women are to be submissive at all times, keeping silent unless their men ask them to speak. Their place is one of service without complaint. Wives will be ruled by husbands in all things and will bow before their desires. Men, being the head of the house, have the right of comfort from a wife or other such women available to serve their needs."

Seriously? Gretchen's brain hurt. She wanted to reject the job, but she'd already started it and had received the deposit. Grimly, she started again.

"Keeping pure blood is the key to the superior man. Only the purest shall breed and make new generations. Separation of the wheat from the chaff is critical. Ham's descendants will be known as chaff and become servants of the wheat. No chaff shall breed. Only the purest of wheat will marry and produce superior children, both of mind and body."

Sounds like a recipe for disaster, Gretchen thought. She'd had enough of working on this for now. It was only midmorning, and she was ready to call it a day. There was a queue of manuscripts from her regular authors on her schedule but no looming deadlines. She descended the stairs into the kitchen and filled a glass with water from the tap. Exiting the house, she walked to the patio area and stared at the moving river. A couple of fishing boats drifted by, and a bigger one appeared as a tiny dot upriver. The morning rain had come and gone, leaving her lawn sparkling with drops. The heat of the day would dry it out in no time, and she'd get out the lawn mower later this afternoon.

A twinge pinged her heart. Rail had been the last person to cut her grass. She closed her eyes and dredged up that memory of him on the riding mower, his shirt off and his tanned skin shining with sweat. His hair tied back in a ponytail, as was his habit when he worked. After the time-consuming chore was completed, he'd come in the house and…

She quivered remembering the shower sex and how hard she'd come from it.

"Marry me."

Those two words constantly came to her when she thought of him now.

"Marry me."

She loved him. No question about that, but was it enough? She had a life back in Connecticut. Friends, a condo, lectures at some of the universities from time to time. She'd have to give all that up to move and live here with Rail. Would she eventually resent changing that much of her life for him? Would he leave his marina and MC for her and come live in Connecticut?

In a book, this was the point in the plot where a character declared undying love and made the great sacrifice of trading their entire life for a happily-ever-after ending. Real life didn't have fairy-tale endings. There was an after. There was the house-kids-growing-older-retirement-health-problems-yearly-taxes-until-we-die life that happened for everyone. What kind of after sat on the horizon for her and Rail?

No way of knowing. Still, the thought of not being with him was equally as repugnant as breaking up with him.

"Marry me."

Damn it, she wanted to. She wanted it bad, but did that equal giving up herself? He hadn't said he loved her.

She tossed the rest of her water on the grass. Her question circled and circled again with no definitive answer. It was as maddening as it was painful to her soul.

She focused her eyes back on the river. The water moved along peacefully, and a few rain clouds drifted over. The boat she'd noticed earlier was coming closer and seemed to be heading toward her pier.

Rail, she thought. He was out testing the repairs

on a boat and came to see her. Her heart jumped, but she kept herself still even though she wanted to run down to the wooden dock and meet him. It was a nice boat. A cruiser that had sleeping quarters and a full galley below deck. She frowned a little as she shaded her eyes. Most of the boats Rail serviced were fishing boats and simpler crafts. It was odd seeing such a luxurious one here.

It was too far away to make out the driver. Gretchen took a few steps forward and squinted her eyes. The figure in the wheelhouse was hard to see.

A hand on her shoulder jerked her around, and she fell into a hard male body. He roughly caught her and pulled her arms together, immobilizing her. Four men surrounded her, but this time instead of bikers, she saw a wall of camouflage, rifles, and sunglasses. The man who held her sneered as he barked in her face too fast for her to read. Without the use of her arms, she had no way of communicating. Or did she?

Gretchen brought her knee up hard and fast between the man's legs. His grip loosened as he doubled over. She shook free and tried to run, but another man slammed into her back, bringing her to the ground. Her head hit the dirt, and she saw stars. She was yanked over onto her back, losing some skin in the process, and the man who tackled her straddled her hips, holding her arms stiffly to her sides.

"Be still!" she saw him say. Sounded like her only option as her head was still painfully spinning from the impact.

He pulled her up and placed her in front of him, crossing her arms at her middle so she had no movement nor escape options. That didn't stop her from struggling and kicking at her captor. That earned her several hard shakes, making her head dizzily whip around.

Another man moved in front of her. He grabbed her chin and forced it up. She stopped struggling when she recognized her memoir client, Matt.

"Be. Still." She obeyed the two words mouthed at her this time. What the hell was he doing here at her house? And why the hell did he have armed guards?

More shock hit her as she finally recognized the man standing behind him. Ezra—or Piglet, as Rail called him—was there. He looked older, thinner, and more haggard than she remembered him to be. The entire Dutchmen MC had spent most of the summer searching for him, and it looked to her like he'd been hiding in the woods, living off the land.

Survivalist cult, farming commune, religious faction. This was where he'd been hiding. Pretty clever in a way, but it also appeared that farm life was much rougher than he'd thought.

Shit, are they here for Rail? Somehow, they knew he

was coming. *Pay attention*, she said to herself and stilled as she tried to follow as much of the conversation as she could. Being deaf had an advantage, as no one expected her to read lips or figure out what they were saying. What she saw chilled her to the bone.

PIGLET WATCHED AS HIS SISTER WAS MANHANDLED INTO submission. He didn't like her much, but it bothered him to see the rough treatment. A bruise was forming on her reddened cheek where she'd hit the ground. Her face was full of anger, but she calmed down after Shem put her in a body lock position.

"I thought you said she wouldn't be here," Matthias said with cold menace.

"Um... I didn't expect her to be here. She's been spending a lot of time up in Red Wing, and I thought...," Piglet started.

"Obviously, you thought wrong." He pointed his chin to another camouflaged man. "Zip her up."

Piglet stayed quiet under Matthias's rebuke as Gretchen's arms were forced behind her and bound with plastic ties. Another man zipped her ankles so she had room to walk but not enough to run or kick. Shem half dragged her to a patio chair and forced her to sit. Piglet saw the fury in her accusing eyes and looked away. "She isn't a threat to us. She's deaf, don'tcha know."

"Of course I know. I've met her professionally several times. If I'm going to publish my grandfather's teachings, I need an editor. She was perfect as she's local. I wasn't aware of her impairment the first time I met her, but she managed to impress me with her skills."

He paused as he regarded the seated woman. "It's true she's defective, but she's smarter and feistier than any of our other women. Her bloodlines are good, and her age isn't so advanced that we can't get a few pregnancies from her. I understand deaf people can still produce hearing children." He turned his reptilian gaze toward her. "She will breed leaders."

Piglet felt nauseous. No way would Gretchen agree to become wife to a brother. The only way it would happen was if she were tied down and....

He coughed to cover up his need to vomit. If he upchucked in front of Matthias and the other men, he'd appear weak, making his status lower.

Some movement from the pier caught his eye. Five girls had emerged from the boat's hull and were strung together on one long rope. They appeared bedraggled, tired, and scared. As they approached, Piglet's gorge rose again. They were so young. Younger even than his so-called wife. Children themselves. A great sense of wrongness filled him, but there was nothing he could do about it. No way he could fight the brothers and help the girls escape the fate that awaited them. He glanced over at Gretchen and saw the horrified look on her face. She knew. She knew what was happening, and it sickened her too.

"All safe and sound." Piglet's blood froze, and he whirled around to see Rebel coming up behind the girls with a smarmy grin slapped across his mouth. "Well, well, well. Here's my old friend, Piglet. Nice to see you again, you fucking asshole."

Desktop followed the girls and sneered in his direction.

Matthias cut in. "All in the past, gentlemen. I have the rest of your money right here. Shem, you men take the girls into the house. Get them cleaned up, fed, and into their new clothes. Everyone here gets a wife, but no consummating unions until the marriage ritual tomorrow night. Understood?"

"You bet, brother."

A few of the girls were crying as they stumbled toward the house. One was so stoic, she seemed out of her head.

Matthias pulled a yellow envelope out of his pocket and handed it to Rebel. "Very good work, gentlemen. I'm hoping I can call on you again for future business?"

Rebel grinned, and Piglet cringed at his brown, rotting teeth. "You got money, I got time. Even if I have to work with fucking scum like him."

"That's not really necessary anymore," Matthias said calmly. He turned to face Piglet. "Congratulations. Naomi is finally pregnant. I can deal directly with Mr. Rebel for future shipments. Therefore, your services are no longer needed."

He pulled out a 9mm, and Piglet gasped as the barrel swung to point to his chest.

"Brother Matthias, I—"

Something hit him, fast and hard. Suddenly, he was on the ground, and blood poured from his chest. *I've been shot! Matthias shot me!* He heard Rebel laughing like crazy as he pointed at Piglet's unmoving body.

"Fucker thought he was special or something. He's not worth the shit I wipe from my ass."

That's when the pain came. He groaned and was trying to roll over when another bullet drilled into his belly.

"Let him bleed out slow. He doesn't deserve a fast death. He needs to lie there with his life dripping out his veins."

Those words came from Desktop. Piglet understood their contempt. He was going to die, and there was nothing he could do to stop it.

He heard a clamor through the white noise in his ears and weakly swiveled his head toward it. Gretchen was fighting two men, kicking and clawing at them with all her strength. Her eyes were on his as she struggled, trying to get to him. All these years they'd never gotten along. He couldn't say one way or another if he ever loved her. They shared half their blood and genetics, but that was it. Still, watching her go at the two men made him proud to call her sister. Matthias was right. She was feisty as hell.

He wished he could stop what was going to happen to her.

The two men finally pinned Gretchen between them. Matthias stepped up and rammed a hypodermic needle into her neck. Piglet watched her eyes roll back in her head and her body go limp.

"Put her in the van. She's going too."

Desktop frowned. "Not a good idea. That's Railroad's woman."

"Railroad?"

"The leader of the Dutchmen MC. Not a man to piss off."

Matthias dismissed the warning with a wave. "I don't know this Railroad, and he has no way of finding out where this woman will be. Our compound is impregnable, and very few know its exact location. We like it that way. Been under the radar for decades, and I don't expect some random biker to change that. He has no power."

Rebel spat on the ground. "Railroad is a stupid shit. Always a fucking bootlicker to Iceman. I'm getting the fuck outta here and finding me some good blow and tight pussy."

He turned to leave, and Desktop followed. Piglet saw one of the camouflaged men throw Gretchen's limp body over his shoulder. Soon, there was silence. He couldn't even hear the river's water anymore.

Dying alone sucks, he thought as his vision faded.

CHAPTER
THIRTY

IT WAS LATE AFTERNOON WHEN RAIL AND NUTTER finished the job. The new roof shingles gleamed in their regimented rows. Opal came out several times to bring them big glasses of ice water. She showed off Pearl to them, beaming as only a new mother could over her offspring.

Rebel is missing out, Rail thought over and over again. He pictured Gretchen holding a baby, cuddling and cooing over the blanket-covered bundle. His baby. His son or his daughter, he didn't care which. A fierce wanting came over him. Gretchen had not agreed to be his wife yet, and the suspense made him crazy. He craved for her to be his. Permanently. He wanted to see her tangle of bed hair across his pillow every morning. He wanted to watch the wrinkles form at the corners of her eyes as they grew older. He wanted to run his hands across her turgid belly as it grew with their children and kiss the stretch marks left behind. He wanted her to be by his side when his hair turned from black to gray and his knees creaked with age. He wanted a lifetime with her, and nothing less would ever satisfy him.

He had named her his woman, his old lady, to the club, but for the world he needed his ring on her finger, not just his patch on her back. If that meant leaving Red Wing, so be it.

He had to go see her. Now. He'd get on his knees and beg her if he had to. Or make love to her until she accepted him and all the love he had for her.

That was it. He hadn't told her he loved her. How fucking stupid could he be?

"I gotta go. See you at the clubhouse later."

Nutter put his tools back in the big rolling box. "You bet."

Mama J came out of the house and into the yard. Her face showed nothing when she walked up to them. Her attitude was cool and remote, but there was a dignity about her that Rail sensed. Even though her stature was short and broad, the air she gave off made her seem ten feet tall.

As she wiped her hand on her flour-covered

apron, she raised her eyes and inspected the new roof. "Thank you for this."

"No problem," Rail said.

Nutter stayed silent. These were the first words Mama J had said to him since the yard incident. "I'm baking for the Red Wing River Walk festival this coming weekend. Opal is coming with me. The baby is coming with us too, but I need a sitter for the rest of the kids."

Nutter spoke with no hesitation. "What time do you need me?"

"Six o'clock."

"I'll be here. Will pick up breakfast on the way."

Mama J's lips pressed together. She nodded sharply and crossed her arms as she strode back in the house.

"Doesn't sound like she's into freezing you out forever," Rail observed.

"I hope she has it in her to love me again. I've never stopped loving her."

There might be more to say, but Rail was in a hurry. "Talk later, brother."

The ride to Wabasha was short, but in Rail's mind it took forever. He pulled up in front of Gretchen's house and killed the engine. No lights shone in the windows, which was odd. She habitually left every light on in the house during the day and didn't turn them off until bedtime. A bad feeling crept into the back of Rail's thoughts. She wasn't home. Something was wrong.

He got off his bike and circled the house, drawing his gun. Twilight was on the horizon, and Gretchen liked to watch the river at that time of day. Maybe she was on the back deck, but the edginess continued in his brain. He slowly made his way around the corner, expecting to see her sitting back and sipping a glass of wine or tea as the day ended.

Instead, he saw blood. A lot of it. And a body.

For a moment he froze. His mind twisted and short-circuited in denial.

Then the body groaned, its voice pain filled, low, and male.

Rail rushed over and found the last person he expected to see. Piglet's white face looked up at him. Red covered his chest and abdomen that displayed two bullet wounds.

"Wail-wroh." Piglet was weak and getting weaker. The blood loss was too great, and the man lay dying.

Oddly, Rail felt nothing. No sympathy for the man who betrayed his club, but also no anger either. He had other feelings on his mind. Ones that, if he let loose with his emotions, he'd lose control of. As it was, he was just on the edge of sheer panic. He squatted down closer to the dying Piglet. "What happened here? Where's Gretchen?"

"They took her. Wasn't s'posed to do that. My wife. Pregnant. Lots of girls."

Rail's thoughts spun in all directions. Piglet's words were slurred and disjointed. Nothing he said made much sense, but a hard-core dread rose in Rail. Suppressed memories he'd been denying from long ago resurfaced, and his blood froze to ice in his veins. He knew what was coming. "Who?"

"Rebel brought 'em. Virgin wives for comfort. He made me do it."

Fuck no!

"He wants babies. New ones."

Rail's body shook as fear set in. "Who?"

"Feisty. Need strong leaders."

"Goddammit, *who*?"

The name echoed in Rail's head before Piglet said it.

"Matthias. Brother Matthias."

Rail reeled back as if struck. Denial, rage, disbelief, pain—a maelstrom of emotions buffeted him as he fought to understand it all. He felt like he and his body had separated, and he was floating somewhere above the scene. His eyes stopped seeing, and his ears stopped hearing. If he had a voice, it was gone too.

He couldn't control it. He crawled to the grass just as his stomach emptied itself. His arms trembled and threatened to collapse. Weakness invaded him, and he was powerless to stop it.

"Now, now, child. It's when we're at our lowest point that the strength comes. You can take the insults, the hardships, everything, 'cause you got a power in your corner that can't be stopped. All you gotta do is call on it, and it will come. Now get on your feet."

Rail squeezed his eyes tight and tensed every muscle in his body. His senses returned. He smelled the fresh grass, heard the *rizz-rizz* of the nighttime insects coming alive in the fading day, saw the dipping sun's light glinting on the river.

"Rail?" The faint call came from Piglet.

Reluctantly, Rail moved back to the man. "Tell me everything you know."

Piglet opened up, and a flood came pouring from his mouth. Rail kept his own mouth closed as the man told him about the farm, the boys, the hunting party, the mushrooms, the women, the breeding barracks, Matthias's future plans—including those he had for Gretchen. Rail's guts threatened to heave again more than once, but he maintained control. His mind whirled with the implications of what he had to do and what he had to face.

"Tell my sister I'm sorry. I'm sorry for Musicman.

The club. Naomi. I'm sorry for everything. Please forgive me. Please for…."

He went silent and limp as the last of his life bled out.

Rail allowed a few seconds of silence for the passing. Then his jaw tightened hard enough to bite through steel. He pulled out his phone. "Get as many weapons as you can find. I'll text you a location map for where to meet me."

"What's going on?" Duke asked, his voice gruff.

"War."

"Fuck. I'm on it."

He hung up, then dialed another number.

"What the hell do you want?" was the growly greeting from a man he never expected to speak to again.

"I need a favor. Listen to me."

CHAPTER
THIRTY-ONE

GRETCHEN WOKE WITH TWIN SPOTS THROBBING IN EITHER temple. She was on her back, and her hands were asleep. Not asleep. Tied. She was tied to a bed of some sort, each arm fastened to a thick bedpost. It was hot, and her clothes were sticking to her. She tried to lift herself, but that only made the plastic bands cut into her skin even more. She took a breath and jerked her arms as hard as she could. She'd seen YouTube videos of how to escape zip ties, but all she succeeded in doing was hurting herself. The worst part was she had to pee. Bad.

She shifted as best she could, taking in the room serving as her prison. The bed she lay on had a draping canopy like something you'd see in a historic colonial house. The few pieces of furniture she could twist around to see were of the same in age and antique look. Quaint was the word she would use. Dim light filtered through lacy white curtains, and she noticed there were striped shadows behind their pretty film. Bars. There were bars on the window.

Where the hell was she, and how the hell would she get out?

Her memory returned to her. Matt at her house. The camouflaged men, guns, the string of young girls, and...

Oh shit!

Tears gathered in her eyes for the brother she didn't really know and hadn't really liked.

Light flared across her face, and she closed her eyes at the sudden burst of pain. She blinked, squinted, and turned her head to see Matt in the doorway.

Her blood turned to ice at his predatory smile. He came to the bed and sat on it, bracketing her rib cage with his hands as he leaned over her. "I don't know sign language, but I know you can read lips well enough to understand me. This is your new life, and you will accept it just as you will accept me."

His gaze drifted down her chest. She wore only a thin T-shirt with no bra underneath and patterned leggings. Being tied spread-eagle left her vulnerable and scared, but she steeled herself. Communication was impossible, but she showed her defiance as best she could through her face. No way would she speak to this man. He didn't deserve her voice.

He laughed at her. "Yes, that's exactly what I expected. You're the strongest and smartest woman I've ever met. The children I will get from you will be exceptional."

Wait? What? Children? She'd caught a few words earlier at her house from the sporadic lip reading she'd managed with the other men. The gist was something about babies. Were those girls kidnapped for breeding stock? It made sense based on the shitty memoir she'd been working on. That was Matt's ultimate plan—producing his own private army of followers? That would take years.

And a lot of women.

She mentally growled and pulled at her bonds, even though she knew it was a useless gesture. She blazed at him, wishing her eyes had laser beams to fry him on the spot. He laughed again and lifted a hand to squeeze her breast. Hard.

"I can make it pleasurable or painful. That part is up to you, but make no mistake, Gretchen. It's going to happen."

If this was a romance book, this was the part where the love-of-her-life hero came bursting through the door, bloody from fighting his way through a horde of enemies to rescue her. Instead, the villain of the story gripped the front of her shirt and tore it down the middle. Gretchen gasped and thrashed in a futile effort to get away. This was really happening, and there was not a damned thing she could do about it.

"Stop fighting. You'll just make it worse on yourself."

She spat at him, determined to fight until she couldn't anymore. If he was set on raping her, she wasn't about to make it any easier. She struggled against the ties, and blood ran down her arms. He tried to pull off her leggings, and she kicked at him, catching him square in the face. He leapt back, clutching his nose. Her victory was short-lived, as his face twisted in anger, and he backhanded her across the face. The blow stunned her for a moment, and she tasted blood in her mouth.

He took something from a drawer and came toward her with a syringe in his hand. His smile was evil as he seized her hair and yanked her head back. "Have it your way. You don't have to be awake for me to fuck you."

She spat in his face again as he made to push the needle roughly into her neck.

Motherfucking asshole! she thought with white-hot rage. *This is the only way you'll get anything from me. I'll never give in, you crazy nutjob!*

The sting of the needle stopped before it penetrated her skin. Someone was at the door, but she couldn't see who it was. Evidently something was happening, because Matt put the cap back on the syringe and tossed it on the nightstand. He left the room.

Gretchen pulled again at the plastic ties, and one of them gave a little. Ignoring the pain, she tried again. And again.

CHAPTER
THIRTY-TWO

RAIL STOOD IN THE CLEARED AREA IN FRONT OF THE Main House, his heart racing and every nerve on edge. He thought he would have to fight his way in, but some of the guards recognized his name and opened the gates. Around him stood a dozen or so armed men. Many of them he knew once, a lifetime ago. He never dreamed he'd be back in this accursed place. No one outside of this compound knew his connection here, and he never expected to be back for it. The men around him were fingering their guns as if they wanted to shoot him and find the ending to the story that started thirty years ago.

He stared at the front door of the Main House, his memories bombarding him. The heavy portal opened, and a man appeared. Tall, strong, and very blond. The white shirt he wore had bloodstains on it, and the man's nose appeared to be broken.

They stared at each other, neither one moving. Finally, the man on the wide porch grinned evilly. "Welcome home, Gideon."

Rail gritted his teeth. "Hello, little brother."

The past rushed up to greet him, and he almost staggered at the onslaught of memory.

Gideon's teeth chattered as he hugged his thin body for whatever warmth he could find. Winter snow had fallen thick all day and coated the ground and trees in a crunchy white layer. Despite his status, he had a job in the commune. He was to keep the firewood stocked in all the buildings, and from early that morning, he'd been trudging through the snow, carrying the heavy split logs to the various houses and stacking them near the doors for easy access. Most of the dwellings were roughly built cabins, and some were no better than shacks. Only one building was an actual house, and it belonged to the High Brothers of their community. They took the most wood.

High Brother Zachariah was his father. They shared the same blue eye color and facial features. Strong high cheek-bones, nose with a little bump at the top, and full lips. The biggest difference was the hair color. Zachariah had the color of fresh wheat on his head, whereas Gideon's hair was almost black. His younger brother, Matthias, had hair the color of new wheat. The wheat boys got to work the land with the brothers, driving the giant farm equipment and learning the ways of the Pure Men.

Gideon never knew his mother. Sometime in his childhood, he found out Zachariah beat his wife to death when he saw Gideon's dark hair. There was no question of Gideon's parentage, as all wives were kept in strict isolation. It was simply her fault that she produced a chaff child from Zachariah's seed. He took another wife immediately, and within a year, she gave birth to a boy, Matthias. Fortunately for this second wife, her son had the gold hair and blue eyes expected of a wheat child. Matthias was coddled in the lap of luxury with plenty of food, warm clothes, and a room of his own. Gideon remained an anomaly.

He was the firstborn son of the High Brother, which gave him some status. He couldn't be made to work the fields like the other chaff boys, but he was also forbidden in the Main House. The only place he could go was into the care of a comfort woman, and his purpose was to serve as Zachariah directed.

Rain or shine, at any time of the day or night, a brother could appear at the one-room cabin Gideon shared with Miriam and her daughter, Rebecca. Whenever a brother showed up, they had to go outside and wait until Miriam finished giving comfort. Rebecca was one of only four surviving children born to Miriam. Gideon thought

Rebecca might be his sister, as she looked a lot like Zachariah. She was a wheat child and had the same eyes as Matthias and he did.

Gideon watched as dusk settled and the temperature dropped. He had no coat, and his shoes were wet from hauling wood all day. He was supposed to stay at the cabin with Miriam, but he was restless. A few weeks ago, Rebecca had bled for the first time. Gideon didn't know what it meant, but Miriam tried to hide it. Somehow, one of the brothers who came to Miriam's shack figured it out. They'd come for Rebecca that morning and taken her away. Miriam cried as they pulled Rebecca from her arms and all but dragged her down the dirt pathway. Gideon only saw the terror in his sister's eyes.

He asked the men to let him come with them. "No one at the house can talk to her like I can. She can't hear well and needs me to help her."

Years of untreated childhood ear infections had left Rebecca with severe hearing loss. She and Gideon made up their own sign language to communicate. Not even her mother could speak to her like Gideon could.

Tears poured down Rebecca's face, and she pulled at the hands holding her and tripped. One man jerked her up roughly.

Gideon tried again. "High Brother Zachariah is my father. I need to see —"

A giant hand lashed out and cracked across Gideon's cheek. His head whipped painfully to the side, and he fell to his knees. Blood filled his mouth as his stinging lip split and swelled. He looked up through pained tears at the man who struck him. He glared, his lip curling up as if he'd just stepped in a horse pile. "I don't give a shit who you are. You're chaff and always will be."

He turned away from the boy and seized Rebecca's arm. The last he saw of her was her crying face as she was forced to walk away.

Gideon stood shivering as he looked at the farmhouse. He should be at home with Miriam, but he had to see if Rebecca was all right. He couldn't erase the look of sheer panic on her face that still burned in his brain. Surely by now the High Brother would see the need for him to be there with Rebecca, acting as interpreter to her voiceless state.

The lights shone from the many windows of the huge house. They were the only ones to have full electricity and running water. Once again, Gideon wished he'd been born a wheat boy instead of chaff. He approached the steps to the long wraparound porch and carefully placed a foot on the first one. It made a light creak, and he froze in place. If he were caught, he would be punished, as no chaff was allowed here. No one appeared. He took another cautious step. Then another. Finally, he stood on the wooden slats of the porch. Eight more steps brought him to the door, and he took each one, shaking from both the cold and fear.

The door gleamed white in the moonlight reflected from the snow. Gideon's mouth dried out, and he bit his tongue to bring some moisture back to it. Should he knock? Would the brother who answered take the time to hear him, or would he be thrown off the porch? Even worse, he could be shunned. Shunned boys never came back.

In the silence of the night, the sound of singing came to him. A chorus of male voices rose in a hymn of praise. He should run. He should run now before they found out he was even there. Something made him turn the knob. He felt the pin release, and the door was freed to be opened. He pushed it slowly, revealing the interior of the house.

Creamy white walls with painted pictures of past High Brothers greeted his eyes. The wood floors shone with wax and were covered with long patterned rugs. Ornate tables were decorated with vases and crosses. Luxuries he'd only heard about but never seen.

The singing echoed down a long hall next to a set of stairs leading to the upper floors. Gideon swallowed, trying not to choke on the dry lump in his throat. If anyone came down those steps or the hallway, his life would be forfeit. The voices rose in jubilation. His mind told him to flee, but he was drawn to the noise. He had to see it.

He crept down the hallway, clinging as tightly as he

could to the wall. An open door appeared, and he could see the backs of a bunch of High Brothers who were singing loudly. Their volume covered up any small noises he made. He didn't dare enter the room, and he didn't dare turn around to run. They would surely hear him then.

He stood as still as a fence post, unmoving, not breathing, waiting in anticipation. Of what, he didn't know and couldn't see. Then a brother moved, and at last he was able to view the room.

A shock wave of emotions rushed over him at what he saw.

His naked sister lay flat on her back, held in place by several High Brothers while Zachariah....

A loud keening burst over the top of the singing brothers, and they stopped their praising. Gideon hadn't realized the anguished cry came from his own mouth. He pushed at the robed bodies, clawing his way toward Rebecca, knowing he wouldn't make it to her but having to try.

Her face turned to him, and he saw her eyes were dull and lifeless. She didn't seem to recognize him. His sister might be alive and breathing, but in all that really mattered, she was gone.

"Sacrilege!" he heard before a slashing pain knocked him down. Zachariah had taken an ornate staff and struck him across his face, opening two deep parallel gashes down his cheek to his jaw. A quarter inch higher and he would have lost an eye.

He had one brief moment when he was free. His eyes found Zachariah's. Next to him was his younger brother, Matthias, staring down at him with a look of contempt on his childish face. The man had stopped taking comfort from Rebecca and looked on his firstborn. Rage so white-hot it burned him black filled Gideon. His ears roared with the overflow, and he screamed at the man in order to release the toxic anger.

Matthias pointed at him and shouted his own condemnation. "Demon!"

The word brought Gideon back to himself and his situation. Hands grabbed for him, but he eluded their frantic grasping and ran. His hands smeared his blood on the walls as he darted blindly to the open door. He stumbled down the steps and tripped, landing hard on his arm. More pain radiated through his body. The brothers were right behind him, but they were hampered by their white robes. That gave him the opportunity to pick himself up and take off into the night.

That was the night some unknown force saved him. That was the night he ran into Flora. That was the last night he was called Gideon.

He shared blood of some sort with most of the men around him. Brothers, half brothers, cousins—they were all tied together in some fashion. He thought the isolated farm would have died out by now, but apparently it had grown into something much bigger. Something evil and more twisted than he imagined it could be. He wondered where his father was, or if he still lived.

"Is Zachariah still around?"

Matthias took two steps forward and leaned on the column next to the porch stairs. He folded his arms and looked down on Rail. "Yes, our father still lives. He had a stroke a few years ago that left him speechless and bound to a wheelchair. I'm the leader of this family now."

"Where's Gretchen?"

Matthias barked a short laugh. "You always did want what you can't have. Nice wide hips, large breasts, smart, and a fighter." He laughed again at some private joke and placed a finger against his nose. "A perfect vessel. She's older than I'd like, and her deafness was a consideration as well, but she is stronger than any woman here. She'll make fine sons."

Rail wanted to be sick. Rage flashed through him, and he wanted to flatten Matthias to the ground. "If you've hurt her, I'll—"

"You'll what?" Matthias sneered. "You've no power here. You're nothing, and you always have been. You should have died years ago."

"I lived despite this place. I'm of the high bloodline, and I demand my right."

Matthias shook his head in disbelief and laughed in amusement. "You demand nothing."

"According to the old writings, any man of the blood can demand his right to challenge." He turned in a circle and met the eyes of the men around him who had their guns loosely pointed in his direction. "No one here can deny my bloodline. Curse me all you want, but I am the firstborn of High Brother Zachariah." He faced Matthias again. "You must accept my challenge."

Matthias stopped laughing. "Have you ever wondered, dear brother, what happened to Rebecca, our dear sister?"

A cold sweat broke out on Rail's forehead. "Tell me."

Matthias shrugged and came down the steps. "She died a few years ago. She never had children by our father. All of them miscarried. Zachariah put her aside and wifed her to me when I came of age. Rebecca still had trouble conceiving, but she did manage to produce one child. A daughter. Naomi."

It took everything he had not to bend over. He felt sucker punched in his gut. The implication made him want to vomit, and his urge to beat something or someone ratcheted up another notch. "You sick bastard."

Matthias gestured to the other men. "We're all

bastards here, but ones with a higher purpose. We have a great vision to fulfill, and this is only the beginning."

A fanatical light gleamed in Matthias's eyes. "I have plans, dear brother. There will be more camps like this one. Careful tracing of family lines to ensure we have enough diversity, but also keeping our progeny pure. My future sons will learn this and go out into the world to lead and become new Highest Brothers in their own camps. Your attempt at a challenge is worthless, chaff boy."

"You think I'm chaff. Not worthy of life," Rail said, letting disdain tinge his words. "Don't forget, little brother, this chaff boy escaped a place that was supposed to be inescapable. I got out, despite all the men searching the grounds and chasing me through the woods. I found a life and thrived in it for decades, and you never found me. I never broke. You can't break me now."

For the first time, uncertainty crossed Matthias's face. "I can have you shot where you stand and bury you in the fields where you should have been all those years ago."

"You could, but that doesn't change anything. I'm not broken, and you wouldn't win."

Matthias moved to stand directly in front of Rail.

They looked at each other with matching blue eyes, but one pair dark and one light.

"I want you on your knees, begging me to end your pathetic life," the blond growled with jagged menace. "Challenge accepted."

Rail lifted a corner of his mouth.

CHAPTER
THIRTY-THREE

THE FIGHT BEGAN SLOWLY. BOTH COMBATANTS STRIPPED to their skins with only their pants in place. No weapons, not even shoes. The rules were to fight until one of them was down, preferably dead. Rail removed his earrings and braided his hair, putting it in a tight bun to keep it from being used against him. They circled each other, waiting for the other to make a move.

"Gretchen has the sweetest breasts, eh, brother? I'll be sure to think of you while I'm playing with them later tonight."

Rail refused the bait. He borrowed his friend Iceman's attitude and let Matthias spew his taunts.

"I bet her pussy is tight. It won't be for long. I intend to seed her as often as I can. Of course, she'll have to be tied down. She doesn't have to like my touch, but she'll have to take it."

Rail seethed on the inside but kept his silent coolness.

"What's the matter, older brother? Cat got your tongue? That won't be a problem after I rip it from your head."

Finally, Rail's patience was rewarded. Matthias lunged, and Rail sidestepped and tagged him on the side of the head. Matthias shook it off and threw a punch, easily blocked by Rail. They traded blows for a while, feinting and moving around each other, but neither making progress.

Rail recognized Matthias's training. Every man in this commune had to learn some degree of hand-to-hand combat, and Rail remembered seeing them train in long rows. Kick-punch-punch over and over again in multiple patterns. Matthias moved in with a thrusting front kick, and Rail anticipated the next two moves accurately. He blocked and shifted on his feet, bringing a chopping hand to the other man's windpipe. Matthias choked but didn't go down. He brought his arm up and landed a backfist to the side of Rail's head. Rail saw it too late and only partially blocked the heavy strike. They separated by a few feet, both of their heads ringing. Rail felt a hot trickle from his throbbing temple. He risked a quick glance at the ring on the man's hand. First blood went to Matthias.

The fight continued on more as a competition in endurance. Each time a blow landed on Rail, there were cheers from the onlookers, just as there were taunts and insults when Rail got in a kick or punch. Matthias's formal training and Rail's biker street skills had them evenly matched, neither one having an advantage over the other.

Then it got dirty.

Someone whistled and tossed Matthias a T-baton. The wood weapon was about a foot and a half long and had a perpendicular handle. It was designed to rest along the forearm with a point jutting out in front to do the damage rather than the wielder's hand. The hard wood protected the arm during blocks, and when spun by the handle, it extended the fighter's reach by a foot or more.

Rail eyed the simple weapon, and icy fingers trickled down his spine. This was a game-changer. He had no weapon, and the chances of him getting one were zero. This crowd wanted to see his mongrel blood spilling on the ground, his body broken, and his life draining away.

He would end up as all those other chaff boys had through the years—buried in the fields with only bones coming up with the seasons' plowing.

He shook his head to clear it of the doomed thinking. He had to win this fight. Gretchen needed him to win—otherwise, her fate would be worse than his death.

The weapon swung in a fast arc toward him, and he instinctually put up an arm to block it instead of stepping back and letting it sweep by. The impact made a sharp crack, and his arm exploded with pain. Fuck, if it wasn't broken, it was at least cracked.

Out of the corner of his eye, he spotted a figure on the porch. He was sitting in a wheelchair with another man standing behind him. Zachariah had joined the crowd. His father. The man who condemned his mother because of his black hair. The man who abandoned him as a child. The man who gave him the lifetime scars, both on his face and in his heart.

He had come to watch his sons fight. Rail didn't have to guess which one of them he expected to win. Matthias had been the golden child of wheat all his life. Rail was chaff and always would be. Unworthy of love. Unworthy of life.

The baton swung again, and Rail moved back to avoid it, cradling his injured arm against his middle. If he could knock the weapon away from Matthias, perhaps he had a chance. It arced toward him on the backswing, and Rail struck down hard on its surface.

He avoided another impact on his body, but he didn't get it away from his opponent.

It was only a matter of time before he went down. He moved only defensively now, trying to keep out of the baton's range. Matthias was an expert with the wooden extension, and his face showed a perverse pleasure in the turn of the fight. He could end it anytime he wanted, but he was obviously enjoying himself. Again and again, he feinted and made Rail duck and move. The jeering crowd got louder with raucous laughter.

Rail miscalculated a move, and the baton hit him square on the ribs. He cried out as he heard several of them give way. Breathing became hard and exquisitely painful. He stumbled as he fought to keep his feet. Matthias grinned and faced away from him, raising his arms in victory. Then he whipped around and brought the weapon down with full power. Rail dove to get out of the way but couldn't move fast enough. The powerful blow caught him across his back, and he went down into the dirt. His sides screamed with pain, and he couldn't get his legs to function. He crawled in desperation. Another blow landed on his body, and he curled into himself. He barely saw the foot aimed at his midsection before it hit his stomach. What breath he had left disappeared.

He was going to die. Beaten to death in the

place he escaped from so many years ago. Perhaps this was payment for the life he led. He rolled onto his back and stared up at the sky. Night had fallen, and he could see the stars glittering in the black sky.

Gretchen, I'm sorry.

Matthias appeared in his line of vision with the weapon positioned on his arm so the sharp pointed end was aimed at Rail's vulnerable chest. This would be the killing strike.

He looked up into the universe. *Please forgive me.*

Time seemed to stop. Someone spoke to him, but it came from inside himself. It had the warmth of his Grams, but it wasn't her. It was more. Bigger. An immensity he couldn't quite comprehend.

"Oh, my precious child, you already have your answer. You've been forgiven. You just have to accept it. All the power and strength you need is there. Just ask for it."

Rail tasted blood on his lips as he lay in the dirt, waiting to die. He closed his eyes and sent out a final plea. *Help me.*

It filled him. Only one other time in his life had he felt this way. The night he ran, something had been with him. Some unseen force or guardian angel had protected him and given him the strength to escape this hellish place. There was a purpose for him. A task he had yet to complete.

I'm ready, he told the sky as an invisible potency touched him.

"Good. Now stand up and do what you need to do."

His pain disappeared, and a divine fire ignited in his veins. Air filled his lungs to bursting, and he rolled, knocking Matthias off his feet. Rail stood up, strong and tall. Whatever gave him this power must have shown, as the crowd of men fell silent, not even whispering.

Matthias scrambled up and backed away with confusion on his face. Rail was supposed to be bleeding out in the dirt, not standing his ground. His expression showed disbelief for several long moments, and then it warped into a mask of sheer hatred.

"Die, you bastard!" He swung the wood weapon again, intending to drive Rail down.

Rail moved fluidly, avoiding the heavy blow, then grabbed the weapon as it passed him, pulling it easily from Matthias, and inertia did the rest. The blond man landed hard against the protruding steps that led to the Main House porch. Audible snaps were heard, and Matthias screamed in sudden pain. The abnormal twist of his leg beneath him showed the limb to be broken, and his shoulder was obviously dislocated.

Rail looked up at the still figure on the porch

who sat in silent observance. He couldn't see the old man's expression or gauge his thoughts. Rail's body was numb and his mind emotionless. He stood over his brother as the man writhed in pain, crying out and cursing. The T-baton sat heavy in his hand. One strike would be all it would take. Only one.

Rail looked at the glittering blue eyes of his father as he heard Flora's voice.

"Forgiveness isn't for someone else, child. It's for you. It's that feeling inside that releases you from your past and frees you to live life fully. You don't have to pay for it. It's always been yours."

He dropped the wooden weapon in the dirt. The quiet roared in his ears as he waited.

A flurry of white darted down the stairs.

Gretchen!

She slammed into him, her hands clutching at him. He heard her muted sobs at the same time he heard the click of multiple weapons being aimed at him.

A sharp command came from the porch. "No." Zachariah's voice sounded deep and powerful in contrast to his frail body. "Let them go."

A collective gasp went through the crowd. Rail remembered his brother saying Zachariah hadn't spoken since his stroke years ago. For him to speak now was a miracle that waylaid anyone from retaliation.

Whether it was him honoring the rules of combat or a tiny bit of fatherly concern, Rail didn't care either way.

Gretchen had a ritual robe tied around her and bruises on her cheeks, but she was alive. He signed quickly to her. "Hang on a bit longer. Let's go."

The crowd parted reluctantly as Rail made his way through them, Gretchen's hand deep in his. He mounted his bike and tipped it so she could settle behind him. He had some concern about her bare skin and the hot pipes near her legs, but they weren't going far. His strength started to fade as he pulled away, and he prayed he would make it out. The security gates were open, and he drove through them with Gretchen holding him from behind. Her body trembled against him with unused adrenaline, and he figured they were both in for a crash.

He saw the flashing lights lining the road where he'd found himself nearly thirty years ago. His knees weakened. Pain bloomed in his broken body, and he could barely keep the bike moving. Several squad cars surrounded them before heading past in the direction they'd come from. An open ambulance and several paramedics were at the scene.

The bike wobbled and almost went down. Duke

caught the handlebar and held it for Gretchen to climb off. "We got all of them we could. There were a few who ran and hid, but most of them are out." He shook his head and cursed. "I can't believe shit like this happened right fucking here under our noses."

While Rail had been fighting to free Gretchen, Duke, Nutter, Camo, and the rest of the Dutchmen had snuck onto the property and freed the women from the breeding barracks and comfort shacks. They also found the children kept in the separate workers' quarters. Boys kept for working the fields until they died and were buried in them. Rail's call to his one contact in law enforcement brought in the authorities needed to make arrests, forcing the long-hidden activities of the farm into the light. There was still so much to do, but Rail was done. The injuries he received during the fight were coming back, and he was having trouble breathing again.

Duke frowned. "You look like you're about to keel over."

Rail's vision clouded. "I am."

He vaguely saw the asphalt as it rushed up to greet him.

CHAPTER
THIRTY-FOUR

RAIL SLOWLY BECAME AWARE OF HIS SURROUNDINGS. All he saw was whiteness, and for a moment he thought he'd died. The beeping noise was annoying, and he quickly figured out that he was in a hospital. Machines came into focus, and he spotted the tubes that hung from fluid bags and attached to the veins in one of his arms. The other one was in a cast. It hurt to move his head much, but he shifted as far as he could. Gretchen was sleeping next to him. She'd pulled a chair close so she leaned her head down on the bed next to his thigh. Her face was turned toward him, and he could see the big purple-and-yellow bruise coloring her cheek. There were dark circles under her closed eyes, and she wore dull green hospital scrubs.

He raised his hand, mildly surprised by his weakness. He touched the tangle of blonde hair on her head, and she woke immediately. Her other cheek was imprinted with mesh marks from the blanket. Rail coughed out a laugh and immediately regretted it.

She sat up, concern reflected in her eyes along with tears. She placed her hand on the muscle of his upper thigh, as it was the only spot free of wires and tubes, and she squeezed it. She picked up the button to call the nurse, but he stopped her.

"Not yet. I just want to look at you for a minute," he mouthed at her. His hands were too immobile to sign. "I love you. I love you so damn much. I was afraid I wouldn't have time to tell you that."

Tears rolled freely down her cheeks. "I love you too. Don't you dare leave me."

"Never. Does this mean you'll marry me?"

"Yes. Now stop talking and let me call the nurse."

He chuckled. "Giving me orders already, eh? You're perfect."

She pressed the button. "I'm glad you think so."

He grasped her fingers as best as he could. "Are you okay? Did he hurt you?"

She shook her head. "No, I'm fine. He never got the chance."

The nurse came in followed by a young female doctor. "Nice to see you awake. I'm assuming you'd like a rundown of your injuries and a prognosis of when you'll get out."

Rail grunted. "That'd be a big yes."

The doctor raised a perfectly plucked eyebrow at him as the nurse wrapped a blood pressure cuff around his arm. "From what was described to me, you're very lucky to be here. Both your arm bones are broken, so how in the world you drove a bike for the length of time you did is a miracle. You have three cracked ribs, one of them bad enough you should have punctured a lung. Somehow, you didn't. One kidney is badly bruised but still functioning." She pointed a pen to the bag hanging by the bed. "I expected this to be full of blood, but it's not." He hadn't realized he had a catheter in his dick, and the thought of someone holding his junk to push a tube inside him made him cringe.

The doctor ignored his wince and kept talking. "By the rest of the black marks on your back and your midsection, you're supposed to have severe internal damage. That didn't happen either. No severe swelling of the brain, only a mild concussion, some lacerations, but nothing life-threatening."

"Gee, Doc. Are you telling me to try harder next time?"

"I hope there is no next time. As I said, you were lucky. You've got an angel watching out for you or something. I'd not take any more risks. We'll keep you here a few more days for observation. Any questions?"

"When do I get the tube outta my dick?"

Gretchen rolled her eyes.

The doctor didn't blink. "When I say so."

Rail examined the woman's face. She was pretty, with dark brown eyes and heavy brunette hair pulled back into a tight braid. Her expression was as no-nonsense as you could get.

"Anything else?"

"Nope."

"Good. I'll check on you during my next rounds." She swiveled on her heel to leave. At the door, she turned. "You did a good thing, Mr. Railroad."

After she exited, Rail shifted his focus to Gretchen. "Please tell me what happened."

She wiped her red eyes and sat on the bed near his hip so he could see her clearly.

"After we got to the place on the road where Duke was waiting, you fainted. That was two days ago. The police rode into the farm and started making arrests. Those camo men broke ranks before any fighting started. It's one thing to play training in the woods. It's another to face the real deal. Some tried to run, but they were easily caught. Your... I mean, Matthias was taken to a different hospital and treated. He's supposed to make a full recovery, but he's also under arrest for a full ticket book of crimes. It's been all over the news about the discovery of a bunch of kidnapped girls and how they were kept for sex and forced breeding. Add trafficking to that, and he'll be away for life. That's not even counting the charges over the children. Statutory rape, abuse, neglect, and a host of other charges have been made."

Rail noticed tears in her eyes, and he assumed they were more for the victims as she spoke of them. She held his hand as she spoke, and he couldn't help but feel pleased at the comfortable way she gave him the gift of her smoky voice.

"No one can find any records for some of them. The ones they called 'chaff boys' were born on the farm, raised, and died there without anyone on the outside knowing of their existence. So far, the police have found parts for over a hundred skeletons in the field and are uncovering more. The kids who've been rescued have no birth certificates or identification, and there's such a mix of DNA going on, it will take months to figure out who belongs to who."

She paused with a frown. "I'm not sure how much that matters. The custody of those children will not be given to anyone at that farm. They're looking for more foster families for them. This whole situation is one big stinking mess."

"Duke? Camo? Nutter?"

She gave him a wry look. "Hiding. The Dutchmen are famous now. Reporters have camped out at the marina, grabbing whoever they can for an interview."

Rail groaned and closed his eyes. There were plenty of people who hated the club. He wondered what they thought now. "Fucking hell."

Gretchen squinted. "I didn't catch that. Say again?"

"Never mind." Fatigue suddenly washed over him. "I may fall asleep. Will you be here when I wake up?"

She smiled. "You have a bad memory. I said I'm not leaving." Her face grew thoughtful. "Although, I might go use the shower while you sleep. I feel grungy as hell."

He grinned. "I think you ordered me not to leave you. That's not going to happen either. You look a little grungy, so be my guest with the shower."

She stuck her tongue out at him. He laughed and screwed his face up at the pain in his side.

"Stop that before you do some real damage."

He sucked in as much air as he could and let it out slowly. His ribs throbbed, but he felt better. He closed his eyes with the intention of taking a brief nap, but it was several hours before he woke again. When he did, a clean and fully clothed Gretchen was the first person he saw, along with Duke and Penny.

"Fucking reporters all over the damn place. Had to sneak in the back loading dock. Fucking cops outside weren't going to let us in here until Gretchen told them it was okay. Penny brought her some clothes and shit. Nothing for you, though. You'll have to leave with your ass hanging out of a hospital gown."

"No he won't, jackass. I brought clothes for him too." Penny gave him a withering look. "Toothbrushes, combs, and deodorant."

"Thanks, Penny. Why are there cops outside? Are they here to arrest me?"

Duke huffed a huge laugh. "Fuck, no. They're here to protect your dumb ass. Some of the shit on the news has got nutjobs coming out in droves. Quoting miracles and signs and all sorts of crap. A couple of the assholes from the farm said they were set to fill your hide with bullets like from that scene in the old *Godfather* movie. Then that guy Zachariah told them to let you go. Scared the shit out of them."

"Why?"

"'Cause that man had a stroke and has been nonverbal ever since. Those were the only words he's said in fucking years. Now he's back to being a mute." Duke shuddered and blew out a breath. "I believe in Jesus and God and all that, but this is real woo-woo shit. Gives me the willies."

Penny sputtered. "Did the big bad biker just say, 'Gives me the willies'?"

He scoffed and threw a heavy arm around Penny's shoulders. "You play your cards right, I'll give you my willy later."

Rail traded glances with Gretchen. She rolled her eyes and nodded at his silent question.

The nurse popped her head in. "I see we have a party going on, but I have to ask you to leave. Visiting hours are almost over."

Duke made a sound of affirmation. "Don't worry about the club or the marina or anything else right now. We got it all handled. Mama J is good. So is Peebles—s'cuse me, Opal—and the baby. Got some bad news, though. Dockhand up in Hastings found Rebel this morning. Overdose. Fucker died with his nose in a pile of meth. Camo's up dealing with the body. Desktop's gone. No cash in Rebel's pockets, so we think he took whatever was there and left the state. Good riddance to that motherfucker. Nothing else needs your attention right now, but I'm not running this shit forever, so get your ass healed and back to work."

Penny blew a raspberry at him. "You're such a jerk sometimes."

Duke grinned. "I love it when you talk dirty to me, baby."

Rail choked a bit before catching Gretchen's attention. "You go with them to the clubhouse. You'll be safe there. Stay in my room and get a real night's sleep."

"I don't want to leave you."

"I'll be fine. You'll be able to help me better later if you're rested."

She frowned but saw his logic. She leaned into him, and his eyes focused on her mouth. She formed the words "I love you" before kissing him.

A sense of rightness enveloped him at her touch. This was it. This was where he belonged.

"You're gonna give me a hard-on even with this fucking tube in my dick."

She half smiled at his words. "Can you repeat that? I didn't quite understand."

"I'm marrying a fucking smartass. Go before I decide to yank this thing out myself."

The room grew quiet after they left. Rail's energy level was low, as was expected. The nurse came in one last time, checked the IV drip, and took his vitals.

"Not gonna lie. If the news reports are correct, you ought to be in a coma. I'm glad you survived.

There are a lot of happy families out there glad to have their girls back all because of you."

Rail was drifting in semiconsciousness. "I had help."

She hummed a noise and left, dimming the lights as she did.

Rail closed his eyes. Gretchen was safe. She would be his wife. As far as where they lived, it would be worked out. She would have his children, and they would grow up with two parents who loved them.

"Thank you, Grams," he murmured as a healing sleep overtook him.

A breath of invisible warmth brushed the loose hair from his forehead.

"Love you, my precious child."

EPILOGUE

SOME MONTHS LATER...

Rail stood and stretched from his crouched position and felt several muscles pull hard before they relaxed. *Fuck, I'm getting old.* The recovery from his injuries had been slower than he wanted, and he still had some trouble with his back.

This boat engine had taken nearly all day, and he was ready to finish it and go home.

He smiled. Home. A real place for him now. Gretchen's complex in Connecticut had emailed her about a hike in rent, which turned into one of the nails in the coffin motivating her to move back. Not that she was considering it, anyway. The fat rock on her left hand had already decided her future living space. The ring he put next to it sealed the deal forever. Duke and Penny had attended the low-key ceremony held in the Hidden Acres chapel. They kept Iceman's old cabin up at Red Wing but, for all intents and purposes, moved their permanent residence to the house on the river in Wabasha.

The weather had turned colder as fall colors started their annual decorations. Already, many of the seasonal boaters had prepped and stored their crafts for the winter months. The Harbor Bar stayed crowded, especially on weekends with the addition of live bands. The Dutchmen's brief flare of fame had died down, but people still came to see the MC that discovered and brought down a cult.

The authorities were still in the thick of investigations, but they did discover that Rail was the only blood relation eligible for inheriting the massive farmland operation. Zachariah Ekstrom passed shortly after the raid, and his will left everything to his firstborn son, Gideon. How and why the name Gideon appeared on the document instead of Matthias remained a mystery. Rail didn't want anything to do with the farm and its legacy of horrors, but Gretchen convinced him to do something different. He signed it over to a nonprofit organization dedicated to taking care of abused women and children. The place of nightmares had been turned into a place of healing and was now called the Flora Jones Home of Grace.

Piglet had been quietly cremated and his ashes scattered in the river. Rail hoped the man had found his forgiveness and peace. Gretchen mourned the brother she hadn't really known. They'd never had a true brother and sister relationship, but when she was in danger, he did step up. That meant something to her, and she grieved the lost chance of getting to know him.

The girl, Naomi, miscarried only a few weeks into her pregnancy and now resided at the Flora Jones Home. The counselors were doubtful she'd ever recover enough from the trauma of her time at the compound to leave. Nathaniel also stayed to serve as a groundskeeper at the only home he'd ever known. As far as Rail was concerned, they both had lifetime rights to live there.

Nutter and Mama J were back on speaking terms, but as far as Rail knew, they would not get back together. Gretchen put it best when she said happy endings were only guaranteed in books. She and Rail had decided they would not take sides and would remain friends with both of them. Even if they didn't have a future together as a couple, they had their children and hopefully would work together as parents to raise them.

His phone beeped in his back pocket, and he slipped it out to see a text from Gretchen that raised his eyebrows.

Gretchen: "I want to lick the sweat from your ball sack." Author wants this as a tagline on her book cover. I don't see this as a turn-on. In fact, I'm kinda grossed out.

He chuckled as he texted back.

Rail: I think you have enough editing gigs to keep you busy. That guest lecture thing up in the Cities still happening?

Gretchen: Yes. Starts next month. I'm not cooking tonight. Bring home some brisket sandwiches? Been craving one all day.

Rail: Sure. See you in a bit.

The days were getting shorter, and darkness was starting to fall when he pulled into Slippery's on his bike. He entered the take-out area and ran into a familiar-looking girl running the cash register. Her makeup-free face showed surprise and slight trepidation when she saw him.

"Um... hi, Railroad. I guess you're picking up an order?"

The tips of her sandy hair showed the remnants of a pink dye job, and her name tag read Kim. Recognition hit Railroad. This was the girl from the club who he kicked out of his bed one night months ago. He hadn't seen her in the club since.

"Hi, Kimmie. It's been a long time. You good?"

She bit her lip as she grinned shyly at him. "Yes, I am. I need to thank you for kicking my ass, so to speak. You told me to go find a better life. I'm doing that. I started a program at the Vo Tech for cosmetology. I'm going to do makeup, hair, and maybe nails. I saw Peebles… oops… Opal there too. She's sad about Rebel, but she's doing okay."

Rail gave her a big smile. "That's great. I hope you and Opal are successful."

She shrugged. "I heard you have an old lady now."

He could hear the wistful note in her voice. She sounded like she still had that crush on him but had accepted that it would never be anything else. Rail thought if it motivated her to do well in school, a little heartache might be worth it. "Yeah, I do. Her name is Gretchen, and she's my world."

Her expression dropped a little. "I'm glad you found someone to love. I hope I have that someday."

"Give it time, sweetheart. You're young, and you have a lot of years left. Don't be in a rush. I'm sure there's a man out there for you somewhere who will love and cherish you for a lifetime. Don't settle for second best. Hear me?"

The corners of her mouth turned up. "I hear you. Thanks for that, Rail."

"You bet."

The house was lit up against the dark sky as Rail pulled into the driveway. *Home.* He would never get tired of the word. He set the food bag on the counter and went upstairs.

Gretchen wore her usual nighttime outfit of tank top and panties, and Rail wondered if she would continue this trend all winter. He didn't mind at all. She sat at her desk, glaring at the computer screen, and he flicked the lights to get her attention.

"Still thinking about sweaty ball sacks?" he joked as she turned her head.

She rolled her eyes, and he laughed at her.

"This author wants to write erotica, but it's way over the top. She's got a scene of seven on one. I had to draw it out with stick figures to see if it was possible. I'm sure someone out there likes this kind of thing, but to me, it reads like a hot mess. Hard to envision and even harder to pull off."

He shook his head. "Seven on one? Where do they put everything?"

"You really want to know?"

"Pass. I prefer one-on-one. As in me on you."

He leaned over and took her mouth in a welcoming kiss. Her mouth opened under his, and her tongue came forward to tease his lips. He groaned and let his hand slip the tank strap down her shoulder, baring one breast.

"Me too," she muttered against his mouth as he plucked at her nipple.

It amazed him how much she spoke out loud to him. Penny told him she didn't like using her voice. With him, she did. A lot.

He pulled her to the bed and replaced his fingers with his mouth, hearing her moan at his suckling. In no time at all, she writhed under him and pulled at his shirt with impatience. "Off. Now."

He stripped quickly and tossed his clothes to the floor. She also finished getting naked and spread her thighs wide as he dropped his head between them. Her moan was louder this time as his lips surrounded her swollen clit.

Fuck, he would never get tired of hearing it, tasting her musky flavor, or making her come. Her hips pushed against his mouth, and he placed an arm across her soft belly to hold her still. He sought her channel with his other hand, and he pushed a finger deep into her wetness. Her cry at his penetration told him she was close. He pulled the finger out, covered in her slick juices, and reached lower to her tight ring. He was in to the first knuckle when she came apart, shuddering with a hard climax.

He moved his body up hers and slid his dick into her still pulsing pussy. She wrapped her arms and legs around him as he began to thrust. They'd been going bareback for a while since she'd started taking a birth control shot. They'd talked about kids but decided to wait at least a year before moving into that phase of their lives. He rocked into her, hearing her breathy catches, meeting her moving hips as she opened and pushed back into his riding body. She licked her own flavor from his lips as he kissed her.

"Coming again," she moaned in her low husky accent.

"Me too, baby."

His speed increased, as did hers. He slammed into her one last time just as he felt the waves of her second release. "I fucking love you so damn much."

She didn't hear him, of course, but the sudden grasp of her hands on his tight buttocks told him she understood.

They ate the cold brisket sandwiches, and he made love to her again before finally calling it a night.

Dawn broke, and Rail woke at the first light coming through the window. The forecast said snow was on the way. He smiled at the sleeping face beside him. He couldn't think of a better way to spend a cold winter than in a warm house with the woman he loved. Quietly, so as to not disturb her, he dressed quickly and left the house to walk down to the pier. The bite in the early morning air heralded the weather to come, and a shiver traced down his spine. Life was good. Real good. He glanced at the sky coming alive with bands of color. He inhaled deep, closed his eyes, and bowed his head.

"Thank you."

A flutter blew by his ear, and he smiled.

"You're welcome, precious."

THE DUTCHMEN ARE JUST GETTING STARTED. CHECK OUT book three, **THE PRICE OF PEACE**, following Angel's story. If you enjoyed THE PRICE OF FORGIVENESS, please consider leaving a review on YOUR FAVOURITE SALES SITE(S), GOODREADS, and/or BOOKBUB. Thank you!

ACKNOWLEDGMENTS

I got my idea for Gretchen's character from an editor friend of mine. I used to be a part of a writing group, and the editor in that group complained several times about working with authors who would send her half-complete manuscripts and then expect her to clean them up. I heard all about some of her worst client problems and worked several of them into this manuscript. Thanks for the inspiration, Sharon Stogner and Adrienne Wilder!

Railroad was tough to figure out. He was an enigma in the first book. It took me a while to find him, and once I did, he spiraled into one of the most complex characters I've written. I can relate to his struggle in life, as he challenged me more than once while I discovered his past and how it shaped him. Now, he's one of my favorites.

Thank you, thank you, thank you to all my beta readers: Brittany Alexander, McKinley Hellenes Krantz, Keely Catarineau, Paula White, Kristen Mitchell, and Chloe Park. You truly made the difference and caught so many loose ends. Becky, Donna, Liv, Lori, and Kristin at Hot Tree Publishing, y'all rock!

ABOUT THE AUTHOR

Thanks for reading *The Price of Forgiveness: Dutchmen MC, book two*. I do hope you enjoyed Railroad and Gretchen's story. I appreciate your help in spreading the word, including telling a friend. Before you go, it would mean so much to me if you would take a few minutes to write a review and share how you feel about my story so others may find my work. Reviews really do help readers find books. Please leave a review on your favorite book site.

Don't miss out on New Releases, Exclusive Give-aways and much more!
Join my newsletter: https://www.mlnystrom.com/contact
Visit my website for my current booklist: https://www.mlnystrom.com/

I'd love to hear from you directly, too. Please feel free to email me at melody @mlnystrom.com or check out my website https://www.mlnystrom.com/ for updates.

facebook.com/authorMLNystrom

twitter.com/ml_nystrom

instagram.com/mlnystrom

bookbub.com/profile/ml-nystrom

ABOUT THE PUBLISHER

Hot Tree Publishing opened its doors in 2015 with an aspiration to bring quality fiction to the world of readers. With the initial focus on romance and a wide spread of romance subgenres, Hot Tree Publishing has since opened their first imprint, Tangled Tree Publishing, specializing in crime, mystery, suspense, and thriller.

Firmly seated in the industry as a leading editing provider to independent authors and small publishing houses, Hot Tree Publishing is the sister company to Hot Tree Editing, founded in 2012. Having established in-house editing and promotions, plus having a well-respected market presence, Hot Tree Publishing endeavors to be a leader in bringing quality stories to the world of readers.

Interested in discovering more amazing reads brought to you by Hot Tree Publishing? Head over to the website for information:

www.hottreepublishing.com

facebook.com / hottreepublishing

twitter.com / hottreepubs

instagram.com / hottreepublishing

9 781922 679161